Readers can't get enough of t!

Going Rogue

"Maggie's world of espionage, heists, and secret hideouts will entice many young adult fans looking for adventure. The characters are well drawn and believable; the plot spirals from one heart-stopping climax to another. Mystery, mayhem, and money blend into a deliciously dangerous cocktail." —*VOYA*

"Filled with intrigue and suspense . . . reader[s] will hang onto its every word." —*LMC*

"Benway has created a loveable cast of characters, a fast-paced plot, and one heck of a fun ride that will leave you smiling and craving more." —My Guilty Obsession

Also Known As

★ "This one is fresh and fun." —*Booklist*, starred review

"Benway offers a rollicking take on the 'spy kids' premise, buoyed by fun characters." —*Publishers Weekly*

"The absolutely delightful cast of characters and snappy dialogue transform this book into a huge success. . . . Plan to have multiple copies of this book available." —*SLJ*

"[Benway] captures the trials and tribulations of growing up with wit and whimsy, humor and perception—making this novel a real joy." —*RT Book Reviews*, 4 stars

BOOKS BY ROBIN BENWAY

Also Known As
Going Rogue

AN
ALSO
KNOWN
AS
NOVEL

GOING ROGUE

ROBIN BENWAY

BLOOMSBURY
NEW YORK   LONDON   NEW DELHI   SYDNEY

First published in the United States of America in January 2014
by Walker Books for Young Readers, an imprint of Bloomsbury Publishing, Inc.
Paperback edition published in January 2015 by Bloomsbury Children's Books
www.bloomsbury.com

Bloomsbury is a registered trademark of Bloomsbury Publishing Plc

For information about permission to reproduce selections from this book, write to
Permissions, Bloomsbury Children's Books, 1385 Broadway, New York, New York 10018
Bloomsbury books may be purchased for business or promotional use. For information on bulk
purchases please contact Macmillan Corporate and Premium Sales Department at
specialmarkets@macmillan.com

The Library of Congress has cataloged the hardcover edition as follows:
Benway, Robin.
Going rogue : an Also Known As novel / Robin Benway.
pages   cm
Summary: When sixteen-year-old Maggie Silver's parents are falsely accused of stealing priceless
gold coins, she must use her safecracking skills to try to clear their names, with help from the
"new team" she has formed as an undercover operative in a New York City high school.
ISBN 978-0-8027-3604-8 (hardcover) • ISBN 978-0-8027-3605-5 (e-book)
[1. Spies—Fiction. 2. High schools—Fiction. 3. Schools—Fiction. 4. Adventure
and adventurers—Fiction. 5. New York (N.Y.)—Fiction.] I. Title.
PZ7.B4477Goi 2014   [Fic]—dc23   2013024934

ISBN 978-0-8027-3786-1 (paperback)

Book design by Nicole Gastonguay
Typeset by Westchester Book Composition
Printed and bound in the U.S.A. by Thomson-Shore, Inc., Dexter, Michigan
2 4 6 8 10 9 7 5 3 1

All papers used by Bloomsbury Publishing, Inc., are natural, recyclable products
made from wood grown in well-managed forests. The manufacturing processes
conform to the environmental regulations of the country of origin.

It seems only yesterday I used to believe
there was nothing under my skin but light.
If you cut me I could shine.
BILLY COLLINS,
"On Turning Ten"

Going in circles, it's a vicious cycle
This is a crash course, this ain't high school.
JAY-Z,
"American Dreamin'"

GOING

ROGUE

PROLOGUE

In September 2004, French police discovered a hidden chamber in the catacombs under Paris. It contained a full-size movie screen, projection equipment, a bar, a pressure cooker for making couscous, a professionally installed electricity system, and at least three phone lines. Movies ranged from 1950s noir classics to recent thrillers.

When the police returned three days later, the phone and power lines had been cut and there was a note on the floor:

"Do not try to find us."

—from www.futilitycloset.com/2005/03/14/underground -cinema/

CHAPTER 1

Roux?"

Nothing.

"Roux?"

Still nothing.

"Roux!"

"Ssshh! I'm thinking!"

I glanced up from my lock and key to see my best friend, Roux, frowning at a tiny magnetic chessboard. "How long does it take to move one chess piece?" I asked her. "You've been sitting there for nearly an hour."

"Did anyone ever ask Catherine the Great how long it took her to take over her husband's army?" Roux asked, her eyes never leaving the board. "Or Elizabeth the First how long it took her to do . . . whatever she did? No. So sssshh."

"But they were royalty. You—"

"I dare you to finish that sentence. Really. I dare you."

I sighed and sat back in my desk, restless and ready to

leave. We had been at an SAT prep class for most of the afternoon (Roux's absentee parents had forced her to register because they read about it in *New York* magazine's "What's Right Right Now" issue while stuck on a plane to Milan; I enrolled because Roux threatened to end our friendship if I didn't), but Roux was in no hurry to leave. We were in some lecture hall at NYU, where the one bright spot was the central air-conditioning. Manhattan had been engulfed in a late-August heat wave for nearly a week, and I was pretty sure that our prep class had a few stragglers that just wanted to escape the heat and had no interest in learning about analogies and test-taking secrets.

Roux was still bent over her chessboard, muttering to herself. Angelo, a family friend and pretty much my surrogate uncle, had taught Roux the rules of chess last spring, and they had been engaged in a summer-long game that seemed never ending. He refused to play online, though, which meant Roux had to keep the game going on her travel chess set.

"Roux seems to be quite good at scheming and masterminding," Angelo had commented soon after their game started.

"And this surprises you how?" I replied.

"Touché."

But Roux also had a soft, mushy side, and she was one of the most trustworthy people I knew. "You're like a Cadbury egg," I had once tried to explain to her. "You've got this hard shell, but inside you're all sweet and mushy and gooey."

She waited a few seconds before socking me in the shoulder.

"Ow!"

"Can a Cadbury egg do that? That's what I thought."

Despite her prickly personality, we'd been friends from the moment we met last year. And she was one of only two people who knew my most secret of secrets, that Angelo, my parents, and I all worked as spies for a secret organization known as the Collective.

I guess you could describe the Collective as a sort of rogue, secretive Robin Hood organization. We try to right wrongs, return money to retirement accounts, expose the bad guys for who they are without ever revealing ourselves. This time last year, I was in Reykjavík with my parents, exposing a human trafficking ring. We've been all over the world, but after a near disaster last fall, we now call Manhattan home.

At least for now.

"Wait a minute," Roux said, sitting up straight with an evil grin spreading across her face. "Waaaait a minute. Oh, you're dead, Angelo. God save the queen because here she comes." She expertly moved one of her pieces, keeping one finger on top of the figure until she was sure, then let go with a triumphant cry.

"He's going to weep when he sees that genius move I just made!" she crowed. "You can tell him I said that."

"Can't wait," I said. "Can we go now?" I gestured toward the lock in front of me. It was complicated, and I had made exactly zero progress on trying to pick it.

"This is frustrating me and I want to throw it out the window."

Roux peered down at the monstrosity. "What the hell is that?"

I sighed. "Annoying locks are annoying. I can't crack it at all, but Angelo told me that I had to try and figure it out while he was gone."

"He's so irritating that way." Roux nodded in sympathy. "When's he coming back?"

"Dunno." I flicked at the lock with my fingernail, but it refused to unlock itself. "He's been gone almost two months, though. Too long."

"I know, right? Do you know what it's like to have to play travel chess with someone out of the country?" Roux sighed in what I'm sure she thought was solidarity. "But c'mon, you're the best lock picker and safecracker that I know. You can do it. Rah, rah, rah and oh, screw it. I can't fake enthusiasm in this heat. I need to save my energy."

I glanced at her. "How many safecrackers do you know?"

She shrugged. "Hundreds, for all I know. You spies are a sneaky bunch."

She had a point.

"C'mon, let's go," I said. "I'll try to figure this out later."

"So where is our assassin friend, anyway?" Roux asked as we got our bags together.

"For the millionth time," I said with a sigh, "Angelo is not an assassin. He handles documents and currency. End of."

"*Suuuure* he's not an assassin," Roux said. "You just can't tell me because you'd be compromising my safety." She gave me a huge, exaggerated wink and then nudged me in the ribs. "I get it."

But I was telling her the truth about Angelo. He wasn't an assassin; he handled the paper trail: phony passports and birth certificates, drivers' licenses, and Social Security cards. Whatever documents my family needed, he provided.

My mom's the computer hacker in our family. She can get into huge computer mainframes, pull up incriminating e-mails that most people would never be able to find, and hide her tracks without even breaking a sweat. My dad's the linguist and statistician, which doesn't sound awesome until you hear him start shouting in German to create a distraction so my mom can drop a tracker into a corrupt businessman's jacket pocket. (You haven't lived until you've shouted German curse words with your dad in a Tokyo airport. It's pretty great.)

I was, as Roux so nicely pointed out, an excellent lock picker and safecracker. Angelo had taught me some tricks of the trade when I was a toddler, but now I had surpassed even his talents. "Go fly, little Jedi," he had said to me after I broke into the safe that he had given me for Christmas last year, which made me happy because it meant he had watched all the Star Wars DVDs I had given him.

My phone buzzed as Roux and I gathered up our bags and chess games, and I glanced at the screen to see two texts from my boyfriend, Jesse. I tucked my phone away without reading them. I don't know why, but I like to read his texts in private. It makes them feel more special, more personal, more *mine.*

"Jesse?" Roux asked. "You have that dopey, love-struck look on your face."

"Shut up some more." I grinned. "You ready?"

"Ready to face that unrelenting, diabolical heat? No."

"You should be a writer."

She snorted out a laugh. "BOOOOR-RING! C'mon, let's go so you can call your boyfriend and say a bunch of gooey, lovey things to him."

"Yeah, because that *really* sounds like me."

"Hey, you're a spy. You have all sorts of secrets."

"Yeah, and you know most of them."

"Thanks, that makes me feel special."

We went down the narrow staircase before getting to the set of double doors, but just as Roux used her hip to shove it open, two girls came through the other side and we all nearly bumped into one another.

"Hey, slut," one of the girls said, and Roux froze, her hip still pressed against the door's bar as they sauntered past, giggling to themselves.

"Rude much?" I yelled after them, but they didn't turn around, and by the time I looked back at Roux, her face had smoothed out into its normal, "what-*ever*" expression. "Do you know them?" I asked her.

"Nope," she replied. "They're probably starting at Harper in September. A new set of ducklings ready to taunt me."

When I first met Roux, she had been the outcast of

Harper School, our private high school in the West Village. She had once been the Queen Bee, the Mean Girl, whatever you want to call it, but karma had reared its ugly head and Roux became a social leper. She rarely talks about it, but the whole experience really hurt her. I had thought things were a little better, but I knew she was nervous about the first day of school this year, and if those two strangers were any indication, she had every right to be.

But the slur was forgotten as soon as we stepped outside, greeted by a wall of hot and humid air. "Forget it," Roux said, starting to step back inside the school. "I'm just going to stay here until Thanksgiving. Maybe Christmas."

I grabbed her sleeve and tugged her outside. "It's miserable, but we're going to suffer together. And it's only two blocks to the subway station."

But we weren't even four steps away from the building before I thought that maybe Roux's idea had been better. "I can feel my hair melting." I moaned.

"I think my skin is bubbling." Roux held up her arm to check. "This has to be super aging, too, right? You can't be exposed to this much heat and not get some serious frown lines."

"I have no idea." I tied my hair up into a messy bun and then fanned the back of my neck. "If I faint, promise me you'll send someone back for my body."

"If I don't go insane from heatstroke first, then absolutely."

"Thanks, you're a true friend."

Roux and I made our way across the street and up

Broadway toward the subway with the rest of the end-of-summer zombies who were staggering around Manhattan. The city had been pretty empty for the past two weeks, as most everyone escaped the city and the heat for the last few days of summer. Even Jesse had bailed to visit his mom in Connecticut. When he and I first met, his parents had just split up, his mom had moved out of their downtown apartment, and Jesse had been barely speaking to her. Things were a lot better between them now, though, so I was super happy that he was visiting her.

"Jesse's coming back tonight?" Roux asked me, slipping Ray-Bans over her eyes.

"Yep. He's gonna call me when his train gets into Grand Central. He might come over later."

"He *better* come over later," she said. "It's almost your first anniversary."

I side-eyed her. "Our anniversary is technically on Halloween. It's two months away."

"Isn't it sooner? You met in late September."

"Yeah, but we weren't *dating*-dating. He was still my assignment then."

So . . . *yeah*. About that. There's really no way to tell this story without making me sound like a terrible person, so I'll keep it short.

Basically, I was assigned to get to know Jesse because his father runs *Memorandum* magazine, which is pretty big. They were going to run an in-depth article exposing the Collective and me, and it was my job to stop the article from running. Only I kinda maybe developed this huge crush on Jesse. And then he started crushing on me right back. And then we sort of made out a lot, and I never told anyone, including Jesse, that I had pretty much become a double agent until we found out that his dad wasn't going to run the story after all. And then when I tried to tell my parents, they realized that I had fallen in love with him and they didn't believe me.

That was sort of a crazy time. I haven't even told you about the attempted kidnapping yet. Or how the bad guys ended up chasing us twenty blocks and Angelo had to fly in on a helicopter to save me and Roux and Jesse from almost being killed.

I don't like to brag, but sometimes my life can be really exciting.

Anyway, Jesse and I are still together, and he's forgiven me for lying to him in the beginning. We both figure that if our relationship can survive all that, then we're pretty good at being together. And we are. He's the only person besides Roux who knows that Angelo, my parents, and I are all spies, and he's never once spilled the secret. (Probably because he also thinks that Angelo is an assassin. Roux can be very convincing.)

"Wanna come over?" I asked Roux as we tried to walk under as many awnings as possible, avoiding the sun. "I think my dad's doing something involving barbecue tonight."

"No, thanks, I have my tae kwon do class."

"Ah, that's right." During our exciting near escape last year, Roux had managed to break the bad guy's nose and now she's all gung-ho on self-defense and putting up a good offense.

"And I think my parents are going to be home late

tonight, anyway," Roux continued, now examining her cuticles. "I should probably be around to guilt them about leaving for five weeks."

"You could probably get a pony out of it," I said.

"The last thing I need is something that neighs and craps all over the foyer." She tossed her hair back over her shoulder and straightened her sunglasses. "Don't worry, I'll get my revenge when they're old and it's time to put them in nursing homes. They'll spend their last days making macramé if *I* have anything to say about it."

Roux's parents are ridiculously wealthy. Like, how-are-you-even-a-real-person wealthy. It might sound amazing, but the real downside is that they're never home. They live in this huge building on the Upper East Side and Roux always seems to have the place to herself. Her dad has meetings around the world, and her mom goes with him. "Someone has to see if all the luxury spas in the world are up to snuff," Roux says, but it's hard to miss the hurt in her eyes. And then there's the Frieze Art Fair in London, Art Basel in Miami, antique auctions in Rome, getaway vacations in Bora Bora, and so on and so on.

It makes my parents insane because they like Roux and feel bad that she's practically raising herself, but what can you do? "We could break into her parents' online accounts and siphon out their money into an account for Roux," my mom answered when I asked that several months ago, and it took an hour for my dad and me to talk her out of the idea.

Once a computer hacker, always a computer hacker.

"Well, tell your parents I said hi," I told Roux as we started to cross the street against the light. "Even though they've never met me."

"Please," Roux said. "I could tell them that you met last year at a black tie cocktail reception for famous chimpanzees and they'd believe me. And maybe I *should* get a pony. I could name it Consolation Prize."

"Brilliant idea," I replied. I had learned long ago that Roux's schemes came and went with equal speed. And sure enough, she was already off on her next subject.

"Are you bored?"

"What? You mean, right now? Not really. I mean, nothing's really happening but—"

"No, I just mean in general. Like, with your life."

I sighed. I knew where this conversation was going and decided to cut to the chase. "No, Roux, I am not leaving on any new missions. I told you, I'm out. At least until after I graduate next year."

"Well, what if you *had* to? Like, if national security was at stake?"

"The government doesn't even *know* about us. I doubt they'd call my dad and be like, 'Hey, you three busy? There's this thing . . .'"

We stopped at the corner across from the subway station at Astor Place as Roux lowered her sunglasses to look at me. "You're lying," she finally said. "Your eyes are going up and to the left."

"That means I'm lying?"

"Yes. I've been studying up on human facial tics."

"Sounds riveting. And I am *not* lying. Are you getting on the subway with me or not?"

"No, I have to go home and get my stuff." Roux stepped off the curb to hail a taxi just as a man cut in front of us. He was wearing an old suit and tie that clearly had not been washed for a few days, and he had a few weeks' worth of whiskers lining his face.

"You!" he said to me, pointing right in my face. His nails were long and dirty, but I didn't flinch. A lifetime of learning how to stay calm in stressful situations often came in handy in New York.

"They're after you next!" he yelled. "Especially you!"

"Excellent, that's great," Roux said under her breath, reaching for my arm and pulling me away from the man. "Let's just step over here and get out of Insane Land, okay? There we go."

I watched as the man staggered down the street, blending in with the late-afternoon crowds. "Well, that was weird," I said.

"Do you know him?" Roux asked.

"I've never seen him before in my life."

"You!" the man yelled again, this time pointing at a nanny pushing a stroller. She didn't even blink. "Especially you!"

Roux just shook her head. "Welcome to Manhattan." She held her arm out for a taxi. "It's almost four, they're all going off duty soon, and I am *not* standing on a subway platform in this heat." She stepped farther into the street so that the next cab would have to hit her or stop for her, not even flinching when one nearly grazed her as he slammed to a halt. I couldn't hear the driver, but I could read lips well enough to know that he was using some pretty unique and colorful curse words.

He and Roux would get along just fine.

"I'll text you later?" Roux said as she climbed into the backseat.

"You better! Enjoy your class! Don't break anyone's nose!"

"I make no promises!" She stopped and pushed her sunglasses up on her head. "You sure you're not bored?"

Now I could hear the cab driver, as well as all the car horns behind them, mad that Roux was holding up traffic. "Definitely not bored," I told her. "Trust me, I'm done. I'm a civilian. I'm out."

And I meant it.

Until I got home and heard the news.

CHAPTER 2

I first knew something was wrong when I rounded Spring Street and our loft came into view. Everything looked normal, just another day in Soho, but there was opera music soaring out, seeping through the cracks in our closed windows and floating down toward me.

It was "Der Hölle Rache kocht in meinem Herzen" from Mozart's *The Magic Flute*.

Translation? "Hell's vengeance boils in my heart."

I ran the rest of the way home.

We've lived in our loft since we moved back to Manhattan from Reykjavík last year. It was just supposed to be a stopping ground, like so many of our houses were. Sometimes they felt like movie sets rather than homes, four walls with actors inside, playing our parts and then moving on to the next set, the next role. I've lost count of all the places we've lived, but we've been on six out of seven continents. (Let's be honest: Antarctica doesn't see a lot of crime-related activity. It's too cold to even *think* about committing a crime.)

I think this is the longest my family has ever been in one place, which is interesting. I've always had wings, never roots, and now I wake up to see the same four walls and have the same name—Maggie—every single day.

Hearing the Austrian aria made me realize how quickly all of that could disappear.

I dashed down the street and hurried into the elevator, yanking its steel door down and jabbing the button until my finger hurt and it finally started to rise. The soprano's voice was staccatoing like rocks across a pond, making my heart match its pace. We never listened to this song, not ever.

This song meant that something was wrong.

The elevator doors opened at a glacial pace, and I finally got so impatient that I stuck my fingers in and practically pried them apart. Our front door was there, the dingy #3 hanging smack in the center, a stark counterpart to the fingerprint scanner that sat next to the doorbell.

The fingerprint scanner had been installed last year, notable not only because it was, you know, a *fingerprint scanner attached to our front door*, but also because the Collective had no idea that it was there. Angelo had it put in as an extra measure of security, along with our new steel front door. If anyone ever tried to sledgehammer through the door, they'd quickly find a half ton of metal waiting to stop them. It was cool if you didn't think about why we needed those things.

This is why we need them:

When I was four years old, a man named Colton Hooper tried to kidnap me because I was apparently a little safecracking genius and he wanted to use me for his own nefarious needs. We didn't know it was him at the time because he hired someone to do it. Luckily, my parents and Angelo got wind of the plan and they flew me out of the country. Colton killed the kidnapper-for-hire to protect his own identity.

That's crazy enough, I know, but what made it crazier was that Colton was a high-ranking member of the Collective. He was our handler—in charge of assigning our missions, providing our multiple identities, and setting us up in our new locations. It turned out he was quite the multitasker, trying to sell information about us to Jesse's dad's magazine. If he couldn't get me, he might as well make some money, right?

Wrong.

Look, I don't like to brag a lot, but I'm pretty proud of the fact that we stopped Colton. And by we, I mean Roux and Jesse and me. I sort of broke code—okay, I *completely* broke code—by telling Roux and Jesse about my family and the Collective. But they responded by being awesome and helping me prove that Colton Hooper was a liar and very dangerous.

And oh yeah, there was also a twenty-block high-speed chase in which Roux, Jesse, and I had to outrun Colton. Then Roux attacked Colton, and Angelo had to fly in on a helicopter and save us. Followed by taking out Colton, which made my parents be all like "What. The. Hell."

It was a long week, I'll tell you. I think I'm still recovering from the drama, even though it happened almost a year ago.

So that's the short version of why we had a fingerprint scanner installed. I don't even know where Angelo got it, or who installed it, but it was there now. I jammed my index finger against it and waited impatiently for the familiar sound of the bolt clicking open. I can crack the lock, of course (what good is being a lock picker if you can't even break into your own house?), but it's faster to wait for the scanner instead.

Still, every second felt like an hour.

I heaved the door open as soon as I could, and the music almost blasted me right out of the loft, it was that loud. There's only two reasons to play music at that volume: one, a party, and two, a secret.

And I was pretty sure that my parents weren't throwing a party.

My mom was the first to see me, arms crossed and brow furrowed as she stood leaning against the kitchen island. Her face totally changed when she saw me, smoothing out into a smile as she stood up straight and uncrossed her arms. "Hi," she said, but I could only read her lips, not hear her.

My dad was standing across from her, the same worried gaze on his face, but it took him a few seconds longer than my mom to hide his emotions. He just waved and then pretended to lip-synch along with the aria, but I was in no mood for dad shenanigans. There was a pot of something on the stove, which was just as bad a sign as the opera. My dad stress-eats when he's nervous: after Colton Hooper was assassinated, he put on ten pounds.

Angelo was standing next to my father, his face as calm and genteel as always. He wore a seersucker suit, a gray-collared shirt, and a pink-and-gray-striped silk tie. How he wasn't melting in the heat, I had no idea, but that's Angelo for you. He's a perfect spy because he's like a mirage, like he exists outside of the world while still living in it. Sometimes it's hard to believe he's even real.

But he was very real, and very definitely standing in my kitchen, and, I knew, very much responsible for the music blasting out of the speakers.

He gave me a small wave and a beatific smile as I ran to hug him. "You're a jerk for being gone for so long," I yelled, since the music was so loud. "You owe me a million espressos."

Angelo just grinned and reached for a remote to turn down the music. "Hello, my love," he said. "Sorry, we were a bit loud, weren't we. Apologies all around."

I crossed my arms and looked at him, trying to figure out where he had been. Pale skin meant north, maybe Russia or Scandinavia. Tan skin meant West Africa, maybe the Mediterranean or Colombia. But Angelo looked the same, impassive as ever.

"Well?" I said. "Is anyone going to explain why we're deafening half of lower Manhattan with our distress signal? I could hear the music all the way around the corner! And isn't this a speech that *you're* supposed to give *me*, your teenage daughter?"

My dad shrugged. "Your parents like to have fun sometimes. Let our hair down. We get crazy."

He may have been trying to be funny (emphasis on *trying*), but the wrinkles were still creased between his eyes and my mom was gripping the dishwasher handle even as she smiled at me.

"How was Roux?" she asked me. "Still Roux-like?"

"She's insane," I replied. "You know that. What's going on?"

Everyone looked in a different direction, desperately trying to avoid eye contact: at the floor, the clock, the window, and I put my hands on my hips and shook my head. "Nope," I said. "Nope, nope, and nope. We *talked* about this, remember? We said we were going to work on communicating as a family so that you're not surprised the next time my best friend, my boyfriend, and I are chased down by a ruthless thug. I thought that was our new rule."

"Sweetheart, it's not that big—"

"Seriously?" I said. "You've been training me since I was two to spot a liar and now you want to lie to me? That is *terrible* parenting on your part. For you, not for me. It's working out pretty well for me."

My parents glanced at each other, then at Angelo. Angelo stayed serene throughout the wordless conversation, but then he picked up the remote and cranked the music back up into cringe-inducing decibels. "Come here," he said, beckoning me over, and I steeled myself and crossed the room into our makeshift cone of silence.

I knew that the loud music was there to screw up any potential bugs. After the Colton Hooper incident, my mom had scoured our loft and made sure it was free of all monitoring devices, but you can never be too careful. Ever. And I knew that this aria, in particular, screwed up bugs because of the pitch changes. Anyone trying to hear voices, or even inflections, would be completely out of luck.

I knew all of this in theory, of course, but not in practice.

My parents, Angelo, and I huddled together in the kitchen, looking like the most ragtag, mismatched football team in history, talking about plays while the clock counted down. My mom put her arm around my shoulders, and I let her because I think she was comforting herself more than me.

"There's been a, um, development," my dad began as the soprano's voice hit a particularly high note. I would probably vomit if I ever heard this song again.

"A development in what?" I asked. "Do we have to move again?"

"No," my mom said.

"Not yet," my dad added.

"Do they *ever* agree?" Angelo asked me with a knowing wink.

"What developed?" I asked again. "Someone tell me before I throw those speakers out the window."

My parents glanced at each other, and I saw my dad reach down to take my mom's hand. "The Collective was here today," my dad said.

"Here?" I gasped. "Here? Like, New York here, or in-our-house here?"

"Our house," my dad replied.

"Our *home*," my mom corrected him, then squeezed my shoulder. "Our home is wherever we are, Mags. You know that."

I did know that. Home is where your family is, blah blah blah. My parents had been saying it since the day I was born.

"Did they find out about the fingerprint scanner?" I asked. "I mean, why else would they be here? And why are we blasting music if they were here?" My stomach was starting to flip and I looked at Angelo.

"They did see the scanner," he said, "but no, love, that's not why they were here."

I thought about Roux, blissfully karate chopping fake enemies in a dojo somewhere uptown, and Jesse sitting outside in Connecticut with his mom, talking about something. Maybe even talking about me. I could feel the change coming, and in that moment I wished I could grab Jesse and Roux and not let go.

"The Collective discovered several discrepancies"—my dad said the word in a way that made me think he didn't believe it—"in some cases that your mother and I did a long time ago. Way back before you were born."

"The Dark Ages," my mother clarified with a smile. "The prehistoric era."

"What discrepancies?" I asked, in no mood to be humored and teased. "And stop treating me like a little kid. You can't bring me into this and then pretend like it's nothing."

My parents looked at each other again and when they looked back at me, it was clear that all the soft-pedaling was over. "They're saying that your mother and I stole some evidence from a case," my dad said. "They're accusing us of lying and they're opening up an investigation."

I stood there trying to process what everyone was

saying. "But it's not true!" I said. "Right? You would never do that! Mom?"

"Of course not," she reassured me. "It's false, it's just a mistake. It's a small mix-up that can be fixed."

"Then why do you look so worried?"

And then it hit me. I knew why they were so worried, why we were blasting opera music on a Thursday afternoon, why my mom hadn't stopped gripping my shoulder.

"It's because of me," I muttered. "It's because of Colton Hooper."

"No, it's not—" my dad started to say, but I shook my head.

"You *know* it's because of me!" I protested. "They're mad because I proved that the Collective screwed up, that they were flawed, and now they're pissed."

Angelo hadn't said a word yet.

"They want us out, don't they?" I continued. "Is that it? They prove that you and Dad lied or whatever, and then they can exile us and no one's the wiser."

No one said anything for a long time, and then finally Angelo spoke up. "Not quite."

I looked at him while my parents looked at me.

"You were not the only one whose life was threatened last year," Angelo said.

"What do you mean?"

"I mean that I've been hearing rumors about a few people that have been . . . disbarred, so to speak, from the Collective."

"For doing a bad job?"

"No. For *refusing* to do a bad job."

I glanced over at my parents. My mom was biting her lower lip. "I—I don't understand," I said. "Why would . . . ? What do . . . ?"

"They're only rumors," Angelo said as my mom put her hand on my shoulder. "I've been contacted by a few people whom the Collective has recently accused of stealing evidence or forging the wrong documents. I thought it was best to investigate."

"That's why you've been gone for so long," I said. "How many people?"

"A few," he said.

"A few?" I repeated. "Like, two or three? Or more? Were they *right*?"

"We don't know," my dad said.

"You knew about this?" I asked, turning around to look at my parents. "You've known about this the whole time and didn't tell me?"

"We didn't want to worry you—" my dad started to say, but Angelo interrupted him.

"You know now," he told me. "You'll always get information when you need it. And they could just be disgruntled employees who were rightfully removed. We don't know yet."

"But it's weird that the Collective is suddenly accusing Mom and Dad of stealing evidence, right?"

"It could be a coincidence or a filing error."

"It's not like they were threatening us," my dad pointed out.

"So that's why you were blasting opera music?" I countered. "Because you just really dig arias?"

"We wanted to talk privately," my mom told me. "Just in case."

"It's a precaution," my dad said. "That's all."

"And what if they're right and the Collective's wrong?" I asked. "Then what?"

No one said anything this time. They didn't have to.

I whirled around and picked up a juice glass sitting on the counter, then threw it as hard as I could. The glass shattered against the brick wall and everyone, me included, jumped at the noise.

"Maggie!" My mom gasped, and she actually looked a little bit scared of me, which only made me more frightened.

"This is bullshit," I said, trying to keep my voice from shaking. "And we can't do anything about it, can we?"

"That is patently untrue," Angelo said. He had barely flinched at the breaking glass or my teenage temper tantrum. "We can always do something."

I looked at him, then my parents. "Like what?"

"Like prove that they're wrong," my dad said. "We can find the missing evidence and prove we didn't steal it."

The glass was glittering on the floor as the sun moved through our windows, and for some reason, it frightened me to even look at it. "It's not really that easy, is it."

"It isn't," my mom admitted. "It was a long time ago and it was a dangerous case. We barely escaped out of it. And that was *with* the Collective's support."

My eyes widened as I realized what they weren't saying. "Are we going rogue?" I whispered. I had heard rumors about spies going rogue, but they had always seemed unbelievable, unstable, completely stupid.

Not anymore.

"Are we going rogue?" I repeated. "Because if so, I'm in."

"No, you're not," my dad immediately said. "This is our problem, not yours."

"Hey," I told him. "This is our home, and home is where your family is. And you're my family and now we're in trouble. I. Am. *In.*"

My mom wiped at her eyes before I could see the tears. "We don't want to put you in any danger."

That's when I knew we were in serious, serious trouble. I love my parents, but they had spent my entire life putting me in danger. It comes with the job. I mean, I was almost kidnapped when I was four! A deranged madman chased my friends and me through lower Manhattan! And *now* they were worried about danger?

"Okay, look, I'm just going to say it," I announced. "I am *really* good at danger. I sort of excel at escaping it. I don't like to brag, but I think it's important to state the facts here."

"You cannot protect her forever," Angelo murmured to my parents. "She's nearly an adult. This is her life, too."

"Yeah, what he said."

"Maggie, we're not trying to prove the Collective wrong," my dad said.

"*Wrong*!" I cried. "I already proved them wrong when Colton Hooper turned out to be a double agent. *Me.* And now they're after you because they want to stop *me.*" Pieces were clicking together even as I spoke, and I wished I had another juice glass to hurl at the wall. "And they want to stop everyone like me."

"We don't know that." Angelo stepped in, a

well-dressed barrier between my parents and me. "All we have are the facts. Those are our best tools. Supposition and worry has never solved anything before and they won't help us now." He raised an eyebrow at me. "Agreed?"

"Agreed," I said, even though I really didn't. "Are we going to be separated, though? Like, if I have to research this? Because I'm ready." I wished I felt as confident as I sounded, and I tried not to think of Jesse's and Roux's faces. "Some kids go to college when they're seventeen. Some kids become *doctors* when they're seventeen!"

"I don't think you're going to be a doctor," my dad said. "Sorry."

"It was just an example. I'm trying to tell you that I can live on my own so you don't have to worry about me."

My mom made a sort of strangled noise in the back of her throat.

"You'll never be on your own," Angelo reassured me. "We have friends all over the world. Maybe you'll get to meet them."

"Yay, new friends." I tried to smile at my parents so they wouldn't look so concerned. Their lack of poker faces was making me edgy, like there was something I didn't know, something they weren't telling me. "Let's do this. I'm in. What's the deal? What's the evidence?"

"Why don't we meet tomorrow and you and I can discuss?" Angelo suggested, straightening his suit sleeves. "It's been quite some time since we've had a tête-à-tête, you and I."

"But—"

"And isn't that lovely boy of yours coming home this evening?" Angelo tapped his very expensive and definitely not a knockoff Rolex. "Might be late."

I glanced down at my phone (producing a sigh from Angelo, who's always trying to get me to wear a watch, that Luddite). "Yeah, Jesse's train's supposed to arrive in, like, thirty minutes. But he can wait. This is important."

"Go," my dad said, gesturing toward the door. "We know you missed him."

I glanced at the door, wanting to stay and wanting to go. "Okay," I finally acquiesced. "But this doesn't mean I'm not taking this seriously. I'm in. Let's do this."

"Maggie," my mom started to say, but I leveled my gaze at my parents and leaned across the counter, as sure as I had ever been.

"I'm in," I said again, and this time, no one argued with me.

CHAPTER 3

Grand Central Station was packed as I rode the subway escalator up to the main concourse. It was rush hour, which meant lots of commuters, and I suspected that more than a few tourists were taking refuge in the air-conditioned hall. I couldn't blame them. I only had to wait on the subway platform for a few minutes before the 6 train showed up, and I still felt grimy from the experience.

Jesse's train was supposed to be in by now, and I stood on my tiptoes and tried to see if he was off the train yet. He had insisted he would just meet me later, that I didn't have come all the way to the station, but it had been two weeks and I missed him. A lot. More than I thought I could ever miss someone. My parents and I had moved dozens of times all around the world, but I had never really made friends and I had definitely never had a boyfriend before.

Leaving doesn't matter when there's no one to leave behind.

I thought of my mom's words as I jumped up again to see over the crowd. "Home is where your family is," she had said. I had thought she was just talking about *our* family, but now I knew what she meant. My family had grown over the past year with Roux and Jesse, and now I knew why spies never made friends.

"Hey!" said a voice behind me, and I turned around to see Jesse standing there, his bag slung over his shoulder, his curly hair in his eyes just like it always was, and his face lit up with the smile that shined only for me. I had looked at him so many times over the past year and yet it never got old. When he smiled, I smiled back. That's how we were.

So it was probably a little weird for him when I flung my arms around him and hung on like a starving python.

"Mags!" he cried, dropping his bag on the ground as I squeezed him tighter. "Mags, um, you're a little—okay, ow."

"I missed you!" I said. "I just missed you, that's all!"

"Yeah, right." Jesse wasn't fooled for a minute. "That's why you're trying to crush me. Here, come here." He managed to extract himself from me, then drew me into a hug, right under the constellations painted onto the ceiling. "What's the matter? Did something happen?"

I shook my head. "I'm just glad you're here. I told you, I missed you."

Jesse kissed the top of my head and I hugged his waist so hard that I could feel his ribs. "Sorry," I said. "I'm all right."

"I don't think this kind of kung fu grip in the middle of a train station counts as 'all right,'" he pointed out. "But maybe that's just me."

"I'm the worst girlfriend ever!" I said. "I was supposed to be all happy to see you and instead you got a clingy person."

"I happen to like *clingy people*," he replied, hugging me a bit tighter. "Especially when they're named Maggie and look as cute as you. C'mon, what happened? Did you and Roux get into a fight or something?"

Roux! I hadn't even thought about leaving Roux behind!

"Maggie?"

"I just really love you!" I cried, my voice muffled against his shoulder. "Like, a whole lot!"

I could feel his laughter vibrating in his chest even as he stroked my hair. "I love you, too, weirdo," he murmured. "No need to strangle me over it."

We stood tangled together for a few minutes, tourists and commuters bumping into us, but Jesse didn't move and I certainly had no plans to stop hugging the hell out of him. He smelled like shampoo and detergent (a different one than when he was at his dad's house) and trains, and I wondered if I was committing him to memory, if I was hanging on so tight because one day soon I wouldn't have anything to hang on to at all.

"C'mon, turn around," Jesse said once my hug started to loosen up a little. "Look at this awesome ceiling with me." He turned me around in his arms and hugged me from behind while pointing toward the blue-and-gold ceiling. "Look, isn't it beautiful? Does that make you feel better?"

It wasn't the ceiling that was making me feel better, it was Jesse, but I nodded anyway. "It's really pretty," I admitted while trying to wipe at my nose without looking disgusting about it.

Jesse kissed the side of my head and held me tighter. "Did you know," he said quietly, "that the ceiling is actually reversed? It's supposed to look like it should if you were standing under the stars, but instead it looks like you're above them. It was this big screw-up, but the designer just said that that's how God sees the sky."

"The God excuse is pretty hard to argue," I allowed.

"Right?" Jesse rested his chin on top of my head and pointed again. "Look. Orion is the only one that's in the right place."

"The hunter," I said softly.

"Just like you and how you used to hunt down the bad guys. Always in the right place at the right time."

I took a deep breath and turned around to face Jesse. "Kind of," I said. "I don't think I'm quite as badass as Orion."

"Well, he was actually killed by a scorpion, so you know." Jesse shrugged. "I don't think that's *really* badass." He smiled down at me. "Better now?"

I nodded and tried to wipe at my nose again. "I'm snotty. Sorry."

"You're disgusting, frankly," he teased. "It almost makes me want to not do this." He bent his head and kissed me and I could taste him on my lips. Coffee and spearmint gum and just *him*. "Missed you," he whispered against my mouth. "A lot."

"Missed you, too." I reached up to kiss him again, harder this time. "You know I love you, Jesse, right?"

He nodded and pushed my hair out of my face. "Of course you do. I'm amazing. Apparently, I'm a *catch*. That's what my grandmother told me last weekend. I don't want to go on about it." He pretended to brush invisible dirt off his shoulder.

"Your grandmother?" I repeated.

"Are you calling her a liar?" Jesse raised an eyebrow. "That's pretty low, calling your boyfriend's grandmother a liar."

I laughed despite myself. Laughing after crying always felt better than just laughing. Why does life have to be so terrible that way? "No, she's right," I told him. "You're a catch. Glad I threw my line out there."

Jesse smiled and kissed me again, and this time, I smiled back at him. "C'mon," he said. "Let's go talk, okay? You can tell me why you're Huggles McGee all of a sudden."

"Our place?"

"Our place," he agreed, then picked up his bag with one hand while putting his arm around my shoulder. "Lead the way, lady."

CHAPTER 4

We stopped at Jesse's apartment long enough for him to drop off his bag, yell hello to his dad, and give his golden retriever, Max, a few tummy rubs before heading out hand in hand to our place, Gramercy Park.

Gramercy Park was the first place I had ever learned to pick gate locks. The only people who have access to the park are those who live directly on its borders, but when I was four years old, Angelo taught me how to crack the lock, and it was the place we met whenever we were both in the city at the same time.

On Jesse's and my first date, I brought him here because he had never been inside the park before, and we just kept coming back. It was our little secret, not only from our friends and family, but from the rest of the city, as well. There aren't many places in New York where you can find privacy, and as a spy I enjoyed some privacy every now and then.

Especially when it was with Jesse.

It took me only a few seconds to pick the lock this time.

"That never gets old," Jesse said after I popped it open. "Seriously, that's really hot. Do it again."

"Maybe I'll just talk to you about cobalt shields and Master Locks," I teased, lowering my voice into what I hoped was a seductive tone.

"What's wrong with your voice?" he asked, then grinned as I laughed and pretended to punch him in the stomach as we made our way to our favorite bench, right under the pagoda birdhouse.

"Don't poop on me, stupid pigeons," I warned them as we got settled. "Little disease-filled wingbags."

"You sound like Roux," Jesse said. "She's got issues with those birds."

"She has raised some excellent points," I countered, then rested my head on his shoulder and relaced his fingers with mine. It was twilight, my favorite time in the New York summer, when the sky looks as purple as the jacarandas in Los Angeles and the buildings are just starting to light up. The heat was still bad, but not as stifling as it had been earlier that afternoon, and I felt Jesse squeeze my hand and rest his head on top of mine.

"So," he said. "What was with all the emotion back at Grand Central? You want to tell me?"

I shook my head. "Not right now. Can we just . . . sit? Just like this."

"Of course." He rubbed his thumb over the back of my hand and I closed my eyes, happy to be still for a few minutes while the city raced around us.

It was almost full dark when I finally spoke again. "How's your mom?"

"She's good. Really into yoga and pottery. I think she's got about ten coffee mugs that she made in class, but only one of them holds water." He laughed a little, a laugh that I heard only when he came back from his mom's house. It was easy and soft, like he could relax now that he knew his mom was happy. "But all the mugs look alike and she won't get rid of any of them, so it takes a while to figure out which mug actually works."

I smiled, pressing my head against his shoulder. "Sounds chaotic."

"And wet. But she's good." Jesse threaded his fingers through mine and lifted our hands up so he could look at them. "I told her more about you. Not the spy stuff, but just . . . you know. About you. And us."

I could feel my heartbeat start to quicken. "And? She was cool with it?"

"More than cool, actually. She thinks you're smart. And pretty. And—"

"Aw, stop it some more." I grinned and kissed the back of his hand. "Did you tell her I'm good at *Jeopardy!*, too? And a whiz in the kitchen?"

"Yes and definitely no. I think that made her like you more." He kissed the top of my head and kept his lips pressed against my hair. "She wants to see you again."

I've been through some scary situations in my life, but making a habit of seeing my boyfriend's mother was not one of them. "Oh."

"Is that okay? Are you allowed to do that?"

"Do what?"

"See her again. Can you meet people twice?"

"Spy-wise? Yeah, I think so. I don't see why not."

Jesse paused before saying, "And Maggie-wise?"

"Maggie-wise, I don't know. What if she doesn't like me this time? What if last time was a fluke?"

"Weirdo. Why wouldn't she like you? You're awesome."

"You're not so bad yourself," I replied.

"Your parents like *me*," Jesse pointed out. "Why wouldn't my mom like you? My dad likes you."

"Your dad's so busy that he probably doesn't even remember meeting me."

"What? How can you even—okay, yeah, you're probably right. But that doesn't mean he doesn't like you. Believe me, if he didn't like you, he'd remember you."

"How completely not comforting."

It wasn't just seeing Jesse's mom again that made me nervous, though. It was the idea of having another tether to the city, another person to leave if we had to go. I knew Jesse had been pretty devastated when his mom moved to Connecticut, and I couldn't bear to hurt him the same way.

"So you'll have dinner with us when she comes into the city next week?" Jesse asked.

"Of course," I said, not letting myself think about whether or not I would actually be in the city by that point. "Hey. While we're talking about important things . . ."

"Hmm?" Jesse squeezed my hand. "You have an important thing?"

"Pretty important, yeah."

"Okay. Out with it."

I took a deep breath. "The Collective is investigating my parents."

Jesse sat up so fast that my head fell off his shoulder. "They're what?" he said. "What?"

"Well, not *investigating* them, exactly. But they're saying that my parents stole evidence after finishing a case, and that's grounds for expulsion from the Collective."

Jesse looked upset, confused, and furious all at the same time. "Does this have to do with . . . *him*, though?" The name Colton Hooper didn't exactly inspire good feelings around us. "I don't get it."

I bit my lip before answering. "Angelo and my parents say it's not true, but I think the Collective is mad that I exposed Colton for being a double agent."

Jesse looked at me as if I was speaking Martian. "What?" he finally said. "How . . . ? Why . . . ? What the *hell* is wrong with them? Why are they mad at *you*? They should be throwing you a goddamn parade!"

"I know," I admitted. "Something's wrong, but I don't know if it's the Collective or something else. I don't know and I *hate* when I don't know something, by the way."

"Believe me, I'm aware." Jesse stood up and started to pace back and forth in front of our bench. "And you can't go to the police."

"Nope. Too many spies would be exposed. It'd be a disaster."

"But Mags, what if Colton Hooper wasn't the only bad spy? What if there are more?"

I looked up at him. I knew I couldn't tell Jesse anything

about the ex-Collective members, about how Angelo was investigating their claims. I had started our relationship by lying to him and I didn't want to do that again.

But if it meant keeping Jesse safe, I would do anything.

"When were you going to mention this?" he said. "Here I am, talking about my mom and dinner and it turns out that you've got all this happening! When did you even find out?"

"Just today. And you're always so happy when you talk about your mom, I didn't want to stop you."

Jesse took a deep breath, then pinched the bridge of his nose. I had seen his dad do the same thing during press conferences or late-night television interviews. The Oliver family gesture. "So what are you going to do?" he asked.

I shrugged. "Prove them wrong and show them that my parents didn't do anything. And hopefully not piss them off. *Again.*"

Jesse stopped pacing and stood directly in front of me. I could see realization moving across his face, the under-standing of why I had been so emotional at Grand Central. "Oh, I get it," he murmured. "You might have to leave."

I bit my lip and glanced at the street, unable to look at his face for much longer. "Maybe."

"Maybe."

"Going rogue sometimes means *going*." I tried to play off the words as funny, but neither of us was laughing. "I don't want to, though. I want to stay here with you and Roux and my . . ." My voice caught and I fought to bring it back. "And my parents. And Angelo and school and everything.

It's our senior year. I want to apply to colleges and go to homecoming with you—is that a thing? A homecoming dance?"

Jesse nodded.

"Well, I want to do all of that. But this is my family and this is who I am. Remember I told you, I have dozens of passports but at the end of the day, all those girls are me." I tried to smile at him, but it felt wobbly. "You fell in love with a spy. Sucks for both of us."

Jesse gave me a small, rueful smile before coming to sit back down next to me. "Can't Angelo just solve it?"

"We're all working on it," I said. "But chances are good that my parents are going to be cut off and everyone in the Collective probably knows that Angelo's practically like my uncle, so they'll cut him off, too."

"Then won't they cut you off?"

"Even if that happens, I don't need technology to do what I do."

Jesse let it all sink in as I curled back up next to him. "If I have to leave," I whispered, "I promise I'll come back."

"What if you can't?" Jesse put his arm around my shoulders and I drew my knees up to my chest. "What if they kill you?"

"Oh my God, they're not going to kill me," I scoffed. "We *stop* killers. It's sort of our thing."

Jesse shrugged. "We already got chased by a madman once, Mags. Weirder things have happened."

He had a point. Unfortunately.

"I'll do everything I can to keep you informed," I

promised him. "But I might not be able to tell you every-thing. I need to keep you and Roux safe."

"Have you told Roux yet?"

I shook my head. "No. I just found out this afternoon and I don't really want to text her about this."

"She's going to lose her mind."

"Oh yeah, she is. It's going to be so ugly."

"I'll probably be able to see the exact moment her head turns into a mushroom cloud."

I started to laugh at the image. "Mount Vesuvius spotted on the Upper East Side." I giggled. "News at eleven!"

Jesse wasn't laughing, though, and he looked down and put his hands in his pockets, avoiding my eyes. "Hey," I said softly. "I meant what I said. I might not be able to tell you everything, but I'll always come back, no matter what."

He nodded and swallowed hard before kissing me. This kiss was different from our train station one earlier. Jesse wasn't comforting me anymore. This kiss was all about us. I ran my fingers into his hair and pulled him closer to me, afraid to let go, afraid of the day when I wouldn't be able to touch him, see him, find him.

"Love you," he whispered when we pulled apart. "I love each and every one of those passport girls."

I smiled and blushed. "You always know just what to say," I said.

"I also know when to shut up." He grinned, then leaned in to kiss me again.

Spy romance. It never gets old.

CHAPTER 5

I slept in the next morning after crashing late. I had been too wired to sleep and had spent most of my night practicing on Angelo's stupid lock. I was so close to cracking it, but every time I almost did it, the pins would collapse back into place and I'd be shut out. I worked until 3:00 a.m., hunched over my desk and probably ruining my posture before dragging myself to bed, and when I finally woke up, the sun was streaming in through the windows and the air already felt steamy.

My parents' bedroom door was still shut, and I could hear their worried murmurs leaking through. I stood there for a minute, trying to listen, and almost fell into the bedroom when my dad yanked the door open.

"Are you spying?" he accused as I righted myself.

"How dare you?" I replied. "Accuse *me* of all people of being a spy." I smoothed my hair down. "I never."

I was trying to make him laugh, but all I got was a muscle spasm that was either a repressed smile or a minor stroke. It's hard to tell with parents sometimes. "You shouldn't be eavesdropping on your parents," he told me. "It's rude."

"Well, you're the ones who raised a spy, sooooo . . ." I shrugged. "What can you do?"

My mom poked her head out from the bathroom where she was brushing her teeth. "Oo nee ta klee or moom."

I glanced at my dad. "All the technology in the world couldn't decipher what she just said."

"You need to clean your room," he translated. "And she's right."

"I didn't know that Mom brushing her teeth was an official language."

I could hear my mom spitting and rinsing. "Clean your room!" she yelled from the bathroom.

"Am I the only one who remembers what happened yesterday?" I cried. "Excuse me, but why aren't we making a plan?"

My dad just pointed at something on our kitchen counter. "Angelo will fill you in," he said.

"I bet none of the Avengers had to clean their rooms," I muttered, but went to inspect the piece of paper.

I would have known it anywhere, a calligraphed *A* printed on heavy cream card stock: Angelo's card. I turned it over and looked at the drawing on the back. It was a statue of a man riding a horse with what looked like an angel standing in front of them. It looked like a thousand statues in Manhattan.

"Angelo." I groaned, dropping my head into my hands. Sometimes he's too clever for his own good.

* * *

An hour later, I had done some sleuthing and discovered that Angelo wanted me to meet him at the northern corner of Grand Army Plaza in Manhattan (not the one in Brooklyn), next to the Sherman Monument. I was showered, dressed, and caffeinated, and ready to kick ass and take names. The first wave of humidity hit me as soon as I stepped outside, though, and before I could change my mind and go back upstairs into our air-conditioned loft, I spotted Angelo out of the corner of my eye.

He was standing next to a light post, reading the French newspaper *Le Monde* and wearing a crisp, white cotton dress shirt with the sleeves rolled up and dark pants. His shoes were impeccably polished, of course, and when he saw me, he gave me a wave and a wink.

"Lovely to see you again, darling," he said, giving me the requisite kiss on both cheeks. "You look as fresh as ever."

"What are you doing here?" I said, kissing him back. "I got your note, I was on my way to meet you."

"Well, that's good. I thought you might not be able to solve this one."

"I'm smarter than you think."

"Yes, Google is a very useful tool, isn't it?"

I pretended to punch him in the arm and he chuckled. "It's good to admit you need help every now and then," he replied, offering me his arm. "And I thought I might escort you there."

My fingers gripped at his elbow as I stopped in the street, nearly causing a collision of people behind me. "Escort me?" I said. "Why?"

"Because it's a beautiful day and I happened to be in your neighborhood."

I raised an eyebrow. "You never escort me."

He shrugged. "I thought I taught you not to ask too many questions. You should get your answers by listening."

"I'm listening now," I said. "Did you follow me last night, too?"

He just smiled and started toward the subway entrance two blocks away. "Let's just say that safety in numbers has never been a bad thing."

"Why do we need safety?"

Just as the words were out of my mouth, a cab came barreling across the intersection, swerving out of the way of a delivery van and nearly coming up on the curb next to us. Angelo's arm immediately cut in front of me, pushing me out of the way like it was nothing, but I didn't miss the look that ghosted across his face: worry, anger, and suspicion all wrapped up in a split-second gaze.

"Asshole!" I yelled. "Sorry, Angelo."

"Well, yes, sometimes certain words do convey emotion better than others." His face had smoothed back into its normal, calm expression, and we continued walking.

This time, I held on to his arm and didn't ask any more questions.

His face had told me everything I needed to know.

CHAPTER 6

Grand Army Plaza was teeming with both tourists and locals alike, which came as no surprise. Angelo was always having me meet him in the most crowded places: the Metropolitan Museum of Art on a rainy school field trip morning, the Statue of Liberty on the Fourth of July, the High Line on the most beautiful spring day. Last March, we held a whole conversation while walking next to the St. Killian's marching band during the St. Patrick's Day parade. (We happened to be next to the bagpipe players. I was hoarse and nearly deaf for a week afterward.)

"So," Angelo said as we made our way toward the statue. "Tell me, darling. How did you sleep last night?"

"Late," I said. "Very late. Too late, actually. I thought it was all a dream at first."

"Some tossing and turning, I assume. That's to be expected. You got quite a jolt yesterday."

I nodded and leaned against the statue's granite pedestals. "You could say that." I turned to look at Angelo and forced a smile. "But that's the game, right?"

"Yes, my dear, but you've been out of the game for some time. I wasn't sure if you still wanted to play."

I bit the inside of my cheek and watched as two tourists, both wearing Statue of Liberty foam hats, took a picture in front of the Plaza Hotel. Someone rushing toward the subway interrupted their shot and they frowned and tried to take it again. "What do you think?" I asked, secretly pointing at them. "Honeymooners?"

Angelo reached out and took my hand in his. "Maggie, my love, you know you don't have to do this."

"And you know that I do," I replied, suddenly feeling the weight of everything we weren't saying. "There's paperwork hidden somewhere, isn't there?"

"Not paperwork, but yes."

"Well, whatever it is, it's probably locked away."

Angelo nodded again. "It is a safe assumption."

"Then I don't have a choice. They're my parents, Angelo. What am I supposed to do, just let the Collective *lie* about them? Kick them out? *All of us* out?" I took my hand away, then felt bad about it. "Sorry. I'm not mad at you. I'm just . . . frustrated, I guess. I'm pissed off. And it's hot. And it smells like horses."

Angelo chuckled to himself. "I thought you loved animals."

I just looked at him. "This is really bad, isn't it, Angelo."

Angelo came over and patted the granite. "You picked the right one," he said. "This statue is the reason I brought you here."

I looked up at it. The bronze was dingy and green in

some places, but it was still pretty impressive. It was of a man riding a (let's be honest here) pretty terrified-looking horse while a winged woman stood in front of them.

"That horse does *not* look happy," I told Angelo. "You should call PETA. They'll regulate."

He smiled and ran his finger over the writing on the plaque. "What do you know about gold coins?"

"Well, if they're filled with chocolate, I love them, and if they're filled with gold, I love them even more. Why, is that what's missing?" Gold coins were a lot more interesting than paperwork and I stood up straight, suddenly intrigued.

Angelo pulled a photo out of his wallet and handed it to me. "Does this look familiar?" he asked.

It was a photo of a gold coin that had clearly been taken from a government file. There was a serial number at the top and the coin itself was being held by tweezers under a harsh light that only served to illuminate it. There was a woman embossed on the front, just under the word LIB-ERTY, holding a staff with her arms flung apart, rays of sunlight shining up at her feet.

"It's beautiful," I murmured. "It actually looks like . . ." I trailed off and glanced up at the woman above me in the statue. "Is that supposed to be the same woman?"

Angelo nodded, a smirk playing at his mouth. He loves when I connect the dots by myself. "The same artist designed both of these pieces," he told me. "A man named Augustus Saint-Gaudens. Quite a talent, don't you agree?"

"I'll say. I think I ate the Play-Doh when I was a kid instead of actually sculpting anything."

"Well, we all have our gifts," Angelo said. "She supposedly stands for victory."

"I like her already." I took the photo from him and turned it over in my hands, but there was no writing, no date, nothing to indicate when it had been taken. "So this coin is missing?"

"Several of them, actually. Many of them. They were created by the US Mint, but President Roosevelt ordered them to be destroyed in 1933."

"Party pooper."

"Yes, well, many people agreed with you. They were supposed to be melted down and most were, but some were sneaked out of the Mint and remain missing to this day. They're incredibly rare, which makes them, of course, *incredibly* valuable. Especially to criminals."

"So they're technically contraband?"

"Stolen property, according to the federal government. The Secret Service has actually set up stings to get these coins back."

"Deeee-*lightful*." I sighed, handing the photo back to him. "So is this the point where I start scanning the trees for snipers?"

"I've already done that," Angelo said, and I couldn't tell if he was just maintaining a straight face for my sake or if he was actually being serious. Either way, I pressed my back against the statue because, hey, better safe than sorry.

"So the Collective thinks my parents have this gold coin."

"Ten of them, to be precise."

"Nice. But what's the big deal about—get away from me, pigeon, I swear to God—these coins?" I narrowed my eyes at a pigeon that was getting too close to my personal safety zone. "I mean, yeah, they were stolen and yeah, gold is great, but how much are these gold coins worth?"

Angelo tucked the photo back into his suit pocket. "The coins we're looking for are from 1933. They're the rarest ones."

"Okay?"

"One gold coin from 1933 sold at auction in 2002 for seven and a half million dollars."

My jaw fell open.

"Shut the front door!" I gasped, then covered my mouth as several tourists turned to stare. (On the bright side, though, my outburst scared the pigeon away.)

"So basically, the Collective is accusing my parents of stealing seventy million dollars worth of gold coins?"

Angelo nodded.

"And they think that we've been hauling them around with us all this time?"

Angelo opened his mouth, closed it, then thought a minute before opening it again.

"I think some members of the Collective know very well that your parents do not have these coins. I also think that there are some members who would like our various coworkers to think otherwise, though."

I leaned against Sherman and his Victory woman and thought about this. "So let's say I find these coins. What's going to stop them from saying that I just, I don't know, dug them out of my dad's sock drawer?"

"Nothing. The Collective has always been able to say whatever it wants. And up until now, they have always told the truth."

"So what's the point then?"

"Because whether or not the Collective wants to do the right thing is beside the point. *We* do the right thing. We do it every day. That is your job, love."

"Yeah, I know we do the right thing, but I'm not going to go out and find these coins and then put them in the hands of someone who doesn't deserve them. What if I do that and then we get kicked out anyway and some evil genius takes them and invests in, like, terrorist activities or something?"

"I know, my love. It would be terrible to see that happen."

I waited for Angelo's inevitable "But that would never happen, darling," or something like that, but it didn't come. "Angelo?"

"Hmm?"

"How many people were kicked out of the Collective?"

"I know of at least six so far. Maybe more."

"Well, that doesn't seem like a lot," I said, relieved. "I thought it was, like, a *hundred*."

Angelo leaned against the statue with me, a rare, relaxed stance for him. "Those six are the ones who refused to bend to corruption, so they say. I'm sure there are more."

"More who became corrupt," I clarified.

"It's possible."

"More than six?"

"Again, very possible."

"But they're just drops in the bucket," I said. "Right? I mean, if it's only a few, then you and I could find them and clean everything up." I pictured Angelo and me, pushing mops and vacuums, literally cleaning the Collective and putting it back in its proper order.

Angelo looked down at me, his gaze steady. "The thing about these drops in the bucket, as you say, is that they build and grow. It might take a while, but many drops create—"

"A flood." I finished his sentence before he could. "Something that could wipe us all out."

"Do you trust me?"

"Of course I do. You swooped down in a freaking helicopter and saved me and my friend and boyfriend. You've got my lifelong trust."

Angelo smiled then, a full smile that showed off all his white teeth. "Then please trust that I will tell you when I know more. All right, darling? I'm still putting a few pieces together."

"Well, can you tell me who has the coins, at least?"

"I am able to do that, yes. It's a man named Dominic Arment."

I sighed. "Of course it is. No one's just named Bob anymore."

"He was the person who last had the coins. Your parents handed them over to him in Washington, DC, years ago." Angelo glanced out at the busy intersection, his face thoughtful. "We all knew each other back in Paris, many moons ago. He was a colleague of your parents even before they joined the Collective."

It was always hard to imagine my parents having a life before me. I mean, I know they did, I'm not that selfish . . . but still. It was difficult to imagine them and Angelo in Paris together. Without me.

"How come they never mentioned Dominic before?" I asked. "Is it because he's the personification of human evil?"

Angelo smirked a little. "Subtle, Maggie. And your parents and Dominic have gone their separate ways, obviously. They have always had different . . . viewpoints, for lack of a better word, on how the Collective should be run."

I crossed my arms over my chest so that Angelo wouldn't see my hands turning into fists. I already hated Dominic Arment. "So where is he now?"

"Apparently here in New York. He has a home . . . and then he has a *home*." Angelo raised an eyebrow at me.

"The place where he takes his mistresses?" I guessed.

Angelo tapped his nose in response, looking a bit disgusted. He's big on moral character, respecting women, all that.

"What a dirty birdie," I replied. "So the gold coins are probably behind Door Number Two."

"We think."

"We think?"

"Darling, this isn't one of our usual cases. We don't have a lot of information. The Collective normally supplies background intelligence for us."

I thought for a few seconds. "Do they know that *you* know all this about Dominic?"

Angelo just smirked at me. "Your job is to look for the coins, if you so desire."

"I so desire. I'm looking for these coins. That's a done deal. Do we have an address?"

Angelo pulled a piece of paper out of his pocket and showed it to me. "Do you see it?" he asked me.

22 Pomander Walk was written on the paper in Angelo's elegant scrawl.

"Yes."

"Good." Then he crumpled it up and tossed it through the bars of a sewer grate.

"Subtle," I said, mimicking him.

He gave me a wink, but his face soon sobered. "This is your biggest case ever, my love. Are you sure you're ready?"

"Are you?" I challenged, trying to lighten the mood even though my heart was pulling a Fred Astaire and tappity-tapping away in my chest. "You trained me, after all."

"Ah, I see. The teacher becomes the student and vice versa." He chuckled and straightened one of his shirt sleeves. "Know this, Maggie. I have always had complete faith in you."

For some reason, that sort of made me want to cry, but I shook it off and wrinkled my nose at him. "This has been a really uplifting conversation, by the way. The Collective wants people to think that my parents are thieves, the Secret Service wants these coins as much as I do, my parents actually *know* the bad guy, and that pigeon is getting *closer*!" I stamped my foot and it scuttled away. "Ugh, disgusting."

"Things are not as bright as one would like them to be," Angelo admitted. "But the sun is out, the birds are singing—I said *birds*, Maggie, not *pigeons*, you don't have to make such a face—and we're having a lovely morning in Central Park." He glanced over at the green trees, then offered me his arm. "Stroll with me?"

I took it because I can never say no to a stroll with Angelo.

And I never will.

CHAPTER 7

Who in their right mind would need to prep for the SATs three days a week during the summer?" I pulled my hair into a ponytail and held it off my neck while I watched an amateur guitarist start strumming in Washington Square Park.

"Stupid people," Roux replied. She was sitting next to me, guzzling her way through a Coke before our midmorning break was over and we had to go back into the classroom.

"Morons," she continued. "People whose parents try to get rid of them for three months under the guise of caring about their education."

I waved my makeshift ponytail, trying to fan myself and failing miserably. "Your parents care about you—" I started to say, but Roux just laughed.

"Yeah, right."

"But didn't they come home two days ago? Family bonding time, yay!"

Roux pulled her sunglasses down her nose just far enough so that I could see her unamused glare, then pushed them back up. "They left again this morning. Something in Bangkok, I think. Or maybe it was Beijing? Biloxi? I don't know. We went to dinner last night but I was too busy ignoring them to listen to what they were saying."

I looked down at my feet. It was always awkward when Roux talked about her parents. Yeah, mine were unconventional and weird and dorky, but at least they were around. "Well, at least now they won't annoy you all the time," I said, trying to cheer her up. "Maybe I could come over. Slumber party!"

"Mags, I love you dearly, but you are the worst slumber party attendee ever."

"I think you're being a little drama—"

"*Ever.*"

"Why? I'm fun! We watched movies and ate raw cookie dough." Several months ago, Roux had been horrified to discover that I had never had what she called "a normal rite-of-passage experience for every teenager residing in the Western Hemisphere."

"You had to Wikipedia 'raw cookie dough' to make sure that you wouldn't get salmonella."

"It had raw eggs! It was a risk!"

"And you fell asleep at ten o'clock."

"I'm an old soul. We go to bed early."

Roux tried to keep glaring at me, but her grimace collapsed into a smile instead. "Anyhoodle," she said. "We could try having a slumber party, see if you've learned anything. Or, you know, maybe I could hang out at your house instead."

"Roux, it's not exactly the safest place."

"Are you kidding? You have four deadbolt locks and a fingerprint scanner! Your windows are bulletproof! It's the safest apartment ever!"

"Could you not say it so loud?"

"This park is one of the weirdest places in Manhattan," Roux said. "No one gives a rat's ass. Here, watch!" Roux stood up and straightened her dress. "HEY, EVERYONE! THIS GIRL HAS A FINGERPRINT SCANNER! SHE'S A SAFECRACKER!"

"What are you *doing*?" I hissed, yanking her back down on the bench. "You are insane! Legimately insane!"

Roux just gestured out at the summer crowd. "See? No one cares. Except for all the pot dealers." I looked where she was pointing and saw several men scrambling out of the park. "Wow. Who knew they could run so fast?"

"You made your point," I said. "Our loft is super safe, yay. Now all of lower Manhattan is aware thanks to the Roux Broadcasting System."

"Now in stereo," she said, not missing a beat. "So when can I come over?"

I sighed and rubbed my palms on my knees, feeling itchy and nervous all of a sudden. "Roux?"

"Uh-oh."

"What?"

"That's not a good voice."

"All I said was Roux!"

"But you said it ominously. Like, with omin." She grinned when I started to crack up. "I'm serious! The last time you sounded like that, you dropped twelve passports in my lap and then I had to run twenty blocks and jump into a helicopter so a crazypants madman wouldn't kill me." Roux sipped at her Coke. "You can see why I'm wary."

She had a point.

"Well, it's not *that* bad," I began, which got Roux's attention. In the worst possible way.

"Are you on a mission?" she whispered, glancing around us. "Are we staking someone out right now?"

"We don't do stakeouts—"

"No, of course not, of course not. That's for less talented spies. Spies in training, that sort of thing. I've been studying up on it."

"You have?"

"You should see the stack of spy novels by my bed." She sighed. "It's exhausting trying to be well read."

"Roux," I tried again. "I'm not on a stakeout. Calm down."

"Phew. 'Cause I *cannot* run in these shoes, let me tell you."

I shook my head. "Can we just focus, please? We only have a few minutes before we get back to class."

"Let's ditch and go buy night vision goggles."

"No."

"Okay."

"The Collective is accusing my parents of stealing evidence."

Well, that got her attention.

"Really?" She gasped. "Did they do it?"

"No!" I cried. "Of course not! My parents are, like, model spies."

"That sounds like an oxymoron. Why is the Collective saying that?"

"Because I think they're pissed at me for showing a gap in their armor." It wasn't the whole truth, and maybe not even a little bit of the truth, but I wanted to protect Roux as much as I wanted to protect Jesse. They didn't need to know everything.

"You mean when Colton Hooper tried to kill you? They should be thanking you!"

I smiled despite myself. "That's what Jesse said."

"Hell yes, he did! Finally, we agree on something." Roux took the last sip of her Coke, then expertly tossed the bottle ten feet into a recycling bin. "So what's the plan?"

"I'm not really sure. I just need to prove that my parents didn't do it because if the Collective finds them guilty, then we get tossed out." It was terrible to even think about it, the fact that my family and I would truly be on our own for the first time in my life. I was already plenty nervous about whether or not to apply for colleges, and that was still nearly six months away. Being kicked out of the Collective would be like losing the only family I had ever known. And what would my parents do for money? A computer hacker and a statistician with no legal work experience weren't exactly at the top of the job postings on Craigslist.

Roux's voice was small when she spoke again. "If

you get kicked out, does that mean you can't go to Harper anymore?"

"I don't know."

"Well, even if you do, I'll homeschool you." Roux dug her elbow into my side, trying to cheer me up. "I'll give you all my quizzes and homework and I'll let you do the reading, too. No need to thank me!"

"I wasn't planning to."

"I don't like to brag, but I am an *amazing* friend." She slung one arm over the bench and looked around her again. I wondered if she had seen Angelo do the same thing whenever he was out in the city. "And you don't have to tell me if you have a plan. I know you have a plan."

"How do you know?"

"Maggie, you have a plan for everything. You always have your MetroCard ready to go so you don't hold everyone up at the subway turnstiles. You carry your keys poking out of your fist so that you can stab someone if you have to. You do homework every day at the same time—from four to six every afternoon, don't even try to deny it. You keep rain boots in your locker in case it rains. Trust me," Roux concluded. "You have a plan."

I had no idea she paid attention to any of that stuff. Roux was usually so busy talking, laughing, flailing, and demanding that I never thought she noticed anything subtle or sly.

"I don't have a plan," I protested, then added, "yet."

Roux grinned. "That's my girl."

"I just have to prove that my parents didn't do anything," I said. "It can't be *that* hard."

"But what if the Collective tries to stop you from proving it?"

"I don't care what they want!"

"That's the spirit!"

"I'm serious. Even if we get kicked out, at least I'll know that I tried to clear their names."

Roux was quiet for a few seconds before speaking again. "What if they want to stop you, though? Like . . . *really* stop you?"

"Jesse's afraid they might try to kill me."

"Jesse has become my psychic twin. The world doesn't even make sense anymore."

"They're not going to kill me," I told her. "You two are just scarred from the whole Colton Hooper experience. That was the first time you ever experienced something like that. Trust me, run for your life a few more times and you'll be able to tell the good guys from the bad guys."

Roux looked unconvinced, but then her face slid into a slow smile. "Hey, remember when I punched him and broke his nose?"

"How could I forget? You *never stop mentioning it.*"

"Ugh, that was so amazing." Roux threw a few small jabs in the air. "So. Getting back to you and your weird problems."

"They're not weird, they're . . ." I couldn't find a word that described the situation.

"They're weird," Roux said. "Trust me. And honestly, I'm not surprised. I could tell you were getting bored."

"I'm not bored. We live in New York. It's not boring."

"C'mon, Mags. It's me, okay? I know you well. You are

so bored. How could you go from being an international safecracker to sitting in history class, pretending to learn facts about cities you've already lived in? I'd die of boredom and I've never even been anywhere."

"Are you kidding? High school is agonizing! Give me a safe any day!"

"Exactly."

I stopped short as I realized my Freudian slip. "I didn't mean it like that," I said. "I just meant that it's difficult. I'm not bored."

"But it's not what you're meant to do."

The certainty in Roux's voice stopped me and for the first time, I admitted to myself that I was bored. I was *so bored*. I loved Jesse, loved Roux, loved my parents, but nothing changed. The scenery was the same, our house was the same, the risk was the same.

"You spin imaginary locks between your fingers," Roux said gently. "You do it all the time. Stop lying to yourself."

I took a deep breath. I was pretty sure we were way late for our SAT prep class. "If I could have everything at the same time, I would," I told her. "You and Jesse and my parents and Angelo and our house, and then I'd just work nights and weekends."

Roux grinned. "Like Batman!"

"Just like him." I laughed. "Same outfit and everything."

"You definitely need those little pointy ears," Roux agreed. "Okay, then, so what's the plan? What are we doing?"

"We?"

"Duh. Of course *we*. What's Jesse doing? Let me guess, standing around and doing that pouty thing he does? Because that's *always* helpful."

"He does not pout! He just . . . okay, maybe he looks a little pouty every now and then."

"Ha! You knew I was right."

"But it's a *cute* pouty thing! And he's doing nothing and *so are you. Nothing*," I added as she started to protest. "You are both civilians in this one. I'm not dragging either of you back into danger." I didn't tell Roux, but I still woke up some nights gasping for breath, seeing Roux and Jesse run behind me and then disappear into the earth below, falling so fast that I was unable to grab them.

I could feel Roux's glare even from behind her sunglasses. "Are you being serious right now?"

"Stone cold serious. Wait, is that a wrestler's name? It sounds like a wrestler."

"You're just going to solve this whole thing by yourself?"

"That's pretty much the plan, yeah."

Roux sat very still for a moment and I steeled myself for the outburst.

Sure enough, I was right.

"That's the stupidest thing you've ever said!" she cried. "So what, you're going to go do your job without Jesse and especially without *me*? What am I supposed to do then? Do you think I *like* reading all those spy novels? If I have to read the word 'Moscow' one more time, I'm going to smother someone with a babushka!"

"It's too dangerous!"

"I know! If Angelo hadn't saved us, you'd probably be dead! We'd *all* probably be dead! I know about danger!"

"No, Roux, you don't. Sometimes people are psychopaths, okay? I have a talent, I have a gift, and I've been trained since I was a little kid. I made a huge mistake by dragging you and Jesse into it last year, I know that, and I will *not* do it again. You deserve better."

Roux sat back against the bench and looked very, very small. "So you go off and do your job and I stay here and do what?"

"You go to school," I told her. "You apply to colleges. You harass Harold! Do whatever it is you enjoy doing! You *love* talking to Harold!"

It might have been just the sun, but I thought for a split second that I saw Roux's lip tremble. "Do you have any idea what it's like?" she said in a near whisper. "What it was like before you came here? Those girls hate me." She pointed over toward our school, which was only a few blocks away. "They *hate* me. I made one mistake and they won't let me forget it. Have you even *noticed* that you're still my only friend? You *know* what they say to me, Maggie. How many different ways can you call someone a slut? Because I think they're trying to set a world record."

Now I knew it wasn't the sunlight. Roux's lip really was wobbling.

"My parents were home for two days and they took me to dinner and talked about themselves," she said. "They asked about school and about friends and didn't listen to any of my answers. Then they taped a note to the refrigerator door this morning and left a thousand dollars cash for emergencies. They don't care about me at home and they hate me at school. The only place I can go where someone doesn't try to shut me down is your house."

I sat dumbfounded. I had thought that nearly everything rolled off Roux's back, that she didn't care what anyone thought of her. She never even blinked when someone in the hall threw a slur in her direction, but I guess if you fire a bullet at someone enough times, eventually they learn not to flinch.

And it made sense now, too, why she thought our loft was safe. Even without the bulletproof windows and high-tech entrance pad, it was still the safest place she had.

"No, it's fine," she said when I tried to reach for her, and she slipped a finger under her sunglasses to wipe at her eyes. "It's cool. I think . . . I think I'm just going to ditch the rest of the class, if that's okay with you."

"I can ditch with you," I offered. "I mean it. We can do something. Do you want to get a manicure?"

She smiled a little. "You're a good friend. But I think I want to be alone for a while. Gotta get used to it again."

And before I could stop her, Roux turned and walked away in the opposite direction of our SAT prep class, not even turning around when I called her name.

CHAPTER 8

And then she just walked off. She just left me alone sitting on a bench like one of those people who feed pigeons and I feel awful."

"Uh-huh."

"Are you even listening?" I stopped walking and turned to Jesse in the middle of the street.

"Of course I am!" He held up his hands in mock-surrender. "Roux left you in the park and you turned into a pigeon. See, crystal clear."

I tried not to smile but my mouth gave me away. "You're horrible."

"I think you mean *hilarious*." Jesse looped his arm over my shoulders as we started to walk again. We were going to Joe's in the West Village for iced coffee and some much-needed catch-up time. I had spent the two days since Roux's outburst researching everything I could about the 1933 double-eagle gold coin, Saint-Gaudens, and Dominic Arment. I also kept working on the lock that Angelo had given me, but I was no closer to cracking it. Jesse had spent those same two days in soccer practice and, after his dad found out that he hadn't done any of his summer reading yet, poring over *The Poisonwood Bible* and *Slaughterhouse-Five*.

Both things were excellent cover-ups for the fact that we weren't really talking. I mean, we were talking. We just weren't . . . *talking*.

"So Roux was upset and left you alone in Washington Square Park."

"Yes," I said. "And she didn't answer any of my texts like she normally does."

"What do you mean?"

"She usually sends lots of emoticons and emojis and exclamation marks. If she could text *actual* fireworks, she probably would."

"Well, I'm really glad now that Roux never texts me. Okay, I'm sorry, I'm sorry," Jesse said, grabbing my arm and reeling me back as I started to stalk away. "Sarcasm off, okay? I'm listening."

"No, you're placating me." I stood on the sidewalk as he held my wrist. "There's a difference."

"Yes, in the spelling. I'm sorry things are weird now between you and Roux."

I was not feeling particularly charitable, though. I had spent two days doing ridiculous amounts of research, but without the Collective's resources, it felt like walking on a tightrope without a net. My eyes hurt from the computer screen, my neck was all wonky from leaning forward to stare at the screen, and now I wasn't even sure how to talk to my best friend.

"No, you're not sorry," I told Jesse.

"Now you're pouting."

"Am not."

He smiled, the corners of his mouth quirking a little. "It's pretty cute. Wanna stamp your foot, too?"

"Yes. Into your crotch."

He drummed his fingertips against the inside of my wrist, making me shiver a little. "You're cheating," I said. "You can't do that. I'm mad at you."

He raised an eyebrow. "Am I? Is this cheating, too?" He started to pull me to him and gently pressed his mouth against my shoulder, working his way up my neck.

"*Such* a cheater," I murmured. "Okay, stop, stop," I added when he started to kiss the spot just under my ear, the spot that he knew made me crumble faster than anything. "Jesse, seriously, we're on the street. That guy by the fruit stand is staring at us."

He gave me one last kiss before pulling away reluctantly. "Forgiven?"

"Perhaps. On one condition: you buy the coffee."

"All men should be so lucky to have these terms," he replied, then took my hand and laced our fingers together.

It was all I could do not to bury my smile against his shoulder.

At the coffeehouse, Jesse waited in line while I reserved a space for us on the bench outside. The city was teeming with people and kids and dogs and I watched from my perch, knees drawn up to my chest.

That's when I saw the man again.

He was the same one who had been watching Jesse and

me from the fruit stand. At the time, I had thought he was just a creeper, but he circled the block twice in front of Joe's, walking with purpose, but not enough to seem noticeable, a newspaper tucked under his arm. Black T-shirt, black jeans, Converse sneakers, nothing distinguishable.

Which, in New York City, made him very noticeable to me.

When Jesse came back outside with our coffee, I stood up. "Let's walk instead," I said, holding on to the crook of his elbow. "We don't get enough exercise."

"What are you talking about? I have soccer practice three hours a day. And we never get to sit on the bench. Someone's always parked here. Remember the time that Philip Seymour Hoffman wouldn't leave?"

"It's really nice out. C'mon, late summer, the heat wave is over. Let's stroll." I had clearly been spending way too much time with Angelo, but there was no way I was going to be a sitting duck while some suspicious guy orbited around me.

Jesse eventually agreed (not before giving me a huge, world-weary sigh, though), and we headed west on Waverly, exactly the direction that the man had headed in not two minutes earlier. "So," Jesse said, handing me my iced coffee. "Have you talked to Angelo lately?"

"I have," I said, trying to keep my voice light. "He says hello."

"Oh, cool, cool. Tell him I said hi." I could tell that Jesse was putting the same amount of effort into keeping his voice light, too. "How is he?"

"Fine."

"Good." Jesse cleared his throat, then took a sip of his blended drink. "Did he, um, say anything? Like, interesting or useful?"

I glanced up at Jesse. "You are terrible at this."

"We can't all be spies, Mags," he said. "I'm trying my best here."

I laughed with him as we both crossed the street. "Yes, Angelo did have something interesting to tell me. And no, I can't tell you."

"Damn."

"That's why Roux got upset. Because I wouldn't tell her anything. See, you *weren't* listening!" I playfully slugged him in the shoulder and he pretended to wince.

"Nothing, though? We're pretty trustworthy, right? We've proven ourselves."

"Of course I trust you." I sipped at my coffee as I dodged an open restaurant basement door. "I just don't want you to know anything because it makes you liable."

"You mean like if we get tortured for information?"

I stopped dead in my tracks. "Jess, don't even joke about that."

"Are you serious? That could really be a thing?"

I didn't want to think about the boatload of problems that could have happened if Jesse and Roux had too much information. "Look," I told him. "It's not that I don't want to tell you, okay? Believe me, I want to tell you everything. I just don't want to risk anything. Last time was . . ."

"An aberration?" Jesse offered.

"Yes. Wow. Good word."

"It's all that summer reading."

"Well, either way, it's not happening again. I'm not letting anyone shoot at you, chase you, or even—"

But I stopped myself when I saw the same man walk down the other side of the street. It was official: he was walking in circles. Large circles, to be fair, but circles nonetheless.

"Let's go this way instead," I told Jesse, spinning on my heel and making a sharp right onto Grove Street. "View's better."

"Why? What'd you just see?"

"Nothing."

"Maggie? I may be a bad spy, but you're a *terrible* liar."

I rolled my eyes, but he was right. Everyone said so. "I just thought I saw someone."

"Someone like . . . ?"

"I just thought someone was tailing me. Or us. Probably me. I don't know. He's been walking in circles for the past five minutes."

Jesse looked around us, which I thought was pretty cute of him. "What does he look like? Do you want me to kick his ass?"

"Oh my God, *no*. Definitely no ass kicking allowed. C'mon, look, there's a bookstore. Let's go inside and see if he follows."

"What if he does, though?"

"Then we pull the fire alarm and I'll go for his knees while you slam him in the face with a fire extinguisher."

"Really?"

"Of course not. See?" I added, poking him in the ribs. "I'm not such a bad liar after all."

I led Jesse toward Three Lives & Company, where we went inside and hovered near the front windows for a few minutes. I kept my eye out for the guy while Jesse thumbed through the fiction section. "More required reading." He sighed. "Do you see anything?"

"Nope," I said, resting one hand on an enormous atlas so I could peer down the street. "I guess it was a false alarm." I wasn't sure if it was or not, but I didn't want Jesse to think otherwise.

"You sure?"

I turned to him and smiled. "Absolutely. Jumpy girl here, I guess. And you can't be too careful."

"Hmm" was all Jesse said, but he picked up my hand off the atlas and ran his thumb over my knuckles. "Hey, I wanted to ask you something."

"Shoot."

"Spy humor. I get it." Jesse didn't exactly look amused as we left the store. "Anyway, my mom's going to be in the city on Friday night. Do you still want to go to dinner with us?"

I could tell from the apprehension on Jesse's face that this was a Big Deal. "Sure," I said. "Of course, I'd love to. Why is she coming back into the city?"

Jesse took a deep breath. "She's thinking about moving back here."

"Jesse!" I squealed before I could help it. "That's amazing! Oh my God, you must be so happy!" I reached up and flung my arms around his neck, hugging him tight. "Does your dad know?"

"I'm not sure. They're not getting back together or anything, but she said last week that she was really missing it here." Jesse's eyes were sparkling a little and I knew how happy he must have been. He didn't talk about his mom very much, but I knew how much her leaving last year had hurt him. It's the words he didn't say that always told me how he felt.

"So you'll come?" he asked. "Seriously?"

"Of course! Even if I'm followed by a thousand creepers, I'll be there! They can't stop me!"

Jesse untangled my arms from his neck and held me out to stare at me. "Please, Maggie, don't bring the creepers with you."

"Okay, no creepers."

"You're sure you're cool with this? I know you've got a lot going on, what with your parents and everything."

"You," I said, poking him in the chest, "are important to me. Yeah, things are crazy right now, but I can handle this. This is all going to be solved and wrapped by the time school starts, trust me. And I'm a spy but I have to eat, too, right?"

"Right," Jesse said, then kissed my nose. "I love you, you know that?"

"Of course you do. I can kick your ass."

He smiled against my mouth and this time, I didn't care who was watching us.

CHAPTER 9

My parents were making dinner when I got back to the loft that evening.

"Thanks, Jeeves," I said to the fingerprint scanner as it let me through the front door.

"Who's Jeeves?" my dad called from the kitchen, where he was chopping onions and getting ready to probably wreak havoc.

"Dad, it's still too hot to cook," I protested. "This is going to be something that you can prepare in the freezer, right?"

"Nope," he replied. "Who's Jeeves?"

"Our fingerprint scanner. I decided to make friends with him."

"Him? How do you know it's a man?" my mom asked. She was attempting to do the *New York Times* crossword puzzle, which inevitably ended with her crumpling it up and tossing it into the recycling bin while muttering that she doesn't need a newspaper to make her feel illiterate, *thank you very much.*

"Because it's cold and impersonal and never asks how I am?"

She grinned. "That's my girl."

"Hey!" my dad protested. "Sensitive male standing right here! Look, I'm actually crying while talking with you, that's how hurt I am."

"It's the onions," my mom and I chorused.

"Perhaps. Hey, don't toss that crossword puzzle. Save it for me."

"So," I said, sitting on a barstool so I could supervise my dad (and possibly get to be a taste tester). "Can I ask you two a question?"

"Of course," my mom said, leaving the crossword puzzle behind. "Is it about today?"

"Kind of," I admitted. "I just saw Jesse."

My parents exchanged a glance that I'm sure they thought I didn't see. They're so adorable that way. "Did you tell him about our new developments?" my dad asked.

"Yes," I admitted. "He needed to know. I can't lie to him again, you know that." I drew a heart with my finger on the concrete countertop. "How did you two meet?"

This time, they didn't even try to hide their shared look. "Well," my dad started to say.

"It was a long time ago," my mom interrupted him. "Details are fuzzy."

"Are you serious?" I scoffed. "C'mon. I remember the very first time I saw Jesse and I'm not even married or pregnant with his baby."

Major, major tactical error.

"Why are you thinking about *pregnancy*?" my dad cried.

"Is *that* what you want to talk about?" my mom screeched.

"Oh my God, no!" I screamed, putting my hands over my eyes. "I was just talking about how you two are married and had me and, ugh, can we please not talk about sex? I think I'm having an aneurysm."

"You think *you're* having an aneurysm?" my dad muttered. "Am I going to need a drink for this conversation? Just tell me now."

"I just wanted to know how you two met!" I said. "That's all! Wow, this went *so* wrong, *so* fast."

I had never heard two sighs of relief as loud as my parents'.

"Much better topic," my mom said, smiling.

"Cancel my martini," my dad added with a weary grin.

"And, like, how did you know you were in love? And how did you know you wanted to be together forever and have me and still be spies and not sacrifice your careers for love, and I guess I'm just confused how you do all this and still love someone."

My parents stared at me before my dad finally spoke. "Is it too late to reorder that martini?"

"I take it Jesse's not exactly thrilled by 'all this,'" my mom said gently while getting a beer out of the refrigerator for my dad.

"Not really," I admitted. "But I have to do it. Was this what it was like when you first met? Were you both spies way back then?"

"Way back then?" my dad repeated. "How old do you think we are?"

"You didn't even have DVRs back then. Or cell phones."

My dad took a swig of his beer in response.

"Your dad and I," my mom said, shooting him a look, "met in Paris. In high school."

"In high school?" I cried. "You were my age?"

They both nodded.

"We were both at boarding school," my dad said. "We were juniors, and your mother did a science project about this thing called the Internet, and I was smitten." He winked at her. "I still am."

She grinned and reached across the table to clasp his hand. "And your dad asked me out in Swahili. I thought it was so romantic."

"Wait, wait, *waaaaait* a minute. Let's back it up a continent. You met in school?"

"Boarding school," my dad clarified. "We were both on merit-based scholarships. I saw your mother in the computer lab, and that was it." He pretended to flutter his eyelashes at her. "It was love at first byte. Get it? B-Y-T-E?"

"That is so cheesy," my mother said, but she was blushing and there is nothing more weird than watching your parents flirt, ugh.

"So then what happened? Did you both want to be spies?"

"We were recruited," my mom said. "Angelo was teaching a course in New World architecture, and he noticed both of our records, and he introduced us to the Collective."

"Angelo knew you as teenagers? Hold on, my brain is exploding."

"Why do you think he's always taking you all over the

city?" my dad asked. "Everywhere you go is an architectural landmark. He loves it."

"So what did you do in Paris?"

My parents looked at each other again. "Watched movies." My mom shrugged. "We watched movies all the time. Explored the city. Went in some of the underground tunnels. Studied hard in school. Maybe kissed a few times."

My dad wiggled his eyebrows.

"Stop, stop, stop!" I said. "Innocent child present here."

"And then after we graduated from high school, we just joined the Collective and that was that," my dad said, adding the chopped onions to the hot oil already in his pot. "Our life was set."

"That was that?" I repeated. "I feel like you just skipped a bunch of stuff."

"We joined the Collective and then had *you*," my dad added. "Exciting times. Sleepless times. It's all a blur."

I thought for a few seconds. "Is that why you never mentioned Dominic Arment?"

My parents both stopped what they were doing and looked at me. "Angelo?" my dad guessed, and I nodded.

"I just think it's weird you knew someone from so long ago and you never mentioned them to me." I wasn't looking at either parent now, choosing instead to trace patterns onto the countertop with my finger. "Why?"

"Dominic wasn't—well, he isn't, I guess I should say, someone who works like us. He's always been a little shady." My dad stirred at the onions before they started to burn. "He was always trying to figure out how to monetize the Collective, how we could make money by doing our jobs."

"I feel like you're not telling me everything," I said. "Like there's more I should know."

"Do you tell Jesse and Roux everything?" my mom asked.

"No," I admitted.

"And why is that?"

I rolled my eyes, knowing what she was getting at. "Because I want to protect them in case someone wants to get information from them," I sing-songed.

"Exactly."

"So you and Dad are trying to protect me?"

"Your interrogation skills are really weak," my dad said, tossing a dishrag at me. "You get information when you need it. Here, dry these dishes."

"Were you and Mom drug smugglers or arms dealers with Dominic or something?" I shot back, ignoring the dish towel. "You're both orphans. Do you have a secret past?"

My parents looked at each other, but I could tell they were amused, not concerned. "*You*'re our secret past," my mom pointed out. "Our little safecracker that could."

I rested my chin on my fists, thinking about that. "You're so lucky," I said. "You were both spies from the beginning. You didn't have to compromise anything."

"There's always compromise," my mom said. "We compromise all the time. For example, I don't like onions."

"And I don't like hearing about how much your mother doesn't like onions." My dad winked at both of us.

"But did you ever want to leave the Collective?" I asked them, now drawing figure eights on the countertop. "Ever?"

There was a pause before my mom spoke up. "We were going to leave after we had you," my mom said. "We didn't think it was the best way to raise a child."

"Are you serious?" I asked, now sitting up straight. "Because of me?"

My dad nodded. "But when you were three, you opened that Master Lock that had been lying on the floor. We were amazed. I mean, our jaws dropped. You had this gift from the very beginning, and you were so talented. You *are* so talented," he amended. "If you were a gifted ballerina or sculptress or mathematician, we would've done everything we could have to foster your talent. It just so happened that your gift is in locks and safes. So we decided to stay."

I couldn't believe what I was hearing. "So if it wasn't for me, you would have left?"

"No. We stayed for you." My mom covered my hand with hers. "Would you really have been happy living a normal life? Going to school, to playdates, living in the same place?"

I squirmed on my barstool. It was like she knew how I had been feeling for the past year, living as a normal teenager instead of a spy. It was hard to admit even to myself, but I felt an itch that I couldn't scratch, a need that wouldn't go away.

"I don't know," I admitted. "But I'm glad I don't know. I like our life, if that makes sense. It's been fun."

"Except for when Colton tried to kill you," my dad muttered.

"Well, yeah, that wasn't fun, but we won," I told him.

"Everything always works out, right? I mean, if you two could meet in Paris as teenagers, anything's possible, right?"

My parents both paused before bursting out in laughter.

"Thank you so much, Maggie," my mom said. "Really, thank you."

"You are so young," my dad added. "So very, *very* young."

"I'm seventeen!" I protested. "I'm practically an old woman!"

My parents fell over in further hysterics.

"Well, this has been illuminating," I huffed, hopping off my stool and going toward my bedroom. "Your onions are burning, by the way."

But when I looked back, I saw my parents kissing over the countertop as the onions smoked around them.

CHAPTER 10

The next morning was Tuesday, which meant yet another day of SAT prep class with Roux. I half considered blowing it off, but then I remembered it was the last one of the session. And also, if I didn't go, my parents would ask why I wasn't going, and I'd have to explain that things were weird between me and Roux, then they'd want to *talk* and I didn't really feel like *talking*.

I wish there was a way for my parents to know what was wrong without me having to tell them. That would make my life *so* much easier.

I dragged myself over to the Main Building at NYU, where the classes were being held, and settled myself toward the back of the classroom, a few minutes late and cranky with lack of sleep. I had spent yet another night holed up in my room, working on the lock that Angelo had given me, still no closer to solving it, while I waited for Roux to call me so we could talk.

The phone never rang. The lock never opened. I went to bed and never slept.

Roux was in the middle of the room, a few rows in front of me, her head bent over her travel chess set. Her cheeks were flushed, and I could tell she was actively not looking at me, her hands balled into fists in her lap.

The teacher (some teacher's assistant that was clearly in it for the summer cash) blathered on at the front of the room about analogies. "Up is to down as light is to . . . ?" he droned. No one responded, even though it was one of the easiest questions imaginable: half of us were surreptitiously tapping away on our phones under the desks and the other half was too shy to answer.

Well, except for me. I was too annoyed. Like, what difference did this really make? Would taking the SAT have any effect on my life, or anyone else's? What does it even matter if someone's good at analogies? How on earth did this become the basis by which intelligence was measured? This, I decided, was why the world's economy was crumbling. Because of stupid standardized tests!

Like I said, I hadn't had much sleep.

"Um, Roux? Roux Green?" The TA was consulting a seating chart as he glanced up at Roux. He pronounced her name like "row," which nearly made me wince. Her head was still down, no doubt planning her next well-strategized move, and I wasn't talking about chess, either.

"You clearly took Spanish in high school," she said, not bothering to look up.

"Excuse me?"

"It's pronounced Roo. Not Row. Anyone with fifteen minutes of French lessons could have told you that. Guess you missed that question on *your* SAT." She still hadn't looked up.

The TA looked flustered as I bit the inside of my cheek and tried not to laugh. I could do a lot of things well, but no one shook up a room like Roux. "Do you have an answer for our question? Maybe you could text someone for the answer?"

Bad move, TA guy, I thought. *Bad, bad move.*

"I'm not texting, I'm playing chess. A knight on the rim is grim, as you know." I had heard Angelo say that several times before about their games, but I had no idea what it meant.

"And as light is to dark," Roux continued. "A chipmunk could have answered that. Those student loans must be pretty hefty for you to take this crap job, huh? Maybe if you had done better on your SATs you could've gotten a scholarship."

This was the old Roux I had first met last year: the one that struck like a cobra in order to keep people from hurting her first. Several other kids were staring at her, goggle-eyed, and one girl leaned over to her friend and whispered into her ear. The second girl glanced at Roux and giggled.

I know I wasn't the best at being a teenager, but I knew that giggle was a mean one. They were gossiping, and I saw the tips of Roux's ears go red.

"She's just cranky because people are being mean to her on Facebook," another girl chimed in, and I could feel my chest getting tight. "Aren't they? Poor Rouxsie. Nobody loves her. Not even Mommy and Daddy."

It was like the air went out of the room, and in the absence of sound, Roux swept her bag up into her arms and stormed out, the desk chair squeaking on the floor and cutting through the tension in the room. I didn't know who those girls were—I was pretty sure they didn't go to our school, either—but they knew Roux.

And that was definitely not a good thing.

"Roux!" I called, grabbing my own bag and running after her. "Roux, c'mon!"

She was way ahead of me, though, not running but not walking, and I had to race to catch up to her. "Stop!" I told her. "Would you just stop already!"

"Leave me alone!" she cried, whirling around, her hair flying like a veil around her head as she spun. "You already made it clear that things are changing, okay? Don't try and act like they're not."

"Roux, things are changing but it doesn't mean—"

"That we can't still be friends? Is that what you were going to say? Face it, Maggie, you and Jesse and me, we're all on borrowed time here. You're not going to stop being a spy for anyone. This is who you are."

"I can be more than just . . . than just *that*," I said. "I can be more than one thing at the same time. Everyone is."

"Really? So you think you're going to graduate and go to college and never once track down a bad guy for the rest of your life?" Roux looked doubtful. "C'mon. That's the stupidest thing I've heard in a long time, and I've heard some really, *really* stupid stuff lately."

I wondered what the Facebook post had said about her.

"Look, Maggie." Roux took a deep breath and let it out slowly, pinching the bridge of her nose, and I realized that she was trying hard not to cry. "Before you got here, I was alone, and if you leave, that's what I'll be again."

"Roux—" I started to protest, but she cut me off.

"I'm not saying that to make you feel guilty or whatever, but it's true, and you know that." Her phone chimed and she glanced at the screen, her face falling. "Another Facebook update," she muttered. "Great."

"Roux, things are changing but it doesn't mean it's a bad thing," I told her, trying to distract her from the screen. "It's not like I'm going to leave tomorrow and never see you or Jesse again.

"I'm late for tae kwon do," she said. "I'll talk to you later, okay?"

And before I could say anything, she had slipped out the door and disappeared into the crowds outside.

"Crap," I muttered, running my hand through my hair. There was no way I was going to go back into that classroom and I didn't want to go home, so I walked up the street to Dean & Deluca, settled myself at a window table, pulled that wretched lock out of my bag, and did what I do best.

I got to work.

Several hours later, I had made a teeny-tiny bit of progress on the lock, almost managing to open the third keyhole before my grasp slipped and it clicked shut. I sat up and sighed, frustrated and somewhat bleary-eyed, and that's when I saw Angelo's card taped to the window outside. I saw what looked like a pen-and-ink drawing on the back, etched along the embossed *A*.

I seriously don't even know how he manages to be so sneaky.

When I got my stuff together, went outside, and plucked the card off the window, I saw a sketch of a stone castle with arched windows and crumbling turrets, surrounded by water and trees.

Belvedere Castle at Central Park.

"Great," I muttered to myself, then started hiking toward the 6 train at Astor Place.

If you ever go to Belvedere Castle, here's a good tip for you: it has a lot of stairs. Do some calf-building exercises beforehand or find an amazing Sherpa to carry you.

I hoped Angelo had a good reason for bringing me here, other than just his love of architecture and old stones. Surely we could have found some old stones closer to downtown.

It took me a few minutes to find him and when I did, my breath caught in my throat. I wasn't sure if it was a good reason, but it was definitely something.

He sat at a small wooden table, a chessboard open in front of him and the pieces strategically arranged. His brow was furrowed like it always was whenever he was deep in thought, but his eyes looked calm and passive. "Ah, careful, careful," he said as his opponent started to move her knight. "Remember, darling: a knight on the rim is grim."

His opponent, however, was anything but passive.

"Why do you keep *saying* that?" Roux demanded as I crept closer, her back to me. "You always say that, Angelo, and I have no idea what you're saying and you're driving me crazy but at the same time, I also want to *be* you and it's infuriating. Ugh." She hadn't let go of the knight yet, her index finger balanced on top. "Is this what trash talking is in chess? A lot of platitudes about knights and grimness?"

"Why, hello there!" Angelo replied cheerfully, looking up at me, and Roux spun around in her seat, eyes red and swollen. It sort of hurt to look at her. "Imagine meeting you here, Maggie, in this castle of all places."

I held up his card between my fingers. "Yes. Imagine that."

Roux whirled back to look at Angelo. "You're a liar," she accused. "You said you wanted to play chess!"

"And yet here we are, playing chess," he replied smoothly. "I would hardly call that a lie." His voice never changed tone or texture, which I knew must have been driving Roux up a wall.

"But you didn't say she was going to be here, too!"

"She?" I said, coming around to stand next to the table. "You know my name. I'm standing right here."

Roux pushed her sunglasses up her nose and started to gather her bag. "Well, this was great fun. I must be going."

Angelo put a hand on her arm and she instantly softened. The two of them, I suddenly realized, were more alike than different. Headstrong, independent . . . and often alone. I wondered what they had talked about before I showed up.

"Listen, my love," Angelo said. "You and Maggie are the best of friends. You have shared many adventures together. You are privy to a great many of our secrets. Friendship doesn't care about geography."

Roux crossed her arms and glared at the chessboard.

"Now sit." Angelo beckoned me over and stood up, giving his seat to me. "I'm going to go buy some water and be back in five minutes. You two should talk."

"There's nothing to talk about," Roux huffed.

"Really? I find that hard to imagine. You always seem able to chatter about something. Little magpie, you are." Angelo tapped her on the head as he walked away, leaving Roux and me in a heavy, leaded silence.

"Sooo," I said, picking up one of Angelo's pawns. "So."

"Yeah. So. And put that down, you're screwing with the game."

I set it down, then picked up the queen just to annoy her.

"I know what you're doing," she said, glaring at me with narrowed eyes. "I invented this game."

"Chess? You're older than you look."

Roux opened her mouth, closed it, sat back and crossed her arms, tapped her foot three times, then opened her mouth again. "I meant manipulation," she said. "And *maybe* I overreacted, okay? I know that must come as a complete surprise to you, seeing as how I never overreact about anything at all, ever."

I rolled the queen across my palm, wiggling my eyebrows at her as she started to get infuriated.

"What are you—? Stop that, put it—! Oh my God, you

have no respect for a classic game of mental warfare, do you? This is just *disrespectful*!"

I set the queen down in the wrong square, then smiled as Roux snapped it back into place. "Roux," I said. "You can't just end our friendship because something *might* happen to it. I won't let you, because that's what friends do."

Roux let out a long, low sigh, then took her index finger and knocked over the king piece. We both giggled. "I hate that guy," she said. "He just stands there and doesn't do anything while the queen hustles all over the board. Useless." When I didn't say anything, she kept talking. "I feel really bad. Ask Angelo. I told him everything."

I looked to where Angelo was standing near a soda vendor, checking his phone. "You did?"

Roux nodded. "I didn't have anyone else to talk to."

Ouch. That hurt.

"It's just weird to not know things about your life," she continued, not noticing my wince. "Like, friends share everything, right? At least we do. And we did all that safecracking together—"

I couldn't help myself. "We?"

"You know what I mean. And now it's like you're about to do something cool again and I'm going to be left out." She shrugged her shoulders and looked really small. "I hate being left out. It sucks."

"It does suck," I agreed, thinking of all the places I had lived, the homes I had had, all the friendships I could never make.

"So you'll tell me?"

I had to laugh. "No. But if it makes you feel better, I didn't tell Jesse, either. And he wants to know just as bad as you do." That last part wasn't entirely true, but what Roux didn't know wouldn't hurt her.

"Well, good, because if you tell that buffoon and not *me*, I will wreak havoc." She sat back in her seat, looking a little smug. "And I can wreak havoc like nobody's business."

"Very aware, thanks," I replied. "And Roux? It's not that I *don't* want to tell you. Angelo's the only person I can talk to about this, too. I know what it's like to feel alone."

"Angelo missed his calling. He should have become a therapist."

"For all we know, he is."

Roux giggled at that. "So can you tell me just one thing about the case?"

"Depends on what the thing is."

Roux leaned across the table, her face very serious. "Do I get to punch anyone in the face this time?"

I laughed. I couldn't help it. "I'll let you know."

Roux grinned, and it felt so nice to have my friend back.

CHAPTER 11

I watched them play chess for a while, then Roux had to go to a massage appointment. "This tension needs to leave my body!" she declared while gathering her bag. "I think I'm getting a seaweed wrap, too. Toxins, begone!" She waved her arm like a sorceress summoning a spell. "Angelo, don't touch that board or this whole game will be invalid and I'll win by default."

Angelo held up his hands in mock surrender. "I wouldn't dream of it, my dear."

She pointed at him warningly, then reached out and hugged his waist. "Thanks," I heard her whisper, and he smiled and patted her shoulder.

"Anytime, darling," he said. "I told you, we always take care of our friends."

After she left, I sank down in her seat and glanced at the chessboard. "It looks the same every time," I told Angelo. "I don't think either of you ever move a piece."

"We dabble," Angelo replied. "So how is Maggie? Your best friend is back, you must be happy about that."

"I am," I said, and I was. "I don't think I'm very good at having friends, though."

"Well, I find that absolutely impossible to believe."

"Some girls were talking about Roux, and I didn't even defend her." It felt good to say that out loud, but I still felt rotten. "What kind of crappy friend does that?"

Angelo was quiet for a moment, rolling the knight back and forth in his palm. (Apparently I had picked up his habit of doing that.) "Sometimes," he said, "it's worth focusing on the bigger picture. You've always been there for Roux, yes?"

"Yes, and she's been there for me."

"So a little misstep is all right. What matters is who shows up when you need them the most."

I raised an eyebrow at Angelo. "We're not talking about Roux anymore, are we."

"No. No, we are not." Angelo set the knight back down and folded his hands primly in his lap. "You should know something."

The hairs on the back of my neck rose when he said that, but I kept my face neutral.

"A few more people have come forward, saying that they were removed from the Collective."

"How many?" I asked.

"Three." Angelo didn't even fidget.

"Can I ask how you're finding this out?"

Angelo glanced over my shoulder, then pushed Roux's untouched water bottle toward me. "Hydrate, please, love. It's quite warm today. And I cannot say. At least, not yet."

Now the goose bumps were traveling down my arms. "How do you know this?"

"It's becoming quite difficult to tell who's a friend or a foe," Angelo murmured.

"Cracks in the Collective armor," I said.

"A bit, yes. But Dominic Arment is definitely a foe." Angelo tapped the water bottle at me, and I picked it up this time.

"Why now, though? Why is Dominic suddenly going all bad guy on us?"

Angelo let out a low, quiet breath. "Apparently, at least according to what I'm hearing, Colton Hooper's death was quite an opportunity for him. Dominic and Colton were enemies—"

"Who wasn't an enemy of Colton?" I pointed out.

"—and after Colton died, Dominic decided to make his move."

"So we killed one bad guy and another one just popped up in his place," I said, feeling defeated.

"Not all bad guys have the same motive," Angelo told me. "To paraphrase Tolstoy, every bad guy is bad in his own way. Dominic has decided he wants to rule the Collective by himself, and if you don't agree, well . . ."

He didn't have to finish his sentence. I understood what he meant.

"Maggie, I'm telling you this because I want you to know something: you only talk to people that I tell you to talk to, is that clear?"

"Of course," I said. "But who am I talking to?"

"No one yet. But if someone tells you they're in the Collective, it doesn't mean they're trustworthy. I'll be the one who decides that."

"What about my parents? Can I talk to them about all this?"

I was only kidding, but Angelo's face stayed somber. "Not unless I tell you."

If I hadn't already been sitting, I would have needed to sit down. "Wait, no, you don't think that my parents are—"

"No, no, darling, sorry. Of course not. But I think that the less information they have, the better. It's safer for everyone."

Angelo had never told me not to talk to my parents about a case before. I knew this was serious. "On a scale of one to ten," I asked, "how much danger are we in?"

"Oh, I'd say a seven, maybe an eight."

"And if I can't break into Dominic's house and find those coins?"

Angelo smiled. "When have you ever *not* been able to pick a lock?"

"Good point. Okay, different scenario: what if I get in and the coins aren't there? Then what?"

"Let's cross that bridge when we get there," Angelo replied, but he said it in a way that made me feel he was convinced the coins were in Dominic's house.

I glanced past the castle walls and looked at the tourists streaming up the stairs. I envied them, their easy lives, and their ability to travel with only one passport, one name, and one identity. "It feels like nothing is happening," I told

Angelo. "I can't open that lock you gave me, I can't go into Dominic's house yet. I don't like this. I want something to *happen.*"

"Oh, my love. Please, whatever you do, be very, very careful what you wish for."

His words hung between us for a minute, neither of us saying anything, then Angelo spoke very softly. "Are you otherwise engaged on Friday night?"

Friday I was supposed to meet Jesse and his mom for dinner, but if I told Angelo that, he would insist I go.

"No, I'm . . . ," I said, my voice equally low.

"Excellent. You can visit Dominic Arment. He has dinner with his wife every Friday night at six o'clock. You'll have two hours."

My dinner with Jesse and his mom wasn't until eight. I could make this happen. If I played my cards right, I could even be early to dinner.

I swear, if they ever give out an award for Best Multitasking Spy, I had better win it.

"I'll be there," I told Angelo.

"You remember the address?"

22 Pomander Walk.

"Of course."

"Lovely. Now, let's move on. You said you can't open the lock. Did you bring it with you?"

"Like a slave," I said, reaching into my bag and pulling the bulky, unwieldy thing out of my purse. "This stupid thing is stupidly stupid."

Angelo tut-tutted at me as he took it into his hands. "How much progress have you made?"

"Not much," I admitted, poking at one of the keyholes. "Look at this. It's impossible. There's four of these holes altogether, with a keyhole on the right and left. The right side opens to a smaller door with two more keyholes, but the one in the middle has to be opened last. And that's all I've got. I can't ever get the last one, and half the time I can't even get the first one to open. Is this really a medieval torture device? You can tell me. I won't breathe a word, I swear."

Angelo smiled ruefully and turned the lock over to glance at it from the side. In his hands, it looked smaller, more manageable. "I don't believe I ever told you where this came from," he murmured. "Did I? I've become an old man, my memory often fails me."

"Oh, stop it. Your memory is fine and you're not old. If you were old, you probably would have fallen on the stairs and broken a hip. And you didn't, so you're fine."

"Your knowledge of the aging process is both frightening and lacking," he teased me, then glanced to his left and right. Anyone else wouldn't have noticed, but I knew he was checking the crowds, looking for new and old faces, making sure all was as it should be. The throngs of tourists were still moving around us, though, and Angelo leaned a bit closer so that he could speak softly.

"This lock," he told me, "is actually from an ancient Greek monastery, Saint Paul's on Mount Athos. Perhaps you've heard of it?"

"I appreciate that, but how often do you honestly think that Roux and Jesse and I discuss ancient monasteries?"

"Excellent point," he said. "Your lack of religious

education aside, the monastery has been around since the thirteenth century. The monks there pray constantly, live in near silence, arise at three in the morning. Very monastic, if you will. It's a shame that they don't allow women to join them. I think you would absolutely love it there."

I smiled despite myself. "Maybe I could take Roux with me, too. Liven the place up a bit."

"Heaven help us," Angelo said, laughing. "But the monks, they also house thousands of religious artifacts and treasures. They're worth millions, perhaps billions."

"There's always money to be made," I murmured, remembering what Angelo had told me last year. "Has anyone ever tried to steal anything?"

Angelo shook his head. "Would you care to guess why?"

I looked down at the lock in his hands. "Oh."

"Exactly." Angelo tapped my nose, then handed the lock back to me. "This is actually just one of a few facsimiles of the lock that guards their most sacred artwork. Only a few monks have access to the keys, and even then, no one can ever have more than one key at a time."

"Sort of like a monk buddy system?"

"I suppose so, yes. This has guarded them against the Crusades, the Nazis, and countless other attempts at thievery."

"How do you know all this?" I asked. "When did *you* become an expert on monasteries?"

"Oh, I have my ways," he replied. "I like to know a little about a lot. I find that it keeps life interesting."

"So you don't have any tips to crack this sucker?" I

asked. "Because this thing is making me insane. I don't like being outsmarted by inanimate objects."

"Yes, you've made that clear over the years." Angelo smirked. "Just keep trying. It will open when you need it most."

I looked at him. "That's it?" I cried. "That's all the advice you can give me?"

Angelo just shrugged. "My love, if I could open locks like *this*, then I wouldn't need you now, would I?"

I just looked at him. "Old man or not, I will seriously break your hip."

He burst out laughing and put his arm around my shoulders. "I can assure you, love, greater people than you have tried before, and all without success."

CHAPTER 12

I didn't sleep at all on Thursday night, too anxious about breaking into Dominic Arment's apartment on Friday evening and even more anxious about the fact that I couldn't tell my parents what I was doing. Ever since my first word, we had always talked about our cases. I had always consulted with them, planned with them, and now I was on my own. Even though they were there, they weren't *there*, and I felt wobbly-kneed and unsure.

Let me tell you, I had a whole new understanding of Roux's predicament with her parents.

All that insecurity, though, just told me what I already knew. I had to find these coins and prove my parents' innocence. Even if the Collective still decided to kick us out, the truth would be revealed.

And I would be the one to hand it to them.

I was so determined that I forgot about one major point: my parents were also spies.

"Where are you going?" my dad asked as I came into the room.

"Roux's, then dinner with Jesse and his mom," I told him. "Roux's helping me get dressed. Something about shoes and not walking like a clod, I don't know." That part was true, at least. Roux had been trying to get me into heels for months and I kept refusing.

But I wasn't going to Roux's.

"Dinner with Jesse's mom?" Now my mom's interest was piqued. "Where are you going?"

"Some sushi place on Bond Street. I don't know, I guess she chose it."

"What time are you meeting them?"

I paused while tugging on my boot. "Is this an inquisition?"

"Why so defensive?" My mom arched an eyebrow.

"You're the defensive one," I shot back. "I'm just trying to put on my shoes."

My dad leaned over so I could hang on to his shoulder and not topple. "You've been staying up late a lot," he replied, trying to sound nonchalant and failing miserably. "Working on something?"

"That lock Angelo gave me. It's insane. It keeps me up worrying about why I can't crack it." Partly true, I consoled myself. I wasn't really lying to my parents.

"Are you sure you're not going out to find these coins?"

Busted.

"I'm going to dinner with Jesse and his mom," I told them. "Call the restaurant and check the reservation if you want."

"You're leaving awfully early, though." My dad was now up and pacing in the kitchen. Never good.

"I told you, I'm going to Roux's! Why are you two suddenly so jumpy?" But I knew exactly why: spies can smell trouble even when they're not involved in it. My parents knew something was up because something *was* up.

They continued to stare at me, both accusing and pleading, and I shrugged my shoulders and hoisted my bag onto my shoulder. "Talk to Angelo if you want to know something," I told them. "He's the one who put me on the silent treatment."

I said it so offhandedly, not even thinking about it, that I didn't even realize why the room had gone quiet. I've done a lot—we're talking *a lot*—of stupid things in my life, but that sentence took the cake. It was like a bomb went off in our kitchen.

"What?" my mom screamed. "He told you what?"

"He can't just order you to do something like that!" my dad hollered. "Where is he? Get him on the phone right now!"

"We are your *parents*—!"

"This is *outrageous*—!"

"HEY!" I yelled, trying to interrupt them. I felt like I should pick up a barstool and use it to keep them at bay, like a lion tamer in the circus. "I told you, take it up with him. But he's right, you two are too close to this. You're too involved."

"Because you're our daughter!" my mom cried. "Of *course* we're involved!"

"Then have a little faith in your gene pool! Remember what happened the last time you didn't trust me? Colton Hooper ended up nearly running me down."

It was a low blow, I admit, but it worked. The tension disappeared as their shoulders sagged, and I felt bad for them. "Just relax," I said. "What are you going to do when I go off on my own? You can't control everything that happens to me. And you won't always get to know everything, either. Is this what college is going to be like? You calling me every fifteen minutes and asking what I'm doing?"

"Yes," my dad said.

"The difference between college and this," my mom added, "is that you won't be risking your life to save ours."

I shrugged and tried to ignore the lump forming rapidly in my throat. "Them's the breaks," I said. "You shouldn't have had a kid who was such an awesome spy. And I told you, I'm going to dinner with Jess. So relax, okay?" I leaned over to kiss my dad on the cheek, then gave my mom a hug. "Watch *Antiques Roadshow* or something. Take a bath. Have some chamomile tea. And don't worry about me."

Because I have enough worry for all of us, I added silently.

"You're going to have to go in blind," Angelo told me. "I don't know whether or not Dominic has surveillance set up and we can't risk it."

"No headset, gotcha," I replied. "You could have mentioned that earlier, by the way."

We were standing in the middle of the Forty-Second Street/Times Square subway station. On an average Monday, it was one of the busiest stations in the city, but on Friday night, it was barely controlled bedlam. We were sandwiched between a violinist playing for change and an opera singer, which kept anyone from overhearing our conversation . . . or their own, for that matter. That opera singer was really hitting those high notes.

"How do we know the surveillance cameras aren't capturing us?" I asked Angelo as he handed me a blueprint. "I'd like to keep my face off of the MTA radar tonight."

"Someone's running interference tonight," Angelo said. "We have approximately three minutes before that camera"—he gestured to one just past my head—"goes back online. Now this," he said, patting the blueprint, "is Dominic's house. Do you have it?"

I stared at it hard for fifteen seconds. "Yep."

"Wonderful." Angelo tucked it back into his jacket. I swear, his jackets were like Mary Poppins's carpetbag. I wouldn't be surprised if one day he produced a hairless cat and a hat rack from his inside pocket.

"Some things to know," Angelo continued. "There is a security code, but we don't know it."

"Excellent news," I drawled.

"You'll have one minute to crack the code before the alarm goes off. If it does go off and we can't infiltrate it and stop the police, you'll have five minutes before they arrive and fifteen before Dominic shows up."

"Good thing I enjoy a challenge. Do we have any idea what the security password is?"

"It changes daily."

I closed my eyes and took a deep breath. *You're fine*, I told myself. *You're the best. You can do this.*

"Don't worry, my love," Angelo said, reading my mind. "You are the best in this business, and everyone knows it."

"Yeah, that's the problem," I said. "*Everyone* knows. Including our enemies."

"Ah, yes, but it keeps them on their toes." Angelo gave me a wink and patted my shoulder. "Always better to chase than be chased."

"Don't I know it."

"Let me know when you're out," Angelo said. "And don't worry, darling. You're like a cat. You always seem to land on your feet."

That was true, but Angelo was missing the bigger point: in order for the cat to land, it first had to free-fall.

I didn't say anything, though, just shook my hands and hopped up and down, a player ready to take the field. I had missed this adenaline rush, the warm sensation under my skin, bringing every sense into hyperalert mode. The opera singer was nearly deafening by now. I could feel the subway's rumble under my feet, the humid subterranean air blowing against my skin. It felt like coming home, and I hadn't realized until that moment just how homesick I had been.

Angelo smiled to see me. "It's lovely to have you back," he said.

"Oh, I never left," I told him, grinning so wide that I felt it in my cheekbones. "Put me in, Coach. I'm ready to crush them."

CHAPTER 13

Pomander Walk was on the Upper West Side of Manhattan, a tiny alley between Ninety-Fourth and Ninety-Fifth Streets. If you weren't looking for it, you could walk right past it. It resembled a little London side street, Tudor-style homes painted in bright colors, surrounded by actual gas lamps and locked security gates. I could see why Dominic had chosen to meet with his mistresses here. Angelo hadn't said whether or not he was British, but you wouldn't have to be an Englishman to appreciate reinforced security on a hidden alley if you were hiding something else, something much bigger than a mistress.

The street was a little busy, nothing too unusual for a Friday night in Manhattan. It didn't matter, though, I knew I could get that lock picked open without anyone noticing. That's the beauty of working in New York: no one will acknowledge anything you do. If I had tried to open that lock with a blowtorch while wearing a Big Bird costume, people would have kept walking by. (Not that I would ever

do that. All those feathers near an open flame? I'd be flam-
béed in ten seconds and definitely earn top ranking in the
Worst Spy Ever contest.)

I pulled a pin out of my pocket and gently started to
scrub at the gears on the inside of the lock. Whatever the
residents at Pomander Walk were paying for security would
have been better spent hiring some Dobermans because the
lock cracked open in less than ten seconds and I slipped
through the gate, looking like just another normal girl on
her way home.

Oh, how looks can deceive.

I knew Dominic's house would be empty, but I glanced
in the window as I crept past, looking for any light or sign
of life. It was dark, though, the only glow coming from the
gas lamp, and I could hear evening sounds coming from
other town houses on the narrow street. Dinner dishes clank-
ing, a baby screeching, a horn in the distance. If that baby
got louder, it would be great, but I knew better than to rely
on an infant for distraction. A crying baby had once kept
my dad from being captured in Milan a few years ago,
though. He still talks about it and my mom and I are like
"WE GET IT ALREADY."

I suspected Dominic's house wouldn't be easy to break
into, and I was right: the lock was way more than just a
standard deadbolt. It had two deadbolts and a paltry lock
that resembled the one on the front gate. Then once I got
through the door, I still had to crack the security system in
sixty seconds before the alarm went off. Apparently Dominic was allergic to dogs so I didn't have to worry about Fido

tearing my leg to shreds, but I knew these locks would keep me busy for at least five minutes. I was lucky that there wasn't a fingerprint scanner like we had at home. Pomander Walk, after all, was supposed to be a quaint residential area, and a fingerprint scanner on the front door would basically be like putting a sign on the house that read: HELLO, THERE ARE VERY SUSPICIOUS THINGS GOING ON BEHIND THESE DOORS! I'm pretty sure the Neighborhood Watch would frown on that.

The first two deadbolts clicked fairly quickly, and I burned through the flimsy lock in mere seconds, but the weight in my bag made me lose my balance for a second and I jiggled the doorknob as I grasped at it in an effort to remain upright. "Crap," I whispered, staying perfectly still for a few seconds just to make sure that I hadn't accidentally started the sixty-second countdown to the alarm going off. I knew I had only one minute and I needed every one of those sixty seconds. My personal best was seven seconds . . . and my personal worst was sixty-one seconds.

I said a quick prayer that I would have a personal best sort of night, then carefully turned the knob and opened the door.

My muscles tensed as I waited for the alarm to start its warning beeps. My heart was racing like a rabbit's, my pulse so loud in my ears, but my hands weren't shaking. They never shake when I'm nervous. It's one of the reasons I'm so good at my job.

I waited a few seconds for the alarm to start beeping, then a few more, but it never did. My heart sped up to a barely manageable pace and I knew something was wrong. Something was very, very wrong. That alarm should have started ticking down. There was no way Dominic would have left the house without setting it, right? He's a professional, a former Collective agent. He wouldn't just leave without setting it because—

Oh my God. He hadn't set it because he hadn't *left*.

Dominic Arment was still in the house.

CHAPTER 14

My brain clicked into survival mode with a surprising amount of speed, considering how long I had been out of work.

Okay. Check to see if anything was weird, different, a little too obvious. Now that my eyes were adjusting to the dimness, I could see a glimmer of light coming from the kitchen and another one from upstairs. If someone wants to trap you, they'll often set up the room so they can grab you fast, take you by surprise before you realize you're even in their trap. There were no trip wires, no laser points zipping across my face, no steel doors falling shut behind me and jailing me inside. Considering I was still standing in the foyer and no one had grabbed or attacked me yet, I was pretty sure that I was the one who had taken Dominic by surprise and not the other way around.

There was a constant shushing sound coming from upstairs, like a waterfall. I stood still and tried to figure out what it was, if Dominic Arment had cleverly decided to

lure me into his house and flood it until I drowned somewhere under the coffee table, when it abruptly shut off.

"Oh, shut *up*," I whispered to myself. All this careful
planning and timing and I had let myself into Dominic's
house while he was in the *shower*?

Well. This wasn't how the job was supposed to go, but
I would have to deal.

I wasn't sure how much time I had before Dominic
came downstairs, so I moved through the foyer and into the
living room. My hair was in a braid that I had tucked down
the back of my black shirt. Wearing it under a hat would
not only be terribly conspicuous but also terribly stifling,
so I had to make do. I had black Frye boots on my feet,
mostly because I hadn't thought Dominic would be home
and wouldn't have to worry about making noise, and I also
didn't want to spend any time lacing up my other boots. I
was wearing the same pair of jeans that I had worn for the
past three days (again, lazy) and my shirt was a plain gray
V-neck. It was a practical getup for prying around in strangers' houses, but it wouldn't work for dinner with Jesse and
his mom, so I had stashed a pair of wedge sandals, a cardigan, and a lip gloss I had "borrowed" from my mom (she
would say "stolen") in my backpack and figured I would
just change in the cab.

Life as a twenty-first-century female spy. It's not easy.

I could hear Dominic humming upstairs, something
vaguely operatic and Italian, and I moved through the living
room, keeping each step as light as possible. Why, oh why,
had I worn Frye boots? If I got out of this situation—when

I got out of this situation—I was definitely going to buy a pair of Repetto ballet flats. Roux could help me, I rationalized. She was good at shopping and price compar—

I came to a halt in the living room. "Oh," I whispered. *"Oh."*

One whole wall of Dominic's living room was covered in shelves, lined with collectibles of all kinds. First editions of books, Depression-era glassware, tiny blue-and-white chinoiserie-style figurines, and what looked like a row of Fabergé eggs. Each shelf held new trinkets, and I realized with grim horror that the coins could be anywhere. It would take hours to go through each book, check behind each shelf for a wall safe, look under each figurine for a secret key or clue.

And I hadn't even gone upstairs yet.

It was hard to tell if any of the walls held actual treasures or if they were all knockoffs, but I didn't have time to start checking because I could hear Dominic's humming moving across the floor and toward the stairs.

More specifically, it was moving toward *me*.

I threw a quick glance around the room, looking over at the dining area and kitchen, trying to find the best hiding spot. I couldn't run out the front door now, and besides, if Dominic left in five minutes, then I'd be stuck outside with no security code and back at square one. Being trapped in a house with a potential madman and a definite criminal was not on my List of Things to Do, but it was better than nothing.

There was a small space between the ceiling and the

wall holding the television. I guess he could have used it for potted plants or other decorative dustcatch-y things, but it was empty. Again, not perfect, but it would have to do.

Dominic started descending the stairs as I silently vaulted off an armchair and grabbed onto the edge of the crawl space, hoisting myself up by my fingers. Roux, I realized as my muscles burned, had been smart about taking up tae kwon do. She probably could have karate-kicked her way up the wall (or whatever it is they do, I don't know one thing about tae kwon do), but I had to settle for wheezing my way into what I now realized was a very small space. I shimmied myself into it so I was lying flat on my back just as Dominic came downstairs, still humming.

I can't lie, the humming was making a bad situation worse. I felt like I was stuck with a large bumblebee. A large bumblebee wearing a lot of cologne. God, Dominic's poor wife and mistress.

I lay flat on my back against the cool drywall, watching my chest rise and fall as I struggled to calm my breathing. *You're fine*, I kept telling myself. *You're totally and completely fine. You surprised him, not the other way around. You're going to get out of here and find the coins and go have dinner with your boyfriend and his mom and it will all be fine.*

Dominic sat down in his chair and picked up the TV remote, turning on the set.

It was *so* not fine.

CHAPTER 15

I lay flat in that tiny crawl space for two and a half hours.

Do you know how I know how long it was? Well, let me tell you.

Dominic Arment, criminal mastermind, potential possessor of ten gold coins worth at least seventy million dollars, owner of potentially priceless antiques, also had *a cuckoo clock collection*.

I thought I was going to lose my freaking mind.

Dominic Arment didn't do much besides watch TV. He got up once to get a drink, but it wasn't enough time for me to climb down and sneak out before he came back. I was stuck, pure and simple. Just me and the cuckoos.

When the birds went berserk at seven o'clock, I started to feel a bit tense. I didn't mind lying still for an hour (I had once spent six hours stuck in a dumbwaiter in Munich, so this wasn't too bad), but I knew that my dinner date was fast approaching. When the cuckoos went off at seven thirty, I felt my heart pick up speed, and when they started crowing at eight, I sighed to myself and looked at the ceiling.

Jesse was going to be so, so hurt. And *pissed*. And *hurt*. And . . . *ugh*.

The only bright spot—and I do mean the *only* one, seeing as how a bird cacophony was scaring me out of my wits every fifteen minutes—was that I had a perfectly sneaky view of Dominic's collection wall. I could see the spines of the books, all of them wrapped in protective plastic covers and faced away from the front window. There was a Faulkner title, a few from Fitzgerald, some Dickens, and even a copy of *Moby-Dick*. I could tell, though, that Dominic wasn't the kind of man who had read the books and bought the first editions because he loved them. He bought them because they were expensive, they were showy. They were things he could hide from his wife so she'd never be able to access them in a divorce. He could show them off to his mistress so she'd think he was well read, worldly.

Every minute that crept by just made me hate Dominic that much more.

The figurines were too far away for me to properly examine, but the Fabergé eggs were closest to me. They really were beautiful, oval and shimmering under the dim light. I had never seen one before, not in all my travels and adventures, and I was disappointed that I couldn't creep over and pick them up and examine them. I wondered how many gold coins it would take to buy one of them, if the coins were already long gone and all that was left were these Russian relics.

The longer I stared at them, I realized that something wasn't right. There was an egg in the row that didn't look quite like the others. It was the same size, but it seemed a tiny bit brighter and bolder than the others. It was a deep golden color, set atop a little wheeled cart pulled by a dark blue figure. It looked bizarre, but no less ornate than the other eggs. From a distance, it sort of looked like a hot-air balloon, and it kept calling to me the way safes call to me just before I break into them. *I have a secret, Maggie. Aren't you just* dying *to know what it is?*

And then the cuckoo clocks went off again, signaling eight thirty, and I almost fell out of my perch.

Apparently they scared Dominic, too, because I heard his glass tumbler suddenly shatter against the floor. "Damn!" he cried, and I stayed absolutely, perfectly, painfully still. He stood up and I could hear him muttering to himself in the kitchen, "Where the hell is the broom?"

This was my chance.

I shimmied out of the crawl space and lowered myself to the floor, trying not to make a sound. (Stupid boots!) There was scotch and glass all over the floor and I leaped over it, nearly losing my balance but righting myself just as Dominic came out of the kitchen.

It's times like this that my brain just shuts off. I don't know how else to explain it. It's like I'm thinking about nothing and my body moves instinctively, going where it needs to go in order to protect me. In a similar way, I do the same thing with Jesse. It's like I know just where to kiss him, when to hug him, almost like we share the same thoughts, the same wants.

I ducked against the staircase, hiding in the shadows as I heard Dominic's shoes crunch into the glass. If he turned, he would see me. If I breathed, he would hear me. All the muscles in my leg were starting to cramp but I bit the inside of my cheek and ignored the pain because there was no way that I was going to be caught in this job and disappoint everyone and ruin my parents' careers. If my boyfriend was going to be angry with me for missing dinner with his mother, I had better have a good reason why I was so late.

Dominic swept up the glass as I crouched not ten feet away from him. I could see only his back, but he looked a bit older than my parents, his shoulders a little stooped and his hair thinning on top. If there's one thing I've learned, it's that criminal masterminds are the most boring-looking people in the world, and Dominic Arment certainly fit that bill.

I spent fifteen of the most painful moments of my life kneeling against that staircase, waiting for the second those cuckoo clocks sounded so I could escape. My heart was racing so fast that I could feel my pulse throughout my body and when I blinked, I could have sworn that I heard my eyelashes tap against my skin. No matter how good a spy you are, you cannot control adrenaline. Your body will always win. All you can do is ride out the rush.

"CUCKOO! CUCKOO!"

"CUCKOOCUCKOOCUCKOO!"

"COOO! COOO! COOO! COOO!"

"HOOOONK!"

I seized the moment and rushed the front door. Dominic couldn't hear my boots on the floor through the incessant noise, nor could he hear the turn of the door, but I knew he'd feel the draft as I shut the door behind me, holding the knob tight in my gloved hands so that it wouldn't click shut. My legs were shaking so badly that I was afraid I'd collapse, but I ducked past the window and vaulted myself out of the gate and around the corner, my lungs taking in huge gulps of air. I knew that Dominic would investigate and I had to get out of there before he came looking for me.

I headed out onto Ninety-Fourth Street, turning on my phone as I did. My breath was still pretty ragged and my legs were going to be sore for days, and when my phone flickered on, I had eleven text messages from Jesse, all variations on the same question:

WHERE R U?????

There was also a missed call from Angelo, which didn't surprise me. He must have heard about the bad intel, but he would never leave that message on my cell phone. Roux had sent her own text message, a photo of her and her doorman, Harold, in the lobby of her apartment building. She had a huge grin on her face, the kind that only meant trouble, and Harold looked like he was praying that wild hyenas would storm through the building and eat him alive. "Harold says helloooooooooo!" the text read.

I called Angelo first.

"Your intel was bad!" I shouted as soon as he answered. Now that night had fallen, the streets were busier than ever and I didn't have to worry about being discreet. To be honest, it felt good to yell. Spending two and a half hours coiled up in a tiny space had left me with too much potential energy and unused adrenaline. I probably could have bounded from building to building like Spider-Man, that's how high I was.

"It was *bad*!" I shouted again, not even giving him a chance to speak. "He was in the house the whole time! *The whole time*!"

"I know, my love. I found out right after you left. I tried to tell you but it was too late."

"And did you know that he has a cuckoo clock collection?" I cried, even though that wasn't really a detail that Angelo needed to know. "He's pathological, Angelo. Who collects those things? A maniac, that's who!"

"Slow down, darling. Are you all right? Did you get—?"

"Of course I didn't get anything!" I turned on Broadway, heading toward Ninety-Fifth Street. The nearby subway station looked vaguely like a spaceship, all sleek surfaces and new design, and I wished that I could just climb into it and fly back in time, back to when things were normal and my family was safe and I knew what I was doing.

"I couldn't get anything because he was in the living room!" I told Angelo. "I got trapped in a crawl space! Who gave you that intel, Angelo? Because they turned on us!"

"I know. We talked about this earlier, love. It's getting harder to tell who's on our side."

"*Why*, though? What's going on?"

"We can discuss later. Did you see anything? Anything weird or different?"

"You mean besides a cuckoo clock collection?"

"Maggie."

I stopped on the corner and rubbed my forehead. I was

exhausted, had a headache, and I knew the night was only going to get worse.

But I had a job to do.

"There's an egg," I said. "A Fabergé egg. It's . . . I don't know if it's fake or real. It just stood out. Dominic has seven of them, but this one is different."

"That's good, that's very good."

"But there's also tons of books and figurines, too. The whole house is like a museum, Angelo. Those coins could be anywhere." Someone jostled my shoulder as they walked past me and I flinched, instinctively turning to protect myself and my backpack.

"And he never saw you leave?"

"I'm sure he felt the air when I opened the door, but no. He didn't see me." I closed my eyes briefly, forcing myself to focus. "Listen, Angelo, I have to go. Jesse's been waiting for me for over an hour. I was supposed to have dinner with his mom and him."

"Wait, Maggie," he said, but I interrupted him.

"No, Angelo. I need. To go. I'll talk to you tomorrow." And then I hung up and yanked out my SIM card before tossing my phone into the trash as I stepped out into the street and raised my arm. A cab sidled to my side, the one stroke of luck I had had all night, and I casually dropped the SIM card on the street as I climbed in and began hurtling toward downtown to find my boyfriend.

CHAPTER 16

It was 9:30 by the time I made it to Bond Street, the sushi restaurant where Jesse had wanted me to meet him and his mom. I was breathless after leaving the cab stuck in traffic and running the last two blocks, shoving my way through crowds of people and throngs of bridge-and-tunnel tourists, and when I got inside the restaurant, I completely ignored the maître d' and stormed into the elevator to take me to the second floor.

It was dark and moody upstairs, the air heavy with the sound of silverware clinking and clattering against plates, the snap of chopsticks echoing right behind. "I'm meeting someone," I said to the second maître d' (seriously, how many do they need?) and went into the dining room.

Jesse was sitting at the table alone, a coffee cup in front of him. The plates had been cleared, a little soy sauce stain on the tablecloth the only evidence that dinner had been eaten, and I came to stand next to him. "Hi," I said. "I am so, *so* sorry."

He looked up at me with angry, hurt eyes. "You missed her. She left to catch her train ten minutes ago."

I sank down into the chair across from him, adrenaline leaving my body with such a *whoosh!* that it felt like it had taken my bones with it. "I'm so sorry," I said again. "I got stuck, I couldn't call. I'm so sorry. Did you have a nice time?"

"No, I didn't have a nice time!" he exploded, and the table next to us glanced over. "You were supposed to meet me here ninety minutes ago! You didn't return any of my texts! I didn't know if you just didn't care or if you were working—!"

"Of course I was working!" I shot back. "Why else would I have missed this? I didn't have a choice, Jess! You think I didn't want to be sitting here with you and your mom instead of being trapped in some guy's house?" I bit my lip, stopping myself from saying too much.

Too late.

"Wait, you went into someone's house while they were still there?" Jesse said. "Do you know how dangerous that can be? You're not invincible, Mags! People could really hurt you!"

"You," I pointed at him, "do not get to tell me about danger, okay? I know. I'm all too aware of how dangerous this is. That's why I can't tell you anything!"

"Your eyes are huge, do you know that? You look like you've been dropping E all night."

"It's just adrenaline," I told him, wondering how disheveled I looked next to all of the other classy diners. "It's fine, it'll go away."

"So you couldn't answer just one text?" he asked, ignoring my response. "Not even one? I even called your parents and they had no idea where you were!"

"You called my parents?" I screeched, and now diners really were paying attention to us. "You know what? We need to go outside. I can't have this conversation in here."

"Fine by me," Jesse said. "I was just getting ready to leave anyway."

We both stormed downstairs, my boots very loud and heavy on the floor compared to all of the high heels, and I was all too aware of my T-shirt and messy hair. I've never been embarrassed by how I looked before, but now I stood out for all the wrong reasons.

The minute we got out on the street, our fight resumed.

"You can't just call my parents!" I yelled. "They don't know about this, either! Oh my God, they're probably freaking out right now."

"What do you mean, they don't know?" Jesse said. "Shouldn't you tell them, Maggie? I thought that was your deal with them! The last time you tried to do something on your own, you almost got all of us killed!"

The air left my lungs. If Jesse had punched me in the stomach, I don't think it would have felt worse than what he just said.

"I'm sorry," he said, his face immediately apologetic. "I didn't mean it like that."

"Yes, you did," I said. "You don't just say something like that and not mean it!" I felt hot tears pricking at the backs of my eyes, but I ignored them. I was too angry to cry. "And I can't tell my parents because this *involves* them, okay? If they knew what I was doing, they would try and stop me and if they stop me, then we're done."

"So you're willing to risk your life and their lives just to be right?"

I took a deep breath, steeling my nerves. "If memory serves," I told him, "you were just fine with me risking my life when I was saving *your* dad's ass. And now that I'm trying to save my parents, you suddenly have a problem with it? Wow, thanks, Jess. Thanks for being such a supportive boyfriend."

I spun on my heel and started to walk away, but Jesse caught up with me in three steps and took my arm to turn me around to face him. "That is not fair—" he started to say, but I cut him off again.

"This isn't about fair!" I yelled. "If this was about fair, then I would be a seventeen-year-old girl having dinner with her boyfriend and his mom, not spending my Friday night squeezed into a crawl space on the Upper West Side, okay? You don't get to talk to me about fair! All you have to do is be normal! I'm the one who has to do all the work here!"

"And you think it's fun to just sit around and wonder if your girlfriend's going to wind up dead or missing?" Jesse yelled back. "You think that's fair? Because it's not, Maggie! It's hell. You're out there doing God knows what and I'm just hanging out. I can't even *help* you and it makes me crazy!"

I pressed my fingers against my eyes, so mad that I wanted to punch something. "This is how it is," I told him, and my voice was so cold that it scared me a little. "You've known this from the very beginning. This is who I am. I can't change and I won't change, especially not right now.

"And if you can't handle it, then you need to go."

I regretted the words as soon as they were out of my mouth.

Jesse's eyes widened in surprise, and then his face smoothed out into something I had never seen before. "That's the thing, Mags," he said, his voice strained and sounding nothing like him. "I can't go. I'm always going to worry about you. Even if we break up tomorrow—"

"You want to break up?"

"No, I'm just saying! Even if we did, I'd still worry about you. I'm going to worry about you for the rest of my life because of this insane job of yours. I can't stand that you're out there risking your life and I can't protect you!"

"Why? Because I'm a girl?"

"No, because I love you!" Jesse suddenly covered his mouth with his hand and turned away from me. His shoulders were bunched together, the tension running down his spine. When he turned back, there were tears in his eyes.

"That's what people do when they love each other, Mags. They protect each other. You looked out for me and Roux, and now you won't let us do the same for you and it makes me *crazy*."

Now the tears were starting to fall and I was too exhausted to try and stop them. "Jesse, wait," I said. "We're both tired. We're both angry. Let's just talk about this tomorrow, okay?"

"When? Can you make time in your busy, world-saving schedule for me? Or do you want to leave me hanging and making excuses to my mom for ninety minutes while you risk your life around town?"

"You didn't tell your mom, did you?" I asked. "Oh, my God, Jesse."

"Of course I didn't!" he cried. "That's what I'm talking about! You can't even trust me and all I've *ever* done is trust you and worry about you and—"

"I can't tell you because it's dangerous!" I exploded. "It's really, really dangerous, Jesse! I shouldn't have even told you and Roux about any of this in the first place, but I did and it was my stupid mistake and now I have to protect you because if I don't . . ." The words stuck in my throat and I couldn't get them out for a few seconds. "If I don't and something happens to you . . ." They were stuck again, not going anywhere this time.

"You don't have to protect me this time," Jesse said, stepping toward me.

"Yes, I do!" I cried. "If you don't have any information, then no one can get it from you. That's what I keep trying to tell you!"

Jesse went quiet for almost a minute as we stood across from each other, both of us trying to catch our breath. He was the first to speak.

"So if you can't trust me and I can't protect you, then how the hell are we going to make this work?"

It's a special sort of pain when someone voices your exact fears, when someone tells you that all the dark thoughts you have about yourself are not only real, but that everyone else can see them, too. It's the sort of pain that drives the tears out of your eyes and shuts down your heart and drops a steel wall in front of it and makes you realize that yes, being alone is terrible, but it will never be as painful as this.

"Maybe we don't," I said, the tears stuck in my throat. "Maybe this is how it ends."

Jesse just blinked. "You seriously want to break up?"

"I don't want to," I said, wiping at my eyes. "I don't know what I'm supposed to do! No matter what I do, I'm going to hurt you!"

Jesse bit the inside of his cheek, his jaw tightening. "Nothing hurts worse than this," he said, echoing my own thoughts.

"Maybe we just need to take a break," I said. "Not break up, but just figure things out."

If a nod could be sarcastic, then that's what Jesse did. "Cool. Fine. Okay." He put his arm up to signal a cab turning the corner, then pulled open the door when it glided to the curb. "Get in," he told me.

"I can hail my own—"

"Just." Jesse took another deep breath and I saw his chin quiver a little. "Just let me do this for you," he said. "In case this doesn't work, let me do one last nice thing for you."

My hands were shaking as I climbed in. We had shared a cab together last Halloween, hauling a very drunk Roux back to her apartment and then heading back downtown after sharing a kiss on an Upper East Side brownstone stoop. It had been our first kiss, and I remembered feeling the cracked pleather seats on the cab ride home, the smell of Jesse's cologne, and the buzzing feeling that I had from kissing someone for the very first time. I had been *in* love with him then, but now it was deeper. Now I loved him.

And I had to let him go.

He shut the door after I got in and I pressed my palm against the window, wondering if I could feel his touch through the glass. He looked away, and I felt my heart sink, but then he wiped at his eyes before pressing his hand up against mine. There was only cold between us, no contact, and when the cab driver pulled away, Jesse's fingers slipped along the glass, leaving tearstains on the window, sending me home alone.

CHAPTER 17

The scene was no less explosive when I got back to the loft.

"Where have you been?" my mom yelled as soon as the fingerprint scanner beeped to let me in. "We have been waiting here, calling your phone—"

"The SIM card in that phone is in pieces somewhere on Ninety-Fifth Street," I told her, then held up my hand. "I cannot fight with you right now. I'm not going to."

"Yes, you are, because we're your parents and we've been in the dark for the past two hours." Now my dad was entering the fray, a small smear of peanut butter on his cheek, a telltale sign of his stress-eating. "Two *hours*, Maggie! We can't even get ahold of Angelo! You need to tell us everything, right now!"

"Can't," I said, opening the refrigerator. I was suddenly ravenous, not having eaten anything since two granola bars at lunch. "You're part of the case, I can't tell you about it. We'd be compromised."

Cue the hysteria.

"We're your parents!" my mother said. "We are not just your assignment!"

I grabbed a yogurt, slammed the refrigerator door, and whirled around. I knew I was being unfair, but it was too late and I was too tired to care. "Angelo's orders," I told them. "He's the only person I can talk to about this."

"Jesse thought you were lying dead in a gutter some-where!" my dad yelled. "And so did we!"

"Well, I think Jesse and I might have just broken up, so don't worry about him anymore," I said, tearing off the lid. It was strawberry-banana flavored, which I personally think is one of the most heinous flavors imaginable, but I was too starving to even notice. "And I'm not dead, obviously, so you don't have to worry about that, either."

"When did you become so flippant?" my dad asked, just as my mom said, "You and Jesse broke up? Why?"

"I don't even know if we *did*," I said, licking the yogurt off the lid and going to find a spoon. "But if we did, it's prob-ably because he's tired of me lying to him. Yeah, that's probably why. Frankly, I'm tired of lying to him, too. It *sucks*. And I became flippant, *Dad*, when I spent two and a half hours stuck in a crawl space while trying to save both of your reputations. You're welcome, by the way. The plea-sure was all mine."

My parents stood there dumbstruck, and to be honest, I felt a little dumbstruck, too. I had never spoken to them like this before. We had never fought like this, this fast and hurtful. It was like the power had shifted and now I was the one in charge, holding information and making decisions. Fighting dirty had apparently become one of my strongest talents, and now I wanted to do it all the time.

The problem with fighting dirty, though, is that it makes you *feel* dirty. I was arguing with the wrong people for the wrong reasons: I was fighting with my parents because they cared about me, I fought with Jesse because he was worried about me, and I was angry at Angelo because of bad intel. But the truth was that I wanted to fight myself. I wanted the two sides of me to clash and only one to win. Either I was a spy or I was a normal girl. I was lashing out at everyone else but in truth, the battle was happening inside me.

And no matter what happened, part of me would end up losing.

"I'm going to my room," I said, very aware of how my voice was shaking.

"No, you're not," my mom said. "What do you mean, you got stuck in a crawl space? Did you walk into a trap?"

"Can't talk about it," I said.

"You *will* talk about it," my dad said.

"No, Dad," I replied, "I can't talk about it. I can't, okay? I just . . ." I took a deep breath that sounded more like a sob. "I want to go to bed. I want to sleep and wake up and figure out what the hell I'm doing, and then we can talk. But I just can't talk tonight because I don't have words for how I feel."

That seemed to hit both of them in different ways. My dad's face softened and he just said, "Okay, baby, we'll talk in the morning."

My mom, though?

"Did Jesse say something to you?" she asked. "Did he hurt your feelings?"

Moms, man. How do they always *know*?

"Mom, this isn't kindergarten," I started to say.

"He did, didn't he. Oh, I knew it. I knew it. Did he say something about you being a spy?"

"Of course he did!" I cried. "What else do you think we argue about? It's the *only* thing we fight about! It's not like you and Dad! At least you two work together and can share information. You didn't have to start off your relationship by lying to each other in Paris. Which, by the way, is still a sketchy story, and I'm really pissed that you won't tell me more about it and about Dominic."

My parents looked stricken. "We don't tell you everything for the same reason that you don't tell Roux and Jesse everything," my dad murmured. "We were keeping you safe."

"Safe from *what*?" I cried. "Does anyone ever just tell the truth anymore?"

I was crying now, really crying, and my dad moved to comfort me, but I stepped back and put out my arm, keeping him at bay. "No, please," I said. "Just tell me the truth or don't do anything."

My mom sank down on a stool at our kitchen island, resting her elbows on the concrete top. "We told you we used to go through the tunnels, right?" she said, and I wiped my eyes and nodded.

"In Paris," I said. "You and Dad."

My dad sat down next to my mom and picked up her hand. "We stumbled across this map when we were around your age," he explained. "It showed all these underground tunnels, so we started exploring, just us and a few other kids from school, and we realized that we could use these tunnels to get into different sites in Paris. We could break into museums or the Pantheon, whatever we wanted, so we started to fix up some of these old building and relics. We didn't steal anything," he added quickly. "Your parents aren't those kinds of criminals."

"I love that you have to clarify that," I said, but my tears were already drying. "Did Dominic go with you?"

"No," my mom said. "We didn't tell him about them. We *wouldn't* tell him, to be more specific. Dominic was always . . . *different* from us. He was sneaky. A couple of students accused him of stealing things from their dorm rooms. He could take things at noon and return them at two and no one would see it happen."

"It was like he was a magician," my dad said. "He could make things just appear. Or disappear."

"You thought he would steal from all the museums if you gave him the chance," I said, putting the pieces together.

My mom nodded. "And he got upset with us, of course. We never agreed with the Collective recruiting him, but we couldn't blame them. And Dominic never did anything illegal, or at least, nothing that we could prove. Not until now."

"So he doesn't know about the tunnels?" I asked.

"Oh, he knows. He just didn't know what we used to

do, or how we used to do it. And again, we were just having fun. We were young and dumb teenagers."

"*Ahem*," I said.

"You'll see one day." My mom smiled at me. "One day you'll be amazed by all the things you didn't know."

"I already feel that way now," I told her. "Why didn't you ever tell me about all this?"

"Because we were afraid that Dominic might try to get the information from you," my dad admitted. "It was such a little thing, but we never knew what he would do. And now . . ." He raised his hands, then dropped them into his lap. "You know."

"I wish you had told me."

"I wish we didn't have to."

My mom's words hung in the air as I contemplated what they told me. "Any other family secrets we need to air?" I asked.

"Not yet," my dad asked. "How about you? Want to get anything off your chest?"

"Not yet," I echoed. The pressure of the night was starting to weigh on me, and I wanted to be alone with my thoughts, both old and new. "Do you mind if I go to bed? I'm really tired."

"Of course," my mom said, coming to hug me, and I let her. "We love you, okay? We love you so much."

"Love you, too," I said, then tried not to wince when she gave me an extra-hard squeeze. "See you in the morning."

CHAPTER 18

I woke up the next morning around 10:00 a.m., still exhausted. I had tossed and turned for most of the night, but I hadn't cried any more after turning off the lights. Crying was too draining, too emotional, and I needed every ounce of strength that I had to figure out this case and get my life back on track. Or at the very least, figure out a new track. Clearly this whole "be a spy and a teenage girl at the same time, yay!" thing wasn't working.

When I rolled over, I saw an *A* card taped to my bedroom door. "Oh, God," I muttered, but dragged myself out of bed and went to look at it. Angelo had clearly been here that morning, doing his sneaky thing with his ever-present cards. I wondered if he had talked to my parents at all, or if they had talked to him. They were no doubt furious with him for not letting me tell them about the case, but I knew Angelo could handle himself. I just didn't feel like getting stuck in the crossfire, which, the more I thought about it, seemed like a pretty good metaphor for the current state of my life.

"So what do you have to tell me today?" I said to the card, turning it over. The familiar pen-and-ink drawing was on the back, stone archways stretched across a small courtyard of trees and grass. It was Angelo's sketch of the Cloisters, a small part of the Metropolitan Museum of Art that was at the very tip-top of Manhattan.

"Oh, joy," I said, then got into the shower.

When I was ready to leave, I opened my bedroom door and stuck my head out. I felt like a rabbit, poking its head out of its hideaway to see how close the enemies are. It wasn't that I didn't want to talk to my parents. I just didn't want to *talk* to my parents.

They weren't there, though, and I found a note on the counter that they had gone to run errands. That seemed dubious at best, and I wondered if maybe they didn't want to talk to me, either. It was too awkward to make small talk and too soon to discuss what was really wrong. It's always bizarre when you realize that your parents don't have a clear solution to the problem, that they're just as confused as you are. It makes them too real, too human, flawed just like you.

"And how was your journey north?" Angelo asked when I approached him at the Cloisters. He was sitting against one of the archways, tiny coffee cup in hand that I knew held a double espresso, and he looked as calm as ever. He had the sort of serenity of a man with a plan, which made me feel a little better.

But not much.

"Oh, you know," I said, clinking my coffee cup against his before I took a sip out of the leaky lid. "Just take the A train for approximately four years, and then you're here! It's so easy."

Angelo smirked at me. "There's a song about that, you know."

"About riding the subway for four years?"

"No, about taking the A train. By Duke Ellington, a wonderful jazz pianist." He shook his head when I stared at him blankly. "Oh, dear. I shall make you a mix. We've been neglecting your musical education."

"You want to make me a mix?" I repeated, incredulous. "Don't you think we're a little, you know, *busy* right now? Also, when did you learn to make a mix?"

"Maggie, love, it's the twenty-first century. Technology does not go backward, so it's best to keep up. And there's always time for a song or two. Now," he said, brushing some invisible dirt off the arm of his suit. "Let's discuss last night."

"Fiasco," I replied. "And cuckoo clocks. There, that's my summary."

"I am very sorry for the lack of correct information," Angelo said with a sigh. "That was my fault. There was a small crack in the system but it's been fixed now."

I gave him the side-eye. "You didn't dump anyone's body into the Hudson River, did you?"

"Of course not, Maggie. Not in this suit." He winked at me and I laughed for what felt like the first time in days. "See? Life is not as bad as you think it is."

"You talked to my parents, didn't you?"

Angelo nodded, running his thumb around the lip of his cup. "They are . . . *concerned*. But I reassured them that things are fine."

"Really? Could you reassure me, too?"

"Why don't *you* reassure *me*? Tell me about everything last night. Start from the very first cuckoo."

So I took a deep breath and launched into my story of Dominic Arment and his bizarre collections and heavy cologne and annoying humming habit. "There's an egg, though," I said. "It's one of the Fabergés. I think it is, anyway. I don't know, I just think it's really important."

"How so?"

"I don't know. It sort of stood out to me. Like it had a secret."

Angelo smiled knowingly. "What's the first rule of being a spy?" he asked in a singsong sort of way.

"Listen," I answered. "And I listened to that egg for two and a half hours. Well, so to speak. I mean, the egg wasn't exactly talking to me, that would be delusional. But there's something with it."

"Do you think it's a real Fabergé? There are some eggs that haven't been accounted for. Eight, I believe."

"I don't know," I admitted. "Maybe? Or maybe it's a fake? I need to get back into that house and figure it out, Angelo. Like, soon. Today. Tonight."

"We'll find a time. But why don't you tell me what happened afterward?"

I glanced out at the small courtyard, at how green the leaves on the trees were against the beige stone of the walls.

"This must be really pretty in the fall," I murmured. "We should come back here. If we're still *here,* I mean."

Angelo sat next to me, always a port in the storm, always hearing what I wasn't saying. "It is quite difficult to do this job when you love people," he said softly. "Don't you think?"

I nodded and swallowed against the lump forming in my throat. "How do you do it?" I asked him. "I mean, you do all this and you still love people, right? Like my parents and me?"

"Very, very much so."

"Then how do you do it?"

Angelo thought a minute, looking out across the park. It was unlike him to not have an answer at hand. "I suppose," he said after a minute, "that I do it *because* I love you. And your parents. And others. The world that we see, Maggie, sometimes it's quite dark and depressing. We meet terrible people all the time."

"But then we bring them down."

"Exactly my point, love. We make the world better. When you love people, you want the world to be a beautiful place for them. If you're lucky enough, you can make their world better just by standing next to them. And if you're very, very lucky, you can work with the people you love to improve things. You're in it together."

"And sometimes . . . ?" I asked, prodding him to give the answer that I didn't want to hear.

Angelo smiled ruefully. "And sometimes you make their world better by traveling far away to save it."

"Do you think Jesse's world will be better if I travel far away?"

"Ah, I should have known," Angelo said. "You and Jesse had a fight, I take it?"

I nodded. "It was really bad. I think we broke up. I missed dinner with him and his mom and then he was upset that I couldn't tell him why I was so late."

"That's to be expected."

I thought for a moment. "This is why spies don't have friends, isn't it? Because of things like this?"

"Sometimes, yes. And sometimes friends can be the very thing that saves you. You never know. If I recall correctly, Roux can land quite a punch. Perhaps she saved all of us that day."

I smiled despite myself. "She'll be the first to tell you that, too."

"Yes, I can imagine," Angelo said. "Maggie, what's done is done. You made choices that weren't for the best when you involved Roux and Jesse and now you must live with the consequences of your decisions. If they're mad at you for not giving them all the information—"

"I'm doing it to keep them safe, though!"

"I know, and I don't disagree with your decision. But they have the right to be upset, too. You can control many things, my love, but you cannot control how people feel."

I nodded. If my parents had said that to me, I probably would've gone all defensive and ballistic, but Angelo always talked to me like an adult. That was just one reason why I loved him so much. "But what if . . ." I had a hard time even forming the words in my mouth. "What if one of the consequences is that Roux or Jesse gets hurt?"

"Listen to me." Angelo set down his coffee cup and grasped my arms, guiding me to look at him. "Listen to me very, very carefully. *I will never let anything happen to Roux or Jesse. Is that clear?*"

I nodded, surprised by the force of his words. "I know," I told him, and I realized with a start that I *did* know that. Angelo would move heaven and earth to keep me, my friends, and my family safe.

I just hoped that I could do the same.

We sat together in silence for a while, watching the tourists and student groups mill around us. "You do remember where we put important things, yes?" Angelo asked.

A chill went through my shoulders and down my ribs as I looked at him. We hadn't talked about that in years. "Yes," I said. "I wouldn't forget something like that."

"All right. Now remember this address." He rattled off an address to me in French. "Do you have it?"

"Of course." I imagined writing it across my brain, tattooing it onto my thoughts and making it a permanent part of me. "But why—?"

"If you ever need to leave, they will keep you safe."

"Wait, wha—?"

Angelo looked down at me and for once, his face was so serious that I knew not to ask any more questions. "Okay," I said instead. "I've got it. Don't worry, I've got it."

"Excellent. And how is progress coming along with your lock?"

"Ugh."

"That well, I take it."

"It's fine, I just can't get the final lock. I'm losing a lot of sleep over this, Angelo."

"You'll be able to open it when you need it most," he said. "Trust me on that." He patted my knee, then picked up his espresso, then set it down again. "You know, darling, there are a lot of people who are upset with us. And there are certain people not very happy with *you*."

I thought of Dominic Arment, of everyone in the Collective who was trying to sully my family's good name. "Well, I'm not very happy with certain people," I replied. "And you can tell them I said so."

Angelo smiled a little. "Duly noted. But we *do* have allies. You must remember that."

I waited until a couple walked past us before speaking again. "I thought I saw someone following Jesse and me the other day. A man."

Angelo nodded. "Yes, that's very possible."

"I knew it!" I said. "Was he a good guy or a bad guy?"

"Funny how you can't tell just by looking at them," Angelo said, then nudged my shoulder when I rolled my eyes at him. "Not every bad guy has the same motives, but either way, I'm not sure, darling. Perhaps he was a little bit of both. Or maybe he was just lost. It's best not to lose our heads wondering about the maybes and what ifs."

"Says the man who just mentioned our secret hiding space and then had me memorize a mysterious Paris address."

"How do you know it was in Paris?"

"Because you hate the suburbs."

Angelo laughed this time. "Fair play. So let's go back to this mysterious Fabergé egg, the one that talks to you."

"I need to see it again," I told him. "I can't stop thinking about it. The only problem is that I don't have anything to compare it to. It's not like I've ever seen a real one. Do you know where we can get one?"

"I might," Angelo said. "But unfortunately they are all an ocean or two away."

"Well, there has to be an exhibit somewhere or maybe a—"

And suddenly it hit me. I knew someone who had a Fabergé egg. Or at least, someone who said she did.

"Oh my God," I said. "*Roux.*"

CHAPTER 19

"**H**arold!" Roux's voice came beaming down the intercom system. "Harold, you shining sun of a man!"

I gripped the granite top of the front desk in Roux's building, my impatience already mounting. Roux's doorman, the long-suffering Harold, barely blinked at me in response.

"Harold, you know it just makes my day when you buzz me. Did you know that? Because you should. Know that, I mean."

"A girl by the name of Maggie is here to see you, Miss Green." Harold's voice stayed calm and monotone.

"Really?" I asked him. "*A girl by the name of Maggie?* You've known me for a *year*. Why can't you just let me go up?"

"Maggie!" Roux's voice sounded positively gleeful. "Magga Ragga!"

"I hate that nickname," I told her. "Will you please just let me in?"

"Harold, it's Maggie! Did you know that things got

super weird between us but we're friends again? Gotta keep up with current events, Harold. Things change every minute around here."

"Roux—" I tried to interrupt.

"Except you, Harold." Roux was on a roll now. "You should never change, Harold. Never, okay? Unless you want to change for the better, I mean. Then you can change. But I would still mourn the man you were and—"

Oh my God.

"Roux!" I shouted into the intercom. "Will you just let this poor man drink his coffee and send me up already? Good Lord!"

There was a brief pause.

"Maggie sounds stressed, Harold. Does she look stressed?"

Harold eyed me. I eyed him right back.

"Oh, never mind. Let her come up, Harold. We'll do some deep breathing exercises together. It's good for the mind *and* the soul."

"Go on up," Harold said to me, gesturing toward the ornate elevator.

"*Thank* you." I could still hear Roux rattling on about the positive effects of yoga even as the doors shut.

The doors opened again at the fourteenth floor, and I hurried out and stalked to Roux's front door, banging on it until she opened it.

"Where's your egg?" I demanded, storming in past her.

"My what?" She grinned. "I was right, you do look stressed. Are you upset about Jesse?"

Wait. What?

"How did you know about that?" I asked her. "Did he call you? What did he say?"

She shook her head. "No, he didn't call. It's online. This girl Sara saw the two of you fighting last night, and she put it on her Facebook page. Did you really flip him off?"

I winced and ran my hand over my face. "No, of course not. It's a long story," I told her.

"I've got nothing but time and a sympathetic ear," she said. "And a drawerful of delivery menus. I mean, *obviously*."

"Roux." I took a huge, deep breath. "Just stop for a minute, okay?"

"Stop what? Oooh, that was a good cleansing breath. You look relaxed already."

"Where's your Fabergé egg?"

Roux froze, her smile slowly slipping off her face.

"Remember?" I said. "When we were breaking into Colton's apartment last year, you said that you got a Fabergé egg for your sixteenth birthday. Were you kidding about that? Because if you were, you need to tell me right now."

I had seen Roux elated, furious, drunk, crying from heartbreak, and determined, but I had never seen that look on her face before. She suddenly looked like an adult, someone who could weigh her options rather than act impulsively, and I wondered if that's how I looked when I was working, too.

"I wasn't kidding," she said. "I was serious."

I took another deep breath. At this rate, I was going to either be completely relaxed or hyperventilating on the floor. "Can I see it? Please? It's important."

Roux went and flipped the deadbolt lock on her front door, then beckoned me upstairs. "C'mon, follow me."

I don't think I had ever seen her be that quiet before, that composed, and the penthouse only seemed to echo her silence. The rooms felt cold as we headed to the stairs, all marble floors and crystal chandeliers, and I wondered if that's why Roux was so loud all the time. Living in relative silence by yourself would be eerie after a while. You would need to stab at it every now and then.

We went into her bedroom, and I followed Roux into her huge walk-in closet. My parents and I once lived in an apartment in Stockholm that was roughly the same size as this closet, and that wasn't even accounting for Roux's massive shoe wall.

"It's over here," Roux said, and she knelt down and shoved a few pairs of jeans out of the way and pulled back the thick carpet, revealing a strong floor safe. "I know *you* could probably break into it," she said with a little bit of apology in her voice. "I made my dad have it installed after I met you."

"Is *that* why you kept asking me about the best floor safe models? You thought that I was going to steal from you?"

"No, no, not *you*. I just learned a lot about protecting things. I figured I probably shouldn't keep the egg in my sock drawer anymore." Roux spun the lock, looking a little embarrassed. "I feel like I'm fingerpainting in front of Picasso," she muttered. "Just don't watch, okay?"

"You flatter me," I said.

"Yeah, well." Roux gave the lock a final twist, then

undid the latch and pulled it open. The safe was deep and vast, and she reached in and pulled out a small object wrapped in red fabric, the only object in there. She unwound it, revealing a tiny clear glass box and a gorgeous green egg inside.

"It's the Imperial Pansy Egg," Roux said, her voice almost reverent.

"Wow," I whispered. It was stunningly beautiful, a marbled jade green color with golden vines twisting around the bottom and winding up its sides. The vines eventually thinned out into individual stems with a delicate pink pansy at the top, all of them connected by a thin gold strand.

"Roux, this is amazing," I told her. "Your parents gave you this?"

"Nope, not my parents. My grandmother. She died a long time ago, but it was in her will that I should get this when I turned sixteen. I liked her. She was really nice. My parents used to send me to her house for the summer, back before they could get rid of me in summer school, and I always used to look at this egg." Roux shrugged as if shaking away old memories. "So she gave it to me. My mom was *so* pissed that she didn't get it instead. I thought her head was going to explode! It was amazing."

I smiled along with her. "That's the spirit. Can I see it?"

"Yeah, sure." Roux handed me the box and I turned it over and over, looking at it from every angle. There was a tiny set of initials stamped into the gold on the bottom. "What are these? Who's that?"

Roux leaned over to peer at it. "Oh, that's the designer's initials. They would stamp them in before firing it in

the oven. Like a business card or the Nike swoosh or something like that."

I just stared at her, my mouth quirking up a little. "Did
you read up on these eggs?" I teased. "Did you actually do
research on a computer?"

"Shut up," she said, but she was smiling, too. "I figured
that I should know what I had. Nothing in this closet is a
knockoff—I got rid of that fake Balenciaga bag as soon as
Bergdorf's got the real thing back in stock, don't even go
there—and I wanted to make sure that this egg was the real
deal."

"And is it?"

A vaguely frightening smile crept across Roux's face,
just like it had after she punched Colton Hooper right in
the nose, satisfied and strong. "Oh, yes," she murmured.
"It's the real deal."

I sat on my heels, giving the egg back to her. "Okay," I
said. "Where's your computer?"

An hour later, Roux and I were sitting on her bed in front
of her laptop, containers of half-eaten Thai food next to us
as we combed through article after article about Fabergé
eggs. "Does your brain ever do that thing where you see
the same word over and over?" she asked, sitting away from
the screen to rub at her eyes. "And then it starts to make,
like, absolutely no sense whatsoever, like it's written in
hieroglyphics?"

I looked at her.

"Yeah, me neither," she said quickly.

"So there are eight missing Imperial eggs," I said. "And one of those missing eggs might be in the United States. And it might look exactly like the one I saw."

Roux pulled the laptop closer to her so she could read the description. " 'A sapphire cherub pulling a two-wheeled chariot containing a golden egg set with diamonds.' Cherubs are *so* creepy, don't you think? Like, why are naked babies shooting poisonous arrows at innocent people a symbol of *love*? Why aren't they a symbol of toddler anarchy instead?"

"Roux," I started to say, but then I paused, thinking about her comment. "That is an *excellent* point," I admitted.

"I blame Hallmark," she said. "Damn them and their anarchist baby uprising. So you think this is your egg?"

"It could be. Or it could be a fake."

Roux sat cross-legged on her bed, picking at the bedspread with her purple fingernails. "I know we sort of had a fight about this," she said, sounding very small, "and I swear I'm not trying to start anything, but it's sort of nice looking up information together. It was fun when you and Jesse and I did that last year. It's like being on a team together."

"It is," I said, clicking through to another link.

"So could you maybe tell me why you need to find this egg? Only because I know people," she added before I could say anything. "Honestly. Swear to God. I'm not trolling for information."

We had been doing research together for almost two hours. She was right, I did owe her an explanation. "I need to find some things that are very important—"

"Well, duh. Isn't that your life motto? Sorry, sorry, go on."

"Anyway," I said. "I need to find something very important and I think this egg has something to do with it."

"Is it hidden in the egg?"

"Maybe? I'm not sure."

I could almost see the wheels turning in Roux's head. "So if the thing you need is in this egg . . ."

"Then it's a knockoff."

"But if it's not?"

"Then I'll end up destroying one of the world's greatest missing treasures for no reason and I still won't have the thing I need to find."

"Oh." Roux frowned a little, then looked up at me. "Wow, Maggie. Sucks to be you."

I stared at her, then very calmly grabbed a pillow off her bed and smacked her right in the head with it. "Kidding!" she screeched, right before I whomped her again. "I was kidding, I swear! Have mercy on the civilian!" But she was laughing too hard to talk and I was giggling, too. In fact, I was giggling so much that I missed her grabbing another pillow and slamming me in the face.

"Ow!" I cried. "When did you become so violent?"

"I'm a quick learner," she replied with a laugh. "Just ask Colton Hooper."

CHAPTER 20

After I left Roux's, I walked along the edge of Central Park for a while, scuffing the toe of my boot along the bricks as I thought about the egg and the missing coins. Was Dominic really that much of an evil genius mastermind to create an entirely fake egg? I knew Angelo was checking his contacts, seeing if anyone had forged a counterfeit egg recently, but the fact that he hadn't called me told me that he was coming up short.

I walked through the melee of Columbus Circle, then went south along the park, patting a few carriage horses along the way. I had only meant to wander around for a while, but I soon realized that I ended up back in the place where it all began: at the Sherman Monument, just under the winged statue of Victory, her arms spread wide as if to say, "How do you like me *now*?"

"Show-off," I muttered, but then leaned against the statue anyway, resting under the safety of her figure as I tried to work things out.

If I broke one of the most valuable creations of the twentieth century, I was fairly sure that my reputation as an expert spy and safecracker would be ruined. If I broke the egg and found the coins, though, I'd save my parents and *their* reputations. I wasn't used to making these sorts of decisions on my own. Usually the Collective told me where to go and what to crack and that's exactly what I did. I did whatever they told me to do, whenever they told me to do it, and I never questioned it. Roux would have asked so many questions that they probably would have kicked her out of the Collective before her first job, but I didn't.

And I was starting to realize what a monumentally stupid mistake that had been.

I sat there for a long time, people-watching as the sun began to finally sink behind the buildings. There were a lot of couples walking hand in hand, which made me feel so lonely inside. I missed Jesse's hand in mine, how it felt when our fingers touched. I remembered the coldness between our palms last night, the tears smearing his fingerprints, and I shook my head, trying to will myself to focus on work.

When it finally got so dark that I couldn't see across the park anymore, I glanced up at Victory. "Any tips?" I asked her. "Because now would be a great time to offer some advice."

She just stared straight ahead, pointing south in the direction of our loft, so that's where I decided to go.

I was just coming up from the R train on Spring Street when my phone (brand-new SIM card in place) started to buzz. I checked it: four missed calls from Angelo.

That was not good. Not good at all.

"Hey," I said, going to stand in front of the Dean & Deluca on the corner so I could get out of the way of the Saturday crowds. It was the same store where Roux and I had met up for Halloween last year, back before she knew I was a spy. It felt like it had been way more than a year ago. It felt like a lifetime. "What's up?"

"You have an hour," Angelo said, his voice oddly breathless. "He's just left. Where are you?"

"Downtown," I said. "Do you have the security code?"

"No, he just changed it again," Angelo said. "You're not going to get another chance, Maggie. Dominic is very suspicious."

"On my way," I said, then hung up and burst across the street. "Excuse me! Excuse me!" I cried, shoving some people out of the way. There were definitely a few angry expletives behind me, but I didn't care. I had sixty minutes to get back into the house, crack the security code, and decide whether or not to break that egg, and I needed every single minute I had.

Twenty minutes later, I raced up the stairs of that spacey New Age station just around the corner from Dominic's apartment on Pomander Walk, my legs still sore from crouching next to his stairs for so long the night before. I didn't care, though. It didn't matter. All that mattered was getting into his apartment and solving this damn case so my parents and I could have our lives back.

I still had my gloves in my bag, and I pulled them on as

I approached the locked gate on Ninety-Fifth Street. No time for subtlety right now: I yanked the lock, scrubbing at it with record speed and it popped open in seconds. I could feel my back molars grinding together as I worked, the crease between my eyebrows deepening as I slipped through the gate and went up to Dominic's door. The lace curtains were drawn this time, reminding me of all the windows I had seen in the French countryside. *Dominic is from France*, I thought, then filed that piece of information away.

I probably had close to twenty-five minutes now, but I didn't dare pull out my phone to check. (I knew Angelo would bring up this fact later: it makes him crazy that I don't wear a watch, especially when I'm working.) The small side street was as quiet as it had been the night before, but no matter. I was about to change that.

It took me only a few minutes to pick the locks on Dominic's door this time and I took a huge breath in, let it out, then used my shoulder to shove the door open. "Here we go," I muttered to myself, just as a loud beep started sounding, making me wince. I made a few halfhearted attempts at trying to guess the pass code, but every single one just buzzed at me, pissed that I couldn't crack its system. Angelo had said the night before that I had one minute before the police were notified of a break-in and five before they arrived. I tried again, but no dice. The beeping sound was getting faster and angrier, letting me know that I only had seconds before there was no going back.

It was time to make an executive decision.

"Screw it," I mumbled. Dominic was already suspicious,

Angelo had said, and no doubt he'd be more suspicious once he found one of his eggs missing. Might as well save some time.

I reached up and yanked the entire alarm box out of the wall.

The cuckoo clocks were nothing compared to the racket the alarm made, and I had to physically restrain myself from covering my ears. *Earplugs*, I thought. *Should have brought earplugs.* It was so strong and shrill and constant that I could almost see it vibrating through the air as it came down to split my skull. It was the first time that a sound had actually hurt my ears, but it only served to make me angrier. You wouldn't install a sound like that unless you had something to protect. Those coins were here somewhere.

I stalked over to the Fabergé egg shelf, my boots crunching against the pieces of the now-shattered alarm box, my eyes going right to that golden mystery egg. If I had had my eyes closed, I would still have been able to find it, that's how strong its siren song was to me. I had felt that way with Colton Hooper's safe, hearing it whisper its secrets. *Come and play with me*, the egg whispered. *We'll have so much fun.*

I picked it up and held it in my steady palm, turning it over to look at it from all sides. It had the same beautiful fragility as Roux's egg, somehow heavy and light at the same time. I only had the description to compare it to, since there were no actual pictures of this egg, but it matched perfectly.

Four minutes until the police arrived.

"Come on, come on, come on," I murmured, turning it

upside-down to see the gold etchwork. Every fake had a tell. There was always something that gave it away. You just had to be good enough to find it, and I knew I was good. But good enough? Good enough to save my family? That was another question entirely.

There was a small mark in the bottom of the egg, and I held it up to the light that ran under the shelf. It was the initial mark just like I had seen on Roux's egg, two small letters that—

Wait.

I peered in closer. These initials were different. The engraving was shallower than Roux's egg, a bit shakier. Roux had said that the initials were carved before the eggs were fired in the oven. So if these weren't as deep, that meant they were carved after firing. Carving into set gold would be nearly impossible.

Seven o'clock. Three minutes until the police arrived.

"CUCKOO! CUCKOO!"

"CUCKOOCUCKOOCUCKOO!"

"COOO! COOO! COOO! COOO!"

The egg was starting to feel heavier in my palm. "Wait," I said, then reached out and grabbed another egg. It was noticeably lighter.

Gotcha.

I set the second egg down and gave Cupid a quick kiss before raising the first egg over my head. "Thanks for keeping them safe," I whispered, then hurled it to the ground.

It smashed open.

And ten gold coins spilled out.

CHAPTER 21

Angelo!" I cried into my phone when I thought I heard him answer, but it was just the drone of an out-of-service buzz. It didn't matter, though. I was so elated that I could have probably flown home and used my happiness to have Angelo teleported right to my front door.

I had the coins in my jeans pocket, hard and flat against my hipbone as I walked quickly through the streets. I couldn't run because the police were no doubt at Dominic's house by now, looking for anything suspicious or weird. Not that a running seventeen-year-old girl would be *that* suspicious in Manhattan, but I wasn't taking any chances. I had the coins and no one was taking them away from me now.

I hung up my phone, grinning like a complete maniac as I tried to flag down a taxi. The coins had looked exactly as the picture had shown, heavy enough to not be fakes, the etching of Victory looking up at me serenely as I scooped her and her nine sisters off of Dominic's floor and hustled them into a small velvet pouch. Ironically, the gold made my heart lighter, my steps softer, and once I got into a taxi, I caught the driver giving me a few weird glances in the rearview mirror as I sat in the backseat and grinned to myself.

I forced myself to not smile so wide, but it was even more difficult after I got a text from Jesse. "Let's talk," it said. "I don't like not seeing you."

My parents were going to be so excited, I thought. Angelo was going to be so proud. I could finally explain to Jesse what had been so important that I had to miss dinner with his mom. School started in less than a week, and everything would be normal and lovely and I would go to college and the Collective would go back to how it used to be and Dominic Arment would be destroyed by karma and an orange jumpsuit and ankle shackles.

I loved my life sometimes. I really did.

I had the cab drop me off five blocks away from the loft just in case, and I blended in with some of the later stragglers in Soho as I took a winding path back to the loft. By the time I went up in the elevator, I was hopping up and down, and when the doors opened, I scanned my fingerprint in record time and shoved my way into the loft.

"I got them!" I yelled. "I did it, I got them!"

My parents came running, and I immediately realized that something wasn't right. My dad looked rumpled and dis-tracted, running a hand over his face as if he could erase his worried expression, and my mom's eyes were red, almost bird-like, her hair up in a messy topknot and her hands wringing together in front of her. There were two half-packed suitcases on the floor, clothes and passports spilling out of them.

I froze. "What happened? What's going on?"

"It's fine," my mom started to say, but she couldn't look at me when she said it, so I turned to my dad, who just shook his head.

"We're fine," he told me, which wasn't the answer to my question and made my heart pick up speed. "It's all right, it's not a big deal."

And then I smelled it: cologne.

"Was Dominic here?" I cried. "He was here! What was he doing here?"

"He just wanted to talk," my mom said.

"About what?" The coins in my pocket felt like they were vibrating against my hipbone. "Did he threaten you?"

Neither of my parents said anything for a minute, then my dad spoke. "He offered to give me 'immunity'"—my dad rolled his eyes—"if I turned in your mother for 'taking' the coins."

"We didn't even recognize him," my mom said, and now her eyes were narrowing, getting mean like a mama bear's whose cubs have been threatened. "He looked insane, not like Dominic at all. I mean, it was Dominic, but not . . ." She trailed off. "Power corrupts, I guess. And he's corroded."

"Wait, what did you get?" my dad asked. "When you came in, you were saying you got something."

"The coins," I said, and my voice was shaking a little. "I was in Dominic's house while he was here with you. Angelo sent me in."

"Did someone say my name?" Angelo said, and I whirled

around to see him standing in the doorway, our door still ajar after I had failed to shut it behind me.

"I got the coins," I said. "And Dominic was here. I tried to call you but your phone was off."

Angelo had an odd look on his face. "My phone's not off," he said, holding it up. "In fact, your parents just texted me and asked me to come here."

"I didn't," my dad said, then turned to look at my mom. "Did you?"

"No. In fact, I just got a text from you, Angelo, saying that you were meeting us here."

"Why is this door open? Does this mean I can't do the finger-scanny thing? This sucks, I love scanning my fingerprint!"

It was Roux.

"Maggie, can you shut the door so I can do the finger-print scanner?" Roux asked, poking her head through the door. "It makes me feel important."

"Sweetheart, what are you doing here?" My mom looked like she wanted to shove Roux right back out the door, and I couldn't blame her. Roux was the last thing we needed in the loft right now.

"Jesse just texted me and said that he wanted to meet us here. Something about making up? I don't know what he's talking about, but if I have to watch him be all swoony and romantical, I will vomit, and that is the God's honest truth. Oh, hey," she said to Angelo and my parents. "Is there any dinner? I'm starving."

My stomach was starting to twist, but before I could say anything, the elevator doors opened again and Jesse stepped out. My heart leaped at the sight of him. It had been only twenty-four hours since our fight, but I realized that I had missed him terribly. His hair was hanging in his eyes again, and he quickly brushed it aside when he saw me, the familiar gesture making me feel even more nervous. "Hey," he said, coming into the loft.

"You texted Roux?" I asked him.

"Why would I text Roux? Hi, Mr. and Mrs. Silver. Hi, Angelo." He was as polite as ever, making my heart beat a bit faster.

"Why would you *not* text me, is the question," Roux said, clearly miffed. "And you said to meet you here. See?" She held up her phone so we could all see the text.

"You texted me, too," I told him, getting out my phone. "You said we should talk."

"I didn't text either one of you," he said. "Mags, you just texted me and said to meet you here. You said it was important."

The six of us stood in the living room, looking at each other. I could see the realization dawning across my parents' faces, the same way I knew it was dawning across mine.

We had been compromised. Our phones had been hacked.

I looked to Angelo to see if he thought the same way, but he was looking past my shoulder and out the window, his face suddenly tight and cold. I turned to look, too.

My heart both sank and swelled as I saw the narrow red light zip along one window, and Angelo was right, be careful what you wish for, because things were about to happen, so many things were about to happen, and, oh, I should have known.

I should have *known*.

"DOWN!" Angelo shouted, grabbing Roux as I yanked Jesse to the floor. My parents hit the ground behind us, and I pressed my cheek against the cold hardwood as the first gunshots shattered the windows wide open, glass raining down, leaving us exposed to the dark, starlit sky and all the demons that were waiting to fall upon us.

CHAPTER 22

I could hear Roux screaming, her voice competing with the sound of glass exploding. There were tiny bits of it in my hair, on my skin, seeping into my clothes, and I could feel Jesse's leg under my hand, my fingers digging into his calf so tightly that I could feel his pulse pounding just under his skin.

But there was no time to explain or reason or even think. Instinct was starting to take over, and my brain was chanting a single word over and over again.

Run run run run run run run.

All the power had been cut in the apartment, leaving us in darkness, and I could only barely see my parents and Roux and Angelo, their outlines hazy and gray. They were all moving, though, shimmying toward the kitchen and its protective center island, and I grabbed at Jesse's jeans as I pushed myself onto my elbows, staying as low as the window frames would allow me. "C'mon!" I yelled to him, my voice nearly lost over the din, but he followed me anyway, staying so close that I could smell soap and shampoo and sweat.

"Are you okay?" my parents screamed as soon as we crawled into the kitchen. From the streetlights outside, I could just make out a cut on my mom's head, but it didn't look terrible. My dad's glasses were broken, but it didn't matter. Roux was crying, tiny little sobs that barely shook her shoulders, and Angelo looked grim and determined and more angry than I've ever seen him before.

"I'm fine, I'm fine!" I yelled before realizing that the gunshots had stopped, leaving us in an eerie silence that was even more scary than the shots themselves.

"Jess—?"

"Fine!" he yelled before I could even ask. He wasn't fine, though, I could see a dark red stain on his T-shirt and all the blood in my body went straight to my heart, making me feel like I had been punched.

"I'm fine!" he said again, seeing the look of terror on my face. "I'm fine, it's just a cut, I'm fine!"

I didn't believe him, though, and my hand went to his chest, shoving away his torn T-shirt. My fingers were freezing, almost buzzing with adrenaline, and Jesse's skin was cold underneath the seeping cut. It wasn't a bullet wound, though, just a cut, but I didn't feel any better. He was bleeding and Roux was crying and *it was all my fault*.

"We need to go!" Angelo shouted, one hand dialing his phone. "Right now!"

"Fire escape!" I cried. "The one in my bedroom!"

And then the bullets flew again, firing directly toward us. I clutched at Jesse's shirt again, and he grabbed my wrist as we both ducked down behind the center island. I could feel Roux pressed somewhere against my back, and

my parents and Angelo were yelling at each other in what I
vaguely recognized as French, only adding to the chaos.

And that's when I smelled the gas.

My parents realized it seconds later, judging from the
way my mother suddenly went stock still and silent. Something very terrible was starting to form in my stomach,
syrupy and acidic and hot, and I looked over at Angelo.

He smelled it, too.

The four of us moved as one, me grabbing at Roux's
and Jesse's hands as we scooted down and around the corner into the back of the loft. There was a brick wall there,
dividing off the bedrooms from the rest of the main living
area, and it held off the bullets for a few minutes.

"What's that smell?" Roux yelled. Her hair was tangled
from dragging herself across the floor, and I could see mascara streaking down her cheeks. Jesse was still quiet, but I
could feel both of our hands shaking together. I squeezed
his fingers as hard as I could, anchoring his skin to mine
before I let go.

"What's that smell?" Roux screamed again, only this
time, the panic in her voice told me that she knew exactly
what it was.

"You need to go!" my mom told me, grabbing my shoulders and shoving me toward the fire escape. "Right now,
you kids need to go!"

The three of us ran toward my bedroom, followed by
Angelo, who immediately grabbed one of my sweaters off
the floor and wrapped it around his arm. I could hear my
parents still speaking French down the hall, yelling at each
other, but the sound of Angelo using his elbow to shatter

my window soon drowned them out. The gunshots were flying in the living room, hitting lamps and picture frames and pillows, and I started to realize that the shooters weren't trying to send a warning. They were trying to kill us and if the guns didn't work, then the gas would.

Angelo used his arm to knock some of the most jagged pieces out of the window frame, then beckoned to Roux. She skittered away from his hand, though, not sure what was waiting for us just outside the building.

"There are people waiting to help you," Angelo said, raising his voice over the sound of gunfire in the living room. "Come, come, you must go! Right now!"

Roux looked back at me. "Maggie?"

"It's fine!" I told her. "I'm right behind you!" I had no idea if it was fine, though. We were in uncharted territory now, and none of our old rules applied anymore. We weren't listening to what we had been told, what we had heard. The concept of "being beige" had gone out the window. Looking back was all I wanted to do. And no matter what was waiting for us outside, there was only one certainty if we stayed in that apartment: all of us would die.

Going forward was the only option.

"Go!" I shouted at Roux as the gas smell started to get stronger. "Do it!"

Something steely flecked in her eyes then, as if she had just gotten a shot of courage as she flung her leg over the edge and stepped out onto the fire escape. It was old and rusted, and she started to make her way down the steps as Angelo beckoned Jesse forward.

"No! Mags first!" he yelled, but Angelo wasn't listening.

This was no longer a democracy, I realized. Angelo was calling the shots, and there was no room for argument. Jesse was out the window, and Angelo grabbed me by the waist and hustled me out behind Jesse. I could see Roux gingerly climbing down the ladder, Jesse waiting for her, and a black car that glided into the alley and stopped, freezing us all.

"It's all right!" Angelo called to them, then helped steady me on my feet. "They're here for you! Faster, faster, do not stop!"

"Angelo—" I started to say, and I was surprised by how bad my voice wobbled.

"Do you remember where to go?" he interrupted me.

"Paris," I replied.

"Yes. Go to our place first and then go there. They will take care of you."

I had no idea who "they" were, but I was willing to trust Angelo with my life and I would have gone anywhere he told me to go. There was just one problem.

"My parents!" I cried. "They're coming, too, right?"

"They're going out another way," Angelo assured me.

"And you? Where are you going?"

"Go, Margaret! Just stop talking and go!"

I grasped the wrought iron and started to climb. My knees were shaking and it was hard to stay steady, but I followed Roux and Jesse. Angelo stayed in the window, watching us go down the ladder, one of his hands concealed in his coat. Roux had always thought he was an assassin, even though I had insisted for the past year that he was only a forger. But I knew that Angelo would always watch out for us, ready to do whatever he had to to keep us safe.

He had promised me that.

Roux hit the ground first, landing on her feet with a soft, "Oh, ow." Jesse followed behind her, not having to drop as far because of his height, then the two of them scrambled into the car. It was a dark town car, much like the one that had driven me around last fall when I was investigating Jesse's father. I flew in after them and slammed the door behind me as the driver screeched out of the alley, gutter water splashing out behind us as he veered around a trash bin and careened into the Soho streets.

The three of us were silent for a minute, Roux glancing behind us to see if anyone was following, but the alley was empty. "Where are you going?" I asked the driver. I knew where he was supposed to go, of course. I just wanted to hear him say it.

"Platform Sixty-one," he replied, turning to glance at me, and I realized with a jolt that it was the same man that I had seen following me the other day in the West Village.

"Don't worry, Maggie," he said, and I detected a bit of an accent. Maybe Russian, maybe Slavic. "We know what we're doing."

"Wait, what's Platform Sixty-one?" Jesse asked, Roux wide-eyed and shaking next to him. "Where are we going? We have to go home, we have to warn our parents, Maggie!"

"Your families are already under our protection," the driver called over his shoulder, blazing through a yellow light. "Do not worry about them."

"I don't even know where my parents *are*!" Roux yelled up at him.

"They are in Berlin," he said calmly, and Roux sat back in her seat, momentarily stunned by the fact that a stranger knew where in the world her parents were while she had no idea.

Jesse twisted in his seat to look at me. Roux stayed silent, watching the streets fly past us and gripping her left hand with her right. "*Who*'s protecting them?" Jesse demanded. "Who, Maggie? The same organization that just tried to *kill* us?"

I didn't know what to say. I was in shock, my mind still spinning and a little fuzzy from the gas. "I-I don't know," I said.

"That's the new us," the driver muttered, hanging a left and going around the corner so fast that he almost took out an older woman pulling a grocery cart behind her. Roux whispered something under her breath and closed her eyes.

"The new us?" Jesse yelled, leaning over the seat.

"Worked for them, twenty years almost. Then they say I stole evidence."

My ears started to fill with an odd, humming sound.

"Did you?" Roux asked.

"Of course not!" he cried. "They want me to turn on friends, I said no. Then they said that paperwork is missing. And then my Social Security number went missing. None of my passports work." His glare seemed to fill the entire rearview mirror as he looked at me. "How much do you know?"

Jesse swiveled in my direction. "Did you know about this?"

"Of course I didn't know about this!" I shot back. "All I know is where we're going now and that I don't trust anyone unless Angelo says so. And he told me to trust him"—I jerked my thumb toward the driver—"so we're trusting him."

"Close enough," the driver said, then flew over a pothole and sent all of us into the air. "And do not worry about your parents," he added, ignoring Roux's tiny yelp. "They are under watch. *We* are watching them, not the Collective."

Roux opened her eyes and looked at me. "The Collective's not watching them?" she repeated. "Is that who he was talking about just now?"

"They're corrupt," I told her, avoiding making eye contact with Jesse and admitting that his suspicions had been right all along.

The driver muttered something under his breath, and although I didn't speak the language, I could tell that it wasn't exactly a polite comment.

"Corrupt?" Roux repeated.

"Yes," I told her. Something sliced through me as soon as I said it, the entire foundation of my life splitting apart. The Collective, which had taken care of me every single day of my life, was no longer to be trusted. Angelo had been trying to prepare me all along for that realization. The strongest force in my life was irreparably broken and neither Angelo nor my parents could fix it.

I saw the orange light reflected off Jesse's face before I heard the sound, a muffled sort of boom that made all three of us turn around to look out the back window. A huge ball of smoke slowly rose into the air, its wispy underside reflecting the explosion, and it felt like a smaller, more potent explosion happened in my heart at the same time, running through me like the flames that now rose in the sky.

"That's . . . that's my *home*," I managed to say.

"Not anymore," the driver replied.

"Are you seriously that much of a dick!" Roux yelled at him as she put her arm around my shoulder. "I'm sure they're fine, Mags," she said, voicing the terrible words that were currently stuck in my throat.

The driver held up his phone. "They *are* fine," he said. "Angelo has sent the text. They got out."

But I couldn't turn around from the window to verify what he said. Jesse had his hand in mine, the warmth between our palms spreading like fire, and I thought about our kitchen table, my mom's laptop, my bed, my clothes, my life, now turning into ash.

There was something dangerous settling in my chest, making it difficult to breathe, and I shook Jesse's hand and Roux's arm off me, not wanting comfort. If they comforted me, I would break down, and I had two people to protect now. There was no time to fall apart.

Jesse just nodded at me when I let go of his hand, and I wondered how much my face gave away. "Hey," I said, leaning forward to talk to the driver. "Can you go faster?"

He smiled and hit the gas.

CHAPTER 23

By the time we pulled up to Park Avenue and East Fiftieth Street, Roux was pale but no longer shaking and Jesse seemed to have calmed down after his outburst. They were being brave, too, I realized, and I wondered how much of it was shock and how much was actual bravery. Not that it mattered, though. Whatever would get us through the next few hours was fine by me.

The car screeched up to the curb and Roux reached down to unlatch her seatbelt. "I'm never complaining about a cab driver again," she said, letting out a shaky exhale, then peered up at the building next to us. "We drove like that just to come to the Waldorf Astoria?"

I reached across her and opened up the car door. "We're going *underneath* the Waldorf Astoria," I told her. "C'mon."

The driver—Markus, I later found out—stood next to the door as we climbed out, one hand concealed under his coat and his eyes looking not at us but at everyone milling around the streets. Jesse started to climb out of the car, then saw Markus and stopped. "Maybe we should wait here?" he said, but I shook my head and gently shoved him out the door.

"I'm not letting either of you out of my sight," I told him. "And I think you'll want to see this."

Markus shut the door behind me once I climbed out, then led us over to two huge silver doors on Fiftieth Street. "What is this, the kitchen entrance?" Roux asked, craning her neck to look up at the building.

Markus and I glanced at each other.

"It's part of Grand Central Station," I told her, digging around in my bag for my tools. "How hard are these locks, Markus?"

"Wait, Grand Central is that way," Roux said, pointing down the street. "This is a hotel. This is not a train station."

"And there's only sixty platforms there, not sixty-one," Jesse added.

I paused. "Why do you two know so much about Grand Central?"

Roux ignored my question. "What are we doing here, Maggie?"

I sighed as I looked back at her and Jesse, both of them very apprehensive and very scared. It was hard to blame them when I felt the exact same way.

"This is our secret hiding place," I told them, then winced. "Wow, that sounds so lame. This is where we keep documents."

"Documents," Jesse repeated, like he was having trouble understanding the word.

"Clock's ticking," Markus muttered under his breath. He was right, we could discuss this later.

"Just trust me," I told them. "Okay? Please?"

"Okay," Roux said, and Jesse nodded at me. I could see in their eyes that I hadn't lost them, that they weren't going anywhere without me.

"Tick tock, tick tock!" Markus yelled.

"All right!" I cried, then took a deep breath. "Everybody look cool for the next thirty seconds."

It only took me twenty seconds to jimmy the lock open, though, which felt even better than it normally did. It was the one thing I really knew how to do well, and in a night of absolute chaos and terror, it was a small comfort to break into something.

Even if that something happened to be Grand Central Station.

"C'mon," I said, opening the door. There was a set of stairs, the light so faint that it took me the entire flight for my eyes to adjust to the dimness.

"Where the hell are we?" Jesse asked.

"It's a secret platform," I said, feeling my way along the wall as we rounded a corner. I hadn't been down here in nearly five years, back when Angelo first brought me and explained the importance of the location, but I hadn't forgotten it. You don't forget something like that. "Franklin Delano Roosevelt had used it when he came to New York City so he could hide the fact that he had polio." I pointed across the musty tracks to an old train car. "That was his."

Both Jesse and Roux looked amazed and I took advantage of the situation. "That's the elevator he used," I told them. "It goes all the way up into the Waldorf Astoria. He didn't want anyone to know that he needed to use a wheelchair, so they created this for him instead."

"Politics." Markus shrugged.

Roux silently fist-bumped him.

"Can you help me?" I asked Jesse, and he followed me across the tracks to the other side of the train while Roux and Markus waited at the edge of the platform. There were tiny scurrying sounds all around us, the rats no doubt uprooted by our arrival and all the construction, and I watched my step as we walked, not especially eager to step on something with rabies and a short temper.

The second we were on the other side of the train, I turned and grabbed Jesse's hands. "You're okay?" I asked. "I mean, I know you got cut, but you're not *hurt* hurt, right?"

"I-I'm fine," he stammered. "I mean, not fine fine, but yeah. No major damage. You okay?"

I nodded, not trusting myself to talk. That syrupy burning feeling in my stomach was still there, but there was no way I could give in to it now. It would consume me if I wasn't careful.

"Mags?" Jesse's voice was softer now and he carefully put his hands on my shoulders. "You sure?"

I shook my head, then took a deep breath and covered

his hands with mine. "I just wanted to say I'm sorry," I said. "It was such a stupid fight, I was stressed and tired and I'm sorry for putting you in danger and—"

Jesse cut me off with a kiss. His mouth was warm and familiar, and I felt myself start to give in to the terror that was racing through me. It would be so easy to stay here, hidden from everything I didn't know and couldn't yet understand, hiding with him and Roux and—

"TICKTOCK, LADIES AND GENTLEMEN!"

"Oh, leave them alone," I heard Roux say. "We almost got *killed* tonight. At least let them make out for a minute."

I pulled away from Jesse and took a deep breath as he did the same. "Not now," I whispered. "I just wanted you to know that I was sorry. I didn't know this would happen."

"It's okay," he whispered back. "I'm glad we're together, all right? It's you and me now. And Roux, too. You're going to figure this out and we're going to help you. That's what we do, right?" He tried to smile, but it was clear that neither of us was in a smiling mood.

Still, it was both the best and the worst thing he could have said, and I bit my lip and nodded. "Okay," I agreed. "Let's find those documents."

Jesse nodded, then kissed me again before taking my hand and helping me up into the train.

It was so dark and dusty that I sneezed three times ("Bless you!" I heard Roux call) before my hand closed on a manila folder, grimy from construction dust and underground soot. It was thick, thicker than I thought it would be. I grabbed the folder and took Jesse's hand so he could help me off the train. A passport fell out and he stooped to pick it up.

"Oh," he said, his voice a little strangled. "Oh, this is . . . wow. Okay."

"What?" I asked, and he held out the passport to me.

It had his picture, the same one that was on his school ID, but it had been Photoshopped to look like a standard passport photo. "Andrew Meyers" it read, along with a fake birth date and "New York, New York" as his place of birth.

I should have known. Angelo said that he wouldn't let anything happen to me, Jesse, or Roux. This was his rainy day stash. "Welcome to the world of international espionage," I told Jesse, then handed it back to him.

"Did Angelo do this?" he asked, shoving the passport in his back pocket.

"Yes, so don't worry, it's the best." I took mine, glancing briefly at the name—Katherine Randall—then handed Jesse his matching birth certificate.

"What'd we find?" Roux asked, gingerly walking over the train tracks to our side. "Markus is super pushy," she muttered under her breath once she was close enough. "He's making me want a cigarette. This whole *night* is making me want a cigarette."

"Dream on," I told her, then gave her her passport. She flipped it open, her eyes widening in surprise. "How did Angelo get this?" she asked, pointing at her picture.

"I don't ask a lot of questions about how Angelo does anything," I replied, then gave her her brand-new birth certificate. "You probably shouldn't, either."

"Got it," she said.

"What's your name?" Jesse asked her.

"My name? Oh, my *naaaaame*. Um . . . Margaux Ellis." Roux thought about it for a few seconds, then smiled to herself. "X marks the spot. Angelo gets me."

I knew we were all bantering to keep the night's sheer horror from seeping into our little circle, and I was grateful for it. Anything that kept the panic of realizing that I had absolutely no idea what I was doing was fine by me.

"Um, Mags?" Roux asked. She was already starting to nervously crease her birth certificate in half. "Why do we need passports? Why don't we just have IDs?" Jesse nodded in agreement next to her.

"Because," I told them, turning to walk back to Markus, "we're going to Paris."

CHAPTER 24

Roux was beside herself. "Paris?" she cried as we climbed back up the stairs. "Paris, *France*, right?"

"Do you know of another one?" I asked, hanging on to the railing as Markus said, "Hurry up, hurry up."

"Paris, Texas," Roux shot back.

"There's a Paris in Vegas," Jesse added. "And probably more. We could wikipedia—"

"It's Paris, France," I interrupted. "When did you two turn into gigantic geography buffs?"

"Well, I *did* win the geography bee in fourth grade," Roux said, her breath a little short as Markus urged us to go faster. "I don't want to brag or anything, but yeah."

Jesse snorted in response but didn't say anything and ignored the dirty look that Roux gave him.

Once we were back in the car, though, Markus continued his daredevil tour of Manhattan. Our conversation died down, and I felt the panic start to creep back in small doses. "Markus?" I asked, leaning forward over the seat. "My parents are coming with us, right?"

"No idea," he said. "My job is to get you three to the airport. That's it."

I sank back against the leather seat, feeling deflated.

"What about Angelo?" Roux asked. The streetlight lit her face every few seconds or so, and I could tell that she was trying very hard to keep the uneasiness at bay.

"See previous answer," Markus told her.

"Can I ask a question?" Jesse said, raising his hand like we were in school. "Why Paris?"

"Angelo gave me an address a few weeks ago," I said, twisting a loose thread from my shirt around my fingertip. The blood started to pulse, making me feel a little better, like I wasn't dead yet. "He told me to memorize it. He said to go there if anything happened."

"Did you know that this was going to happen?" Jesse asked.

"I knew that it was more dangerous than I expected," I admitted. "But I thought that if I found what I was looking for, then we would be okay."

"And did you find what you were looking for?" Roux's voice was tight and I knew she was thinking about how she and I had researched the Fabergé eggs.

"Yes," I admitted, hesitant to say too much about the coins. As of right now, Angelo, Dominic, my parents, and I were the only ones who knew I had them, and until I knew who to trust, it would stay that way. "I can't say what I found," I added quickly, "but I found it."

"And is that why a bunch of men just tried to shoot at us and blew up the loft?" Roux asked.

"Very possibly," I said. "Very, very possibly. Yes."

Jesse let out a low whistle and then slumped down in his seat. "So this thing you found, do you still have it?"

I nodded just as we passed under a streetlight, now cruising through Queens on the way to JFK International Airport. "I do. I need it. I can't let go of it. It's what will help my parents prove that they're not guilty." Even as I said the sentence, though, I knew it wasn't true. This new Collective didn't care if I had the coins or not. They just wanted to gain power, and the more I was around, the less chance there was of that happening.

A huge rush of energy hit me when I realized that. *Screw them*, I thought. The Collective was *my* family, *my* home, not theirs. It had introduced me to Angelo, Roux, and Jesse. I wasn't going to let anyone take that away from me.

Not without a fight, at least.

"Listen," I said, leaning forward so I could talk to Roux and Jesse. "I trust Angelo with my life. He told me the other day that he would never let anything happen to me or to either of you, and I believe him. So if I trust *him*, then you have to trust *me*, okay?"

"Okay," Roux said. It was as if I had asked her to borrow her history notes or something, she agreed so easily. (Not that she ever takes notes in history, though. Or math. Or any class ever.)

"Do you even know where we're going?" Jesse asked. "I mean, besides just an address."

I shook my head. "We never know. This is how a job works, and now you're working with me." Just saying it out loud made me feel better. "We did it before, right? We can do it again."

Underneath the streetlight, I saw Roux's face break into a cautious smile. "Be careful what you wish for," she murmured. "If that's not the truth."

"No kidding," I replied, remembering Angelo's words from a few days before, then held on to the armrest as Markus made a huge swerve into the British Airways terminal at JFK.

"I thought you said we were going to Paris," Roux said, looking out of the tinted window. "Not London." Then she looked at me. "Is Paris code for London or something? Is there a whole list of words we should know? Is there a secret signal?"

"You *are* going to Paris," Markus said, screeching to a halt and forcing all of us to hang on to something to keep from flying forward. "Our journey has come to an end. Everybody out."

"Thank God," Jesse muttered. "Who taught this guy how to drive?"

"Well, we don't exactly get our licenses from the DMV," I told him as Markus got out of the driver's seat and came around to open our door. Again, he stood next to us, one hand placed protectively to his hip as we climbed out.

It looked like a normal airplane terminal, travelers milling around with overstuffed suitcases, the smell of exhaust and jet fuel heavy in the air. I wondered how Markus knew who was a friend and who was a foe, then decided that I didn't *want* to know. If Angelo had put us in his hands, then he had a reason. (Bad driving abilities aside, of course.)

Roux hoisted her bag up onto her shoulder, holding her new passport. "You're coming with us?" she asked Markus, and I could tell from her voice that she wasn't exactly thrilled with the possibility.

He shook his head and pointed toward the check-in desk. "They'll take care of you from here," he said, then shook hands with Roux and Jesse. When he got to me, he put his hand on my shoulder. "I know you don't feel like it," he said quietly, "but you've done a wonderful job tonight."

I felt tears rushing up, and I stuffed them back down just as fast. There was no time to break down. "You're right," I told him. "It doesn't feel that way at all." I glanced over at Roux, who was running her fingers through her hair. Two tiny bits of glass fell and bounced onto the curb. "Ugh, *lovely*," I heard her say.

Markus just shrugged. "What, did you think this was going to be easy?"

He had, unfortunately, an excellent point.

Jesse walked through the sliding glass doors first, followed by Roux and me. "So long, crazy driver," Roux said as Markus peeled away from the curb. "I hope he has a first aid kit in his car."

"Where are we going, Mags?" Jesse asked as we looked at the check-in desk. "Do we have tickets?"

"I have no idea," I admitted. "Maybe in our bags? I don't—"

"This way, please!" a voice called, and I looked up to

see a flight attendant beckoning us to the first-class check-in desk. She looked familiar, so familiar that I couldn't take a step until I could place her face.

"Thank you, Zelda," my mom had said.

Zelda. The Collective had tried to turn her, too. I wondered if she had suffered the same way that Markus had, suddenly a citizen with no country.

"I know her," I whispered. She was the flight attendant that had accompanied my parents and me from Reykjavík to New York last year. At the time, I had been so ready for Manhattan, ready to leave beautiful and boring Iceland and land in a city that offered nonstop excitement. I had been ready for something to happen, and as I looked at Zelda and saw the recognition in her eyes, as well, I realized that I had been so, so stupid.

"This way!" she called again, her voice brisk and efficient. Roux glanced at me and I nodded, leading our little ragged group over to her.

"You're taller," Zelda said to me by way of greeting, but I could tell that it was something she said because she thought she should, not because it was the truth.

"You know each other?" Roux asked, but Jesse elbowed her in the arm and she stopped talking, but not before elbowing him right back. "Watch it," she muttered, rubbing her arm.

"Passports," Zelda commanded, and the three of us handed them over. I got the distinct feeling that no one ever directly disobeyed Zelda. At least, no one who lived to tell about it.

"Do you know where my parents are?" I whispered to her. There was no need, though. There was hardly anyone nearby and certainly no one close enough to wonder why I was asking a flight attendant about my parents' location. Still, I couldn't bring myself to raise my voice. The question was scary, but not as scary as the potential answer.

"My job is you, not them," she replied, but her voice was a bit kinder this time. "Angelo does such excellent work." She scanned my passport with a satisfied nod. "The man's an artist."

"Do you know where *he* is, at least?" I asked, but Zelda just shook her head again as she scanned Roux's and Jesse's passports, then printed out our boarding passes. "Follow me," she said, and we did only because we had nowhere else to go.

She led us through the maze of JFK and into the hustle and bustle of airport security. Her heels clicked on the floor almost like she was firing warning shots with every step, and I noticed a few security guards following behind us, bringing up the rear. Roux and Jesse were both glancing nervously at them, but I knew they were working with Zelda. Otherwise, there was no way she would have let them be so close to us. I had no dossier to tell me where to go, what to do, who to be. All I had was my training and instincts.

And my instincts told me to follow Zelda.

When we got to airport security, I saw the metal detector and froze so quickly that Roux bumped into me. "What is it, Mags?" she asked.

I ignored her. The ten gold coins were pressed hard against my hip in my jeans pocket, and I forced myself not to cover them with my hand.

"I can't go through that," I told Zelda.

"Me, either," Jesse piped up, and both Roux and I looked at him. I had no idea why he said that, but hey, safety in numbers.

Zelda raised an eyebrow at Jesse, but when she looked at me, I realized that she knew exactly why I couldn't go through the metal detectors. "This way," she said, beckoning us over her shoulder as she turned around, and we followed her like rogue ducklings to the first-class security line. There was a man there in a uniform, watching bags go through the scanner, and when he saw us, he and Zelda exchanged a glance that was so fast no one else would have caught it.

I saw it, though. I knew he was working with us. On one hand, I felt relieved, but on the other, it just made me more nervous. How many of them were there? How many people had been betrayed by the Collective? How many more were in danger?

Zelda went through the detector first, looking like she did this sort of thing every day. Jesse went after her, putting his bag on the scanner as he took a breath and went through the metal detector. It didn't let out a single beep, and the security guard never checked his bag or even looked up at us. Roux followed, again with no response or reaction, and I held my breath as I stepped through the gate. The gold coins almost felt like they were bruising me, their presence was so overwhelming. There was no way that they wouldn't set off the metal detector, that they wouldn't bring everyone running, that Dominic himself wouldn't suddenly appear and—

I stepped through without a sound.

Zelda raised an eyebrow at me when I looked in surprise at her. *See?* she seemed to be saying, then beckoned us with one finger as we scurried through the airport. It was after nine o'clock by this point, and the airport was still busy. I hadn't been in an airport terminal in years—we always flew private planes after 9/11—and I gazed around me as we hustled to keep up with Zelda. "They have Starbucks in here now?" I whispered.

"Are you serious?" Roux whispered back. "You're an international spy and you don't know that there are Starbucks in airports?"

"I've been sort of busy doing other things," I shot back.

"You can't swing a dead cat without hitting a Starbucks," she replied. "That's just the way the world works now." Then she grinned at me, a shaky one but a grin nonetheless. "Better keep up, Maggie."

"Katherine," I corrected her.

"Oh, right, right."

I felt Jesse's fingertips brush at my palm, and I reached out to take his hand. His fingers were cold, nearly as cold as mine, and neither of us even looked at each other as he caught up with my steps. We were walking in rhythm, Zelda a few steps ahead and Roux a few steps behind, two new security guards suddenly tailing us, and I realized that we were like a little army going into battle. We had already survived one shootout, and who knew what lay ahead, but we were a team now. Roux and Jesse were in this just as far as I was, and I couldn't tell if that made me feel better or worse.

CHAPTER 25

Zelda led us into the Concourse Room, which was a lounge area for first-class passengers. The furniture looked new and comfortable, and the lighting was soothing and dim, almost like a hotel lobby. It was quiet and nearly empty, and as the doors zoomed shut behind us, I felt safe for the first time in what felt like hours. All I wanted to do was sink into one of the plush sofas and not think about anything, but Zelda *clack-clack-clack*ed us over to a spa.

"There's a spa at JFK?" Jesse asked in surprise.

"What, were you raised in a barn?" Roux asked, but I could tell that she was as surprised as he was. I had always imagined Roux as well traveled, her (real) passport full of stamps from around the world, but it suddenly occurred to me that her parents were the ones who traveled, not her. In fact, it was entirely possible that Roux had never been outside of the United States. It seemed like such a mean thing that I shoved the thought out of my head. I could think about that later, I decided. There was only enough room in my brain for so many broken things.

"There are showers," Zelda pointed, then positioned herself by the door. "I'll wait here."

Jesse disappeared into the men's side of the spa while Roux and I shuffled off into the women's side. There was soft music being piped in through the speakers, and Roux and I glanced at each other before cracking up despite ourselves.

"This is the least relaxing music I've ever heard!" she giggled.

"Jesse must be loving this," I added, which set Roux off again. "Why do we even have to shower? Can't we just get on the plane and—"

Roux and I were suddenly confronted with a large wall mirror.

"Oh," I said.

"So that's why." She sighed.

We both looked like disheveled orphans from a nineteenth-century novel. Roux's hair was all tangled, and my braid was falling apart, leaving pieces everywhere. There was a tear on my sleeve, and Roux had a small cut on her forehead. It wasn't enough to attract attention, but it was obvious that we had been through something. It wasn't just our clothes and hair: it was the looks on our faces. I already knew that Roux was wide-eyed and pale, but what I hadn't realized was that I looked worse than her. My lips were sort of bluish-white, and all the color was out of my face. I looked like a ghost of myself, in shock from the evening's events. *Pull it together*, I thought. *You have to get everyone through this.*

"You know her?" Roux asked, jerking her head back toward the spa's entrance.

"Zelda? Yeah, I saw her about a year ago. I think she works—well, *worked*, I guess—for the Collective."

Roux watched me for a few seconds, then glanced at herself in the mirror. "Do you think she could, you know, *kill* someone?"

"Of course," I said, then reached for a towel and pulled the elastic out of the end of my braid. "Why else would she be here?"

"That's what I thought," Roux murmured, then followed me down the hall.

I remained in the shower for a long time, putting my hands against the tile and letting the water run down my hair and bead on my nose as I stood still and tried to breathe. Now that I was away from Roux and Jesse, I let the panic swell a little bit. What was I going to do with ten priceless gold coins and two innocent people? I had told them that I trusted Angelo and I did, I really did. But it was harder to hang on to that trust and believe everything would be okay, now that I didn't know where he was, or worse, if and when I would see him again.

The water stayed hot longer than I thought it would considering that I was in one of the biggest airports in the world. My fingertips started to prune, and I could see pink splotches rising up on my arms and legs, my skin protesting against the heat. I didn't adjust it, though. The water cut through the numbness and forced my brain to think instead of just float.

I didn't know when our flight was, but it didn't matter. I was pretty sure that Zelda would reach in and yank me out of the shower if she thought we were going to be late. I wondered what Angelo had told her, how much she knew. She knew about the gold coins, that much was obvious from the look she gave me at airport security. They were still in my jeans pocket, a tiny glimmer peeking out from the denim, and I kept one eye on them as I rinsed the soap away. I had double locked the door, of course, but still. I had no idea who was an enemy anymore. I wasn't taking any chances.

Finally, once the water ran cold, I stepped out and swaddled myself up in towels. They were itchy and smelled like bleach, but they worked, and after I dried off, I went through the bag that Zelda had given me. There was a toothbrush among other toiletries, two pairs of jeans that were the exact size and make of the ones I had been wearing that night, and the two shirts and sweaters that I had been missing earlier. Angelo, I realized. He had stolen them from me, for me. I held them to my nose and smelled detergent, our loft, Jesse's cologne, my dad's cooking.

"Knock-knock!" I heard Roux call, and I quickly got dressed and opened the door for her. Her hair wasn't wet, but her eyes were red. She smiled, though, waving away my concern. "If a girl can't have a breakdown in a steam shower, where can she have it?" she asked. "Don't freak out, I feel better now. Cried it out. Salt water cures everything, right?"

"Right," I said slowly. "Roux, are you sure—?"

"Does it matter?" she asked. "Really, does it? I'm in this now. It doesn't matter what I think about it." She didn't sound upset, just thoughtful. "Although I wish Angelo would have packed some better clothes for me." She gestured to her black long-sleeve T-shirt and jeans and sneakers. "It looks like the Gap threw up on me."

"Lovely imagery," I said, smiling despite how guilty I felt.

"Isn't it?" she agreed. "That's what AP English will do to you. And he didn't even pack mascara or anything. Do you think I could borrow some from Zelda? She looks like she knows her way around a Sephora or two."

"I'm pretty sure Zelda would stab you with her mascara wand," I told her, running a brush through my hair.

"Good point. Or her stiletto heel. That's another thing that Angelo didn't pack, by the way."

"You really think you're going to need a pair of stilettos?"

"We're going to Paris, Maggie." Roux sounded reproachful. "I wish I could have packed for this trip. I would have done a much better job, no offense."

"None taken," I told her. "I'll let Angelo know that the next time someone tries to kill us, please consult about our wardrobe first. Priorities."

"Exactly," Roux said, then smiled at me in the mirror. "C'mon, let's go check on Jesse and make sure that Zelda's not trying to seduce him."

The mere image of Jesse being seduced by Zelda made me laugh. "I would pay good money to see that."

"You don't have any money," Roux teased me.

I thought of the gold coins and said nothing.

Jesse, of course, was not being seduced by Zelda or the two businessmen who were sitting at the far end of the lounge. His curly hair was still damp from the shower and he was wearing a plaid button-down shirt, jeans, and sneakers.

I know that we had a lot going on, and I know I should have been focusing on bigger things, like, oh, I don't know, finding the people who tried to kill my family, best friend, and boyfriend, but when Jesse looked up at me, my breath caught in my throat a little. The plaid shirt brought out the green in his eyes (thank you, Angelo) and the shower had made his hair so curly that it was corkscrewing over his forehead and into his eyes. "Hey," he said when he saw me, then reached out a hand so I could sit next to him. I perched on the arm of the loveseat and he wrapped his arm around my waist as I draped mine over his shoulders.

"Scoot, scoot," Roux said to him. "It doesn't say JESSE'S SEAT, NO ONE ALLOWED on it, you know."

Jesse rolled his eyes but moved anyway, and Roux plunked down next to him. None of us said anything, but it was pretty obvious that no one wanted to sit by themselves just yet.

A huge flat-screen TV was airing the local news, the screen filled with pictures of our building in flames and nearly a dozen firemen trying to stop the blaze. "So far, police suspect a gas leak," the anchor was saying, "but they're unclear if anyone was in the building at the time and are currently trying to locate the owners."

"Yeah, good luck with that," I muttered. It didn't seem

like the fire had spread to any other buildings, which was good. "Can you turn it off, please?"

Jesse got up and jabbed at the button, then came back and settled in next to me. Zelda eyed us as we all squished together, but if she thought anything, she kept it to herself.

"I need your phones," she told us, "and you—"

"Jesse," he said.

"Jesse, yes, of course. You need to call your parents and tell them that you'll be gone for a while."

Jesse just blinked at her and then started to laugh. It wasn't an "Oh, ha-ha, Zelda, you're a scream" laugh, though. "Are you serious?" he said, the smile starting to fade from his lips. "Just call my parents and tell them I won't be home for a while. Do you know who my dad is? That's not exactly gonna sit well with him."

"I'm wildly aware of who your father is," Zelda replied coolly, and Jesse sank back a little against the couch. "You're going to tell him that you're visiting your mother in Connecticut."

Jesse pressed his mouth into a tight line, then glanced up at me. "How do they know that my mom's in Connecticut?"

"Hell, they knew my mom was in Berlin." Roux shrugged. "It's a brave new world, my friend. Better go along with it."

I nodded in agreement, squeezing Jesse's shoulder, his skin warm under his shirt. "They'll believe you," I assured him.

"But what if my mom calls my dad and—?"

"It's not like they talk to each other, anyway," Zelda

interrupted him, which was possibly the least helpful thing anyone could have said at that moment.

"*Really?*" I said to her, raising an eyebrow.

"*Seriously?*" Roux added.

Zelda just shrugged, raising her hands in a "what can you do?" gesture.

"Fine," Jesse said, then dug his phone out of his pocket. "So . . . what exactly am I telling them?"

"That you're staying with the other," Zelda said, a little more politely this time. "Don't worry, we'll have you call them every few days to reassure them."

"How long are we going to be gone, exactly?" Roux asked. "School starts in, like, four days. Not that I'm in any hurry to get back to that prison, of course. Paris is really fine by me."

"You'll be gone until it's safe to come back," Zelda replied, then turned her gaze to me. "That's your job."

I nodded.

"Mom, I'm staying with Dad. Dad, I'm staying with Mom." Jesse sighed and put the phone to his ear. "Good thing they hate each other."

"Good thing mine hate *me*," Roux added, and she didn't sound that disappointed about it, either.

"Roux, they don't hate you, they—hey, Dad."

Zelda, Roux, and I tried to look like we weren't listening as Jesse spoke with his dad, then his mom. I gazed down the hall as I heard Jesse explain to his mom about staying in the city, my eyes falling on the two businessmen at the bar. "They're fine," Zelda said quietly, not even looking at me, and I nodded. That's not why I was looking at them, though. I wondered where they were going, what they did for a living, if they had any earthly idea how lucky they were. For a few fleeting seconds, I even found myself wanting to follow them to their destination, far away from the maelstrom I had started, but then I heard Jesse take a shaky breath and I yanked my attention back to him.

"Well, that was terrible," he said, trying to smile and failing. "Lying to my parents used to be a lot more fun."

"I'm sorry," I whispered, rubbing my fingers over his shoulder blades the way he liked. "I'm really sorry, Jess."

"Yeah, well, what are you gonna do?" He sighed, then squeezed my thigh and took another shaky breath. I knew he had already forgiven me, that I didn't need to apologize to him, but I wasn't quite ready to forgive myself.

"Now I need your phones," Zelda said, and we handed them over without question. After that, she told us our flight was at ten thirty and then gave us a few minutes to ourselves.

Jesse, Roux, and I all looked at each other. "Well, this is swell," Roux said, sinking back against the loveseat. "My first time in Paris. I never thought I'd be traveling quite like this."

Jesse looked up at me. "You okay, kid?" he asked.

"You're only two months older than me," I protested. "You can't call me that, it sounds weird."

"Yes, because that's *definitely* the issue to focus on right now, Maggie," Roux said, examining her fingernails. I didn't know whether or not she was faking her nonchalance, but it was nice to see her acting like herself again. Her crying jag in the shower must have done her some good.

"You okay?" Jesse asked again, a bit softer this time, stroking his hand over my knee. "You're pretty pale."

"I'll get you a snack," Roux offered, then hopped up to go examine the food offerings. "Something doughy sounds good. Or sugary. Or maybe salty. Do they have french fries? I'll see what I can do."

"I'm fine," I told Jesse after she wandered off. "Aside from the racking guilt I have about getting you two involved in this."

"You sort of didn't have a choice," Jesse said. "And it's not like you were the one who tried to kill us."

"I know, I know. I just . . . you could be back home dating Claire instead," I told him, mentioning his previous girlfriend, the one he had broken up with right before my family and I moved to New York.

"Yeah, no offense to Claire, but I'd rather have someone try to kill me than date her again." He grinned at me, wider than necessary so that I would smile back. "It's not your fault, Mags. I'm serious. I told you, we're in this together now. You're the one who pulled me down even before they first started shooting, remember?"

"Like I'm going to forget that anytime soon."

"You saved my life. You have amazing instincts. So don't worry. And your parents are going to be fine and Angelo is Angelo, right? They've probably been through way worse than this."

"I just wish I knew where they were," I admitted, tracing a loose thread on his shirt. "I like this shirt on you, by the way. It makes your eyes look really green."

"Dodging death and looking good in clothes? Pretty sure that makes me James Bond right about now," Jesse said.

"Like your Halloween costume that first time we met."

"The first night we *kissed*, you mean."

I looked at him, my heart swelling so painfully that it seemed to move my skin and bones, then leaned down and kissed him. "Love you," I whispered against his mouth.

"Now you know what it's like to kiss a spy," he replied, then kissed me again as I gave him a slow, sad smile.

CHAPTER 26

We flew all night to Paris.

When we first boarded the flight, there were only a few businessmen in the first-class cabin with us. I came to a halt when I saw them, though, which caused Jesse to bump into me and Roux to bump into him. "Great," I heard her mutter. "We're the Three Stooges now. Wonderful."

"Do we—?" I started to say to Zelda, but she cut me off with a nod of her head.

"They've all been vetted," she said. "Take your seats, please. The plane is about to depart."

Jesse and I were across the aisle from each other, with Roux seated between me and the window. We settled in, but my hands wouldn't stop moving. They unbuckled and rebuckled my seatbelt three separate times; moved my hair off my face, then pulled it back over my shoulders; flipped through the safety card until I could have recited the whole thing from memory. "Maggie?" Jesse said. "You're a little, um . . ."

"You're twitchy," Roux said. "Where's the champagne? Don't we get champagne on this flight?"

As if on cue, Zelda came down the aisle with a tray of champagne. "Look, I'm psychic," Roux said, then flagged Zelda over to us.

"Forget it," Zelda said when she realized what Roux was after. "You are underage in both the United States and Europe."

Roux's face smoothed out into an eerie facsimile of her normal expression and I braced myself for what was about to come. Across the aisle, Jesse was more succinct. "Here we go." He sighed.

"Look, Zelda," Roux said in a very quiet voice that I recognized as the calm before the storm. Three business-men were getting settled into their seats and paying absolutely no attention to us, which was a good thing. "I don't know how your evening went, but a madman tried to kill me tonight. And my best friend. And her parents. And her beloved older friend."

Jesse looked on in disbelief. "*And?*" he asked. "Who else was there, Roux?"

"I was getting to that," she said. "And Jesse. And I don't know about you, Zel, but that sort of put a strain on my mental health. I just had to shampoo glass out of my hair. I'm a little—oh, how do the French say it?—*on the freaking edge* right now, so if you don't mind, I'm going to take a glass of champagne and hopefully—fingers crossed, Zelda!—it'll knock me out for the flight so I can temporarily forget that we're all on the run from an insane lunatic who tried to kill all of us. Okay? Does that sound good to you?"

I glanced up at Zelda, wondering if she would just put Roux in a sleeper hold before moving on to the rest of the passengers, but her mouth quirked up a little and I saw a brief glimmer of something pass through her eyes. Recognition? Respect? I couldn't tell.

Either way, she handed Roux a glass of champagne. "*À votre santé*," she said.

"You betcha," Roux replied, then raised her glass in a mock salute before knocking half of it back in one gulp.

"I thought you cut back on drinking," I said to her after Zelda continued her path up the aisle.

"I did. Consider this a cheat day. Here," she added. "It'll put some color in your cheeks."

I hesitated for a minute, then took a small sip. It burned a little and then warmed my stomach, but it didn't calm me down. I was pretty sure that the only thing that would have calmed me down right then was an elephant tranquilizer, but I was too scared to ask if Roux had any of those on her. If she did, I didn't want to know about it.

Jesse shook his head at Roux. "You always have to make a scene," he said, but he was smiling a little. "We can't just fly to Paris after nearly being killed in a hail of gunfire like normal kids."

"Can't hear you," Roux trilled. "I'm floating away on a sea of bubbles to Paris."

"You know, not to burst your bubble—no pun intended— but this isn't exactly going to be your run-of-the-mill vacation," I told her. "We're kind of on the run."

"I know," Roux said. "But we're on the run with a huge network of subversive criminals. Could be worse." She grinned at me, and now I knew that she was trying her hardest to cheer me up.

"Good point," I told her. "What could possibly go wrong?"

"I'm sure you have an alphabetical list," she replied, but before I could answer, the captain's voice came on and told us to prepare for departure.

I looked over at Jesse as we began to taxi down the runway. There had also been a hoodie in his bag and he was wearing it now, the hoodie pulled up over his hair and almost concealing his face. "Hey," I said across the aisle, then extended my hand when he looked over. He reached out and took it, his fingers warm around my cold ones, and I reached around the divider between Roux's and my seat and took her hand, as well. She squeezed back three times, a brave reassurance, and when I looked back at Jesse, he blew a quick kiss in my direction. "Relax," he said as the plane started to rise into the sky. "We're going to be fine."

We landed in Paris around noon, the skies cloudy and rainy. Roux, true to form, slept like a rock through the entire flight and even Jesse slept for a few hours, but I stayed awake the entire time, looking out the window, watching some stupid movie with English subtitles, and thinking. It took a few hours for the shock to wear off, but now that it had, I discovered that my brain was going into full-blown work mode.

The first thing I had to do? Find out where my parents

and Angelo were. I was hoping that they would be waiting for us in Paris, but I knew that wasn't possible. It was way too dangerous for everyone to be in the same place at the same time. So I needed to find them. A tinier, darker voice kept reminding me that I would have to find out if they were alive first, but I couldn't think about that. Of course they were alive. Markus said they got out. Of course they did. That wasn't even a possibility.

I also had to figure out how to get us to the address in Paris. Angelo had sent me there, of course, but I had no idea where it was. I knew that someone would get us there, but then what? Were we supposed to just wait for news? Were we supposed to go into hiding? Angelo hadn't said what we were supposed to do while we were there. I knew this, though: if I had sit in some small apartment with Roux and Jesse and play Parcheesi while Angelo and Zelda and my parents and everyone else got to fight against these maniacs, I would lose my mind in less than a day.

Both Roux and Jesse woke up before we touched down, and by the time our plane landed, we had taken turns freshening up in the plane's bathroom. I avoided looking into the mirror as I brushed my teeth, though. I didn't need to see what I already could feel: pale skin, drawn face, dark circles, frozen eyes.

When we landed, Zelda held us back as the other passengers departed, then we followed her off the plane and out into DeGaulle Airport. "I haven't been here in a few years," I said as we followed Zelda toward baggage claim. Jesse walked next to me, his hand back in mine, his stride surprisingly assured for someone who had just flown halfway around the world.

"Same here," he said. "I came with my mom and dad when I was twelve. We did the tourist thing."

"Everyone's been here but me." Roux pouted. "This is embarrassing."

When we got outside, the air was warm and humid, pressing down into our clothes and hair. Zelda cut through a line of passengers and led us to a black Mercedes with tinted windows that was idling at the curb. "*Au revoir,*" she said as she opened up the back door. "My journey with you is done."

"Wait, but what about—?"

"Hurry, hurry," she said, waving us inside the car. "*Bonne chance,*" she said to me just before she closed the door, and the slamming sound made my heart jump.

The driver pulled away from the curb, our eyes meeting in the rearview mirror. He gave me a quick nod and a curt, "Hello, Maggie." I didn't recognize his voice but I nodded back, realizing that I had no choice but to trust him. What else was there to do?

"Roux?" I asked.

"Yeah?"

"Have you ever had an anxiety attack?"

"Of course I have. I'm seventeen and I live in Manhattan." She leaned forward on her seat to look at me. "Are you having one now?"

"I don't think so," I said. "But I might."

"Um, not to add any extra anxiety—" Jesse began to say.

"Why do I get the feeling that this is going to be one of the least helpful comments ever?" Roux said.

"—but do you know where we're going, Mags?"

"The address that Angelo told me," I said.

"And the guy driving us knows where that is?"

"Yes," I said, even though I wasn't one hundred percent sure. "He does. This is how we work, Jesse, okay? Just . . . please just trust me."

He took a deep breath and pushed his hoodie off his head. His curls were a riotous mess, almost like they were rebelling from his scalp, and Roux giggled before she could stop herself.

"What?" Jesse snapped at her. "I have bedhead, okay? At least I still don't have pillow creases."

Roux kept giggling. "It's cute!" she protested. "You look like you're five years old! Adorable!"

I bit my lip so I wouldn't start laughing, too, but it was hard.

"Oh, you too?" Jesse asked me. "*You*'re going to make fun of my hair now?"

"It's cute," I admitted, starting to giggle with Roux. "Here, let me just . . ." I reached up to flatten it with my hand, stroking the curls back into place.

"Do you have a hairnet?" Roux asked, barely able to keep her voice from shaking. "Or maybe a shower cap? That might work. We could just lasso it maybe . . ."

Jesse just groaned and buried his face in his hands. "I can't believe that I'm on the run with you two," he grumbled. "This is so not okay."

"There there," Roux said. "You'll always have your hair for company."

That was all it took to send both of us into hysterics.

We calmed down as the car took us into Paris, though, and by the time we were gliding through the sixth arrondissement, the three of us were silent. Even Jesse's hair seemed to sense the seriousness of the situation because it wilted a little back into its normal position. The city was as gorgeous as I remembered and across the seat, Roux was glued to her window. "It's so much better in person," she said softly as we passed by a small park, and I felt a small stab of anger at her parents for never taking her to Paris or Bora Bora or probably anywhere else, for that matter. And then I thought of my parents and that stab quickly spread into worry. "They're fine," I whispered to myself.

"What?" Jesse asked, glancing down at me.

"Nothing," I replied. The car was slowing down at the curb as my heart picked up speed and when we came to a stop, the driver said, "Wait here," before he came around to open the car door, his eyes glancing up at the buildings around us. I knew what he was looking for, but I didn't want to say it out loud.

When we opened the door, we tumbled out in front of a set of large black lacquered doors. Each door had a golden lion's head door knocker, the ring tight in the lion's mouth, and there was a brass doorknob directly in the center of the door on the right.

I looked at the driver. He looked at me.

"Okay then," I said, then went up and knocked on the

door. The sound echoed, which told me that there was an empty hallway just on the other side.

"Uh, I'm pretty sure they're not going to open the door," Jesse said, his hoodie pulled back up because of the steady rain that was falling. Roux had shoved her hair down the back of her sweater and was standing next to him with her arms crossed, glancing skyward just as she had seen our driver do.

"Who's they?" Roux asked him. "Like you know who's back there. Maybe there's no one."

"A really comforting thought," I said.

"Sorry."

"Try the door," Jesse said, gesturing to the knob. "Maybe it's open."

I looked at him. "Even less comforting."

The driver was no help, still watching the buildings around us, and I took a deep breath and pulled on the doorknob. The door stayed shut, but a tinier one built into it swung open, almost like something from *Alice in Wonderland*.

And then I saw what was behind the door.

"What's that?" Roux asked.

"That looks medieval," Jesse added. "Like full-on bubonic plague medieval."

"Lovely imagery," Roux said.

"Well, I'm just saying . . ."

"It *is* medieval." I sighed.

Sure enough, it was the lock that had been frustrating me for the better part of six months. The lock that Angelo kept encouraging me to open, the lock that I could *never* open, was the only thing standing between us and getting through the door into safety.

"Wait," Roux said slowly, recognition dawning across her voice. "Isn't that the lock that you were working on last week? The one you couldn't open?"

"Way to be positive, Roux," Jesse whispered to her.

"Excuse me, we're standing next to a man who's scanning for snipers, probably!" she hissed back. "Forgive me if I'm not Little Mary Sunshine." Then she looked at me and smiled. "Good luck, Mags. No pressure, okay?"

"None at all," I agreed, then took a deep breath, knelt down, and got to work.

CHAPTER 27

Opening that lock on a good day was difficult. But in Paris? In the rain? Six, twelve, eighteen (my time zones were all screwed up) hours after being shot at and going on the run? Let's just say it was challenging.

Our driver, Mathieu, was nice enough to offer me a little lock-picking kit. I eyed him, then pulled my own out of my pocket, where I had stashed it a million hours ago when I broke into Dominic's house for the second time. Mathieu nodded, a sign of respect. I wondered how good he was at breaking into safes.

I hoped I was better.

I readjusted my stance in front of the door. The street was empty, the sounds of traffic far away, and I wondered if that's why Angelo sent me here. If people were gone during the day, it was always easier to sneak in and out of a location.

Or, in my case, to break into one.

The wet ground soaked the knees of my jeans almost

instantly and it became painful a few minutes later. The
first of the four locks was always the easiest, the second
one was a bit more difficult, but by the time I got to the
third one, my muscles were starting to shake. It wasn't easy
even during the best of times, but I hadn't eaten or slept in
a while.

"Shit," I whispered when the third lock slipped away
from me. "Damn it, okay. Sorry, I just have to start over."

"Take your time," Roux said, but she was shivering a
little in the rain. It was still humid out, but colder than it
had been at the airport.

It will open when you need it most, Angelo had said,
but his words just hurt when I thought about them now.
I needed a lot of things right now, and part of me wanted
to fling the tools away and stop opening the lock until
someone—anyone—explained what I was doing here and
why someone tried to kill us and where in the world my
parents were. As soon as I had answers, then maybe I might
open the lock, but until then, no deal.

But none of that was going to happen, so I kept
working.

The third locked slipped again, then once more. The
rain wasn't helping either, and our driver Mathieu eventually herded Jesse and Roux back into the car. I couldn't
blame him. Having two people standing around staring
at me breaking into someone's apartment was not incon-
spicuous.

"If he drives away with us, I'll go ballistic on him,"
Roux assured me as she slid into the car.

"You do that," I replied, then shoved my hair out of my face and tried for a fourth time.

By the tenth time, I was near tears. Sometimes opening a lock is like a sprint, other times it's a marathon, but now I felt like I was in some never-ending Ironman competition. My arms were starting to tense up, but when I loosened my grip on my tools, the lock would slip and I'd be back to square one. My legs shook from squatting in the same position for so long. My hair was now getting wet, not just damp from the light rain, and above all else, I knew that my best friend and my boyfriend were waiting for me in what was probably a bulletproof car, waiting for me to open this door and get them inside to safety.

I hated this lock. I hated Paris. I hated my job, I hated being a spy, I even hated Angelo for teaching me how to pick locks in the first place. I hated my parents for not following me for the first time in their lives. I hated myself for wanting them to give me more space, more responsibility, more independence. Now that I had it, the world felt too big, like I would never find my way home again. "Our home is wherever we are, Mags," my mom had said, but now I didn't even know where they were.

I gritted my teeth and anchored my biceps, trying to get that third lock again. Sometimes you use talent to break into something, and other times, you have to use emotion instead.

"I hate you so much," I whispered, then pushed at it one more time. "I just want to go home."

I felt the third lock suddenly jolt into place and I gasped

when my tool moved forward, anchoring it open. "Oh!" I said, then carefully let go and moved on to the fourth lock. I had never gotten this far before. I had never wanted something so badly before.

The fourth lock was tiny, barely big enough to fit the jimmy in, but I managed to wiggle it open. Even though my thigh muscles were trembling, my hands were still as steady as always, which made me feel a bit better. Steely McGee, my dad used to call me, and I could hear his voice now as I carefully slipped through the gears and moved them apart. I held my breath, scared that even a puff of air would make everything fall apart. It was like building a house of cards, when one wrong movement could destroy everything.

I could feel Roux's and Jesse's and even Mathieu's eyes on me as I turned the lock one half turn to the left. If this didn't work, we were screwed. There was no Plan B, no other location, no backup situation. We either got in or we didn't.

With a loud popping sound, all four locks clicked open.

We were in.

I sat back on my heels, letting out a whoosh of air and feeling my heart pound. Behind me, I heard Roux let out a whoop before Jesse shushed her, then she shushed him right back. I was exhausted and starving and emotional, but at least the lock was open. Once again, Angelo had been right.

"C'mon," I said to them, "let's go in."

Mathieu handed us our bags, then went back to the driver's seat, ready to bid us good-bye. He idled at the curb until I waved him away, and then he drove off, leaving the three of us alone for the first time since the attack. "What is this place?" Jesse asked.

"I have no idea," I told him. "But we're going in."

The door was surprisingly heavy, and when we opened it, we were in a dim hallway, lit by a single crystal chandelier. There was a table against one wall and a mirror above it, almost like the lobby of an apartment building. "Is anyone else getting *The Shining* flashbacks?" Roux whispered. "Just me? Okay then."

There was an elevator at the end of the hall and we went in. It was old, too, and creaky, a lot like the one we had in our loft.

I pulled the gate shut and pressed the up button. "It's probably just an empty building," I told Roux and Jesse, trying to convince all three of us. "Angelo has places like this all over the world. Probably."

Neither of them replied. They didn't have to.

The elevator came to a sudden, jolting stop on the second floor, and we carefully climbed out. There was a door waiting for us and when I turned the knob, it opened without any trouble. My heart was pounding faster than it had been downstairs when I worked on the lock, and my hands were definitely shaking now. I could hear Jesse's raspy breath behind me, and I couldn't hear Roux at all.

The door opened into an apartment, all warm light and wooden parquet floors and crystal chandeliers. There were several gray couches and a loveseat, and raw silk curtain framed the windows and flowed to the floor. Bookshelves lined the wall behind the dining room table and I caught sight of a Gauguin painting on one wall.

Angelo, I knew, loved Gauguin.

"Well," said a voice from the living room, and Roux, Jesse, and I all tiptoed forward to see a guy and a girl standing there. "Took you long enough."

They were probably only a year or two older than us, but they looked amused, even almost surprised that the three of us had managed to get into the apartment. He was pretty average height and had on dark jeans rolled at the cuff to reveal thick-sole boots. He wore a black sweater with holes in the wrists and elbows, only they look artfully arranged, not moth-eaten. She stood next to him in leggings and ballet-style shoes and an oversized Rolling Stones T-shirt, her dreadlocked hair piled into a dark jumble on top of her head.

"It is nice to finally meet you, Maggie," the girl said, smiling at me. "We have been waiting for you."

CHAPTER 28

Roux, Jesse, and I stood in the doorway, not moving.

"We weren't sure you were going to be able to open the lock," the guy said. His English had a heavy Australian accent, and I realized that his thick, black-frame glasses had no glass in them. "We heard you struggling with it."

"Thank you so much for that," I said. "How do you know me?"

"Angelo sent you here, yes?" the girl said. Her voice had a French accent, but not as thick as his Australian one. "He said you would be arriving."

"You talked to Angelo?" I said. "Is he here? Where is he?"

"Not here," he said. "I'm Ryo, by the way. This is Élodie."

She waved a little. "Hi."

"I like your hair," Roux piped up behind me.

"Thank you."

"Wait a minute," I said, waving my hands in front of me. "Let's back up a few steps. Who are you?"

"Ryo and Élodie," Ryo said again, pointing between them.

"No, I mean, who *are* you?" I said, gripping the back of the chair for support. "What are you doing here? How do you know Angelo?"

"What, you think you are the only young person in the Collective?" Élodie said, a smile playing at her mouth.

"You're in the Collective, too?" Jesse asked, and Élodie smiled at him.

"You're Jesse," she guessed. "And Roux."

"Hi," Roux said. "Nice place."

"It's Angelo's," Ryo told us. "We use it sometimes for . . . refuge."

"Refuge," Jesse repeated. "Are you on the run, too?"

"Not exactly, mate," he said. "At least, not right now. Who knows? Tomorrow is a brand-new day." He smiled at Élodie. "Right?"

She grinned back at him, then turned to us. "Are you starving? Do you want some food?"

"Wait!" I said again. "Back to the topic at hand. Where's Angelo? Where are my parents?"

Ryo and Élodie glanced at one another. "We don't know," Ryo said, his tone cautious. "We just got a call from Angelo saying to meet you here."

"Mags," Jesse said behind me. "You should sit. Or eat something."

He was right, of course, but I ignored him. I was starting to shake again, the exhaustion and stress of the past day making its way through my bones. "I want to talk to them," I said. "Call Angelo right now. I want to talk to them."

"We cannot do that," Élodie said. "He calls us. We don't know how to find him."

"Then why are we here?" I yelled. "Get him on the phone right now! I want to talk to my parents! I want to know they're all right!"

I don't think I had ever thrown this loud of a temper tantrum in my life, but I certainly was now. I felt Jesse try to grab my arm, but I shook him off and stalked around the table into the living room, planting myself directly in front of Ryo and Élodie. "You need to tell me right now if my parents are dead," I said, tears building up in my eyes. "And if you lie to me, I'll kill you myself."

"They're not dead," Ryo said. "I promise, Maggie. They're not dead. We wouldn't lie about that."

I looked at both him and Élodie, looking for any sign of treachery. Their faces were honest, though, and a little sad, and that's when I burst into tears. "I want to go home!" I said. My voice was choked and I didn't sound like myself, which only made me cry harder. "I'm out, I'm done! I don't want to do this anymore!"

Jesse's hand was on my waist, reeling me back. "Mags, c'mon," he was whispering, and I tried to shove him away, but he was stronger than me. "It's okay, we're okay."

"It's not okay!" I cried, and the full truth of the words slammed into me. "It's not okay! Nothing about this is okay!"

Despite my struggles, Jesse managed to pull me into his

arms. He still smelled familiar, like home, and I buried my face in his plaid shirt and started to sob. "I'm sorry!" I wept. "I just want . . ."

"I know," he whispered, his mouth close to my ear. "Nothing to be sorry about."

The tears were so strong that they almost hurt, racking my ribs and lungs as they tore their way to the surface. Everything ached and I was so tired and jetlagged and I missed my parents so much that they felt like phantom limbs, parts of me I could no longer find.

Jesse was still there, though. His hand cupped the back of my head as he held me, his fingers smoothing over my tangled hair, and I could hear the rumble of his voice in his chest. He was talking to someone, maybe even me, but I couldn't understand the words. All I could do was cry.

After a few minutes, I felt him gather me up and start to guide me out of the room. I was still a sniveling, teary mess as I stumbled along with him, but he held on to me so I wouldn't fall. "C'mon," he said soothingly. "Let's lie down."

"I'm not tired." I sniffled.

"You're such a liar," he said, but his voice was affectionate and warm. "You can be stubborn tomorrow, okay? Let's take a break for now."

I could hear Élodie talking as we walked down the hall and into a bedroom. It was plain, just a table and mirror and a bed covered in a white duvet, with one window that showed the stormy skies outside. Jesse pulled back the covers and set me down on the bed, then tugged my shoes off before pulling off his sneakers and wriggling out of his hoodie. "Here," he said, slipping it around my shoulders. I pulled it around me and clung to the sleeves as I lay down and scooted over to make room for Jesse.

He crawled in and pulled the duvet over us, wrapping me up in his arms. I was still hiccuping a little and Jesse's shirt was cold and wet from my tears, but it felt good to be in a real bed with someone who loved me. "Go to sleep," Jesse whispered. "It'll be okay, I promise."

"You don't know that," I said. My throat was scratchy and sore and my chest hurt, like someone had stepped on it.

"Of course I do," he murmured, resting his chin on top of my head. "Things always work out when you're around. Haven't you noticed?"

I was quiet a long time, thinking about that. Jesse's heartbeat was slow and steady in my ear, a tiny measure of time, our breathing soft and even. "Jess?"

"Hmm?"

But I was already asleep.

CHAPTER 29

When I woke up, the sky was gray and the room was dim. I still had Jesse's hoodie, but it was tangled around my waist. When I went to reach for him, his side of the bed was empty but still warm, like he had just gotten up a few minutes before me. I felt better, though, almost satiated. I had been running on fumes and when they gave out, so did I.

I looked out the window for a few minutes, seeing only the sky and the old pale Parisian buildings across the street. Their windows were arched and wide, just like the ones in Ryo and Élodie's—or Angelo's?—apartment, and I saw figures moving past the window, winding up their day, living their life.

The bedroom door opened and I looked over to see Roux peeking her head in. "Hi," she whispered. "Are you awake?"

"Mmm-hmm," I mumbled, stretching my arms over my head, and Roux took that as an invite to plop herself down next to me.

"So," she said. "Better?"

I nodded as I sat up. "How bad is my hair?"

"Atrocious," she replied cheerfully, which made me smile.

"What time is it?"

"Almost six thirty. At night," she added. "Jesse just got up a little while ago, too. He's talking with Ryo and Élodie. They're pretty cool. Élodie's going to dye my hair for me."

Called it.

"Are you hungry?" Roux continued. "There's food. And coffee, of course."

"There's always coffee," I said. "Wait, though. Are you okay?"

Roux just shrugged. "Yeah. Yesterday wasn't exactly my idea of fun, but we're okay now. And I like it here. I like Paris. I mean, I haven't been outside yet, but I still like it. What about you? Are you okay?"

"I think so," I said. "Just needed to have a psychotic breakdown, that's all."

"I highly recommend them." She grinned at me. "Next time, though, definitely break something. Otherwise you just look like an amateur."

"Noted," I said. "Maybe smash a plate?"

"A plate, maybe a few glasses if someone else will clean up the mess." Roux's eyes gleamed wickedly in the dark room. "I'll show you a few things when we get back to New York."

"So you're not mad that we had to leave?"

"What, and leave behind a bunch of people who called

me names and two parents that wouldn't know my name if they saw it on my birth certificate?" Roux rolled her eyes. "The world's bigger than one city, right? It's just nice to be doing something for once, rather than sitting around and waiting for someone to do something to *us*."

I smiled back at her. "So it's better than SAT prep?" I teased.

"So much better." She laughed. "At least *this* will be useful in life. C'mon, let's go eat. There's cheese!"

After she left, I went into the bathroom and washed my face and brushed my teeth using one of the new tooth-brushes that was laid out next to the sink. The water was surprisingly cold and it made me shiver, but it woke me up, too, and I finger combed my hair before padding down the hall and into the kitchen.

Ryo, Élodie, Roux, and Jesse were all around the large wooden table. There was a French press in the middle of the table, half-full with coffee, and some bread and cheese and cold roast chicken and figs. "She's alive," Ryo said when he saw me.

"Nice hair," Jesse added, winking at me. I had it coming after all the grief I had given him about his curly hair, though, and I smiled a little as I slipped into the chair next to his.

"Sorry about . . . *that*," I said, waving my arm back toward the living room. "I was just tired. And stressed. And pissed. And I won't kill you, Ryo."

"I wasn't worried," he said. "And don't sweat it. No one's dead, so it's fine."

"You should have seen me after our last debacle,"

Élodie said, rolling her eyes to the ceiling. "Ask Ryo, I was a mess. But then *he* fell apart after—well, we are getting ahead of ourselves."

Roux shoved some cheese at me. "So good," she said, her mouth full. "Try it."

I took it, then poured some coffee into a chipped china teacup. It was strong and hot and made me feel more like myself.

"I know I asked this earlier," I said, "but I probably missed the answer if there was one. What do you *do*? Who are you?"

"We should wait for Ames before we explain," Ryo said. "He'll be here soon. It's somewhat easier to explain with him here."

Élodie laughed under her breath and said something to Ryo in French before grinning at him. He smiled back, but what was surprising was that Jesse smiled, too.

"Wait, Jess," Roux said. "Did you understand that?"

His eyes widened in realization. "Wait. No. Wait, say something else in French again."

Élodie rattled off a string of words that I didn't understand, but to my absolute amazement, Jesse responded in perfect French. "Holy shit!" he cried, then looked at me in surprise.

"You speak French?" I cried. "Since *when*?"

"Since I don't know!" he said. "I mean, I've been learning French since kindergarten, and I know that I like to go with *mes amis* to *la plage* and drink *limonade*, but I thought it was just stupid things like that. Wow, my expensive education actually *works*!"

"Drink lemonade with your friends at the beach,"

Élodie scoffed. "Tell me, do you see a beach around here? What do they teach you in those textbooks?"

Jesse was still laughing to himself, though, not listening to Élodie at all. "I can't believe it!"

"I wonder what *I* can do if Jesse can speak French," Roux mused. "Does anyone have a ninja star I can throw?"

"No," we all said immediately, but it did nothing to squash Roux's enthusiasm for Jesse's newfound talent. "You should totally take AP French when we get home," she told him. "You'd smoke everyone in that class."

"Good plan," I said. "Now I have a non–language related question. How's Ames going to get in the front door? He can't crack the lock."

"Of course he can." Élodie shrugged. "We all can. It's easy."

"Easy?" I cried. "I almost lost a finger trying to get that thing open! I've been practicing for nearly six months and it was still difficult."

"Ames made a tool that makes it simple," Ryo said. "And besides, that's how we know someone is worthy of getting in. If you can't do the lock, you don't deserve to be here. Lucky for you, you passed the test."

"Luck had nothing to do with it," I said. "More like blood, sweat, and tears. Literally."

"Well, that sounds like a party!"

We all turned to see a guy walking through the living room into the kitchen, a huge grin across his face and a motorcycle helmet under his arm. He wore a leather jacket and his boots were heavy on the parquet floors, and he had the sort of flushed cheeks that made him look like he was perpetually embarrassed or pleased.

"Oh," I heard Roux murmur behind me.

"Howya?" He nodded at Ryo and Élodie, dropping his helmet down on the table and giving Élodie a kiss on the top of her head before doing the same to Ryo. "Someone said something about blood? Who are these strangers? Why haven't we boiled them in a pot yet?" He winked at me. "Just kidding. I'm a vegetarian. I only eat my enemies. For breakfast." His Irish accent was broad and deep. Roux hadn't stopped looking at him.

Ryo gestured to me, ignoring the guy's bravado. "Ames, this is Maggie."

Ames's face split wide open in a smile. "Maggie," he said. "We've heard so much. How's high school? Waste of time, yeah?"

"My own personal hell on earth," I said. "I'm sorry, how do you know I'm in high school?"

"We were waiting for you to explain, Ames," Élodie said, patting the chair next to her. "Way to take your time, by the way. We love waiting for you."

"You know what I like best about you, Él?" Ames said, and Élodie wrinkled her nose at the nickname. "You use sarcasm to hide your true emotions. It's so human." He looked at Jesse. "You must be the boyfriend. Falling in love with a criminal, yeah?" He winked at Jesse in a knowing way. "It's great craic."

Jesse looked a bit confused but still shook Ames's hand. "Hey," he said.

"I'm Roux," Roux said, offering her own hand, and the Ames Charm Tour came to a halt when he took her hand in his. The two of them froze for only a second, but it was clear that something had changed in the room. Roux's shoulders, which were always somewhere around her ears due to her constant nervous energy, fell a little, and the blush in Ames's cheeks grew a little, along with his smile.

"*Enchanté*," he said to her. "I'm sure."

Roux grinned, but it wasn't her normal smile. It was the smile she got when someone paid attention to her, when they noticed her. It was real and warm and I almost felt like I should look away, like Roux and Ames should have this moment for themselves.

Ryo, apparently, felt differently.

"So you're here," he said. "Finally. And Maggie's here, along with her two rogues. Can we please get to work?"

"Right," Ames said, plopping down between Élodie and Roux. "So. Maggie. We heard you almost got shot. Good work not dyin'."

"Um, thank you?" I said.

"About that," Jesse said, his hand cupped around his coffee mug. "So we're all cool just sitting in front of these large windows?" He pointed at the arched windows that lined one of the kitchen walls. "No one's worried about a follow-up attack?"

"They're bulletproof and tinted," Élodie said. "Please do not worry."

"Yeah, no offense," Roux said, "but I've heard that before. Let me guess: the Collective put the windows in. Because if so, that won't make me feel any safer."

"The Collective," Ames scoffed. "You still trust them after all they did to you?"

Roux and Jesse both looked at me, and I took a deep breath.

"I don't know what to believe," I said, "but it would be a lot easier to figure out if you told me what we were doing here and who you were."

Ryo, Ames, and Élodie all looked at one another. "We used to be part of the Collective, too," Élodie said. "Until they tried to turn us, then erased our identities."

I felt both Roux and Jesse look at me.

"And some other things," Ames added, pulling off a piece of chicken with his fingers.

"Care to elaborate?" Jesse asked.

"It's complicated."

"You know what's *complicated*?" I said. "Flying all night to Paris after someone opens fire on your family. *That*'s complicated."

Ames grinned and pointed at her and Élodie. "You two, you love to make it all woo-woo-y."

"Well, it's not like we explain it that often!" Élodie protested. Her hair was in her face, and she twisted it back into a hasty bun. "We don't have open membership, Ames."

"Can we back this up a moment, please?" I interrupted them. "Let's go back to that ex-Collective part."

"That's the best part," Ames agreed, then popped the chicken in his mouth and leaned so far back in his chair that I was afraid he would fall.

"I'll start," he said. "They recruited me when I was in

high school in Dublin, said I had a gift for mechanics and locks and such."

I tried not to bristle with jealousy.

"And then when I turned eighteen, they wanted me to go further, do more dangerous things."

"Which you probably loved," Élodie muttered.

"'Course I did!" Ames grinned. "But there's dangerous and then there's what they asked me to do. Spying on other members of the Collective, hunting down people who tried to leave." He shrugged. "That's not what I do, mate. I don't turn on friends. When I said no, they tried to kill me. So I ran."

He told the story like he was describing a trip to the supermarket. Jesse's posture was ramrod straight next to me, Roux's eyes were wide, and I realized that I had my hand over my heart.

"Tell 'em your story." Ames nodded at Ryo. "That's a good one."

"I was in Tokyo," Ryo said, rubbing his hand over his face. I wondered how much sleep they were getting. "The Collective came to me and interrogated me about Élodie for hours."

"I was in Dakar, in Senegal," she interjected. "I had no idea about any of this. Things had been so slow with work lately, you know. The Collective said we should take some time, go visit our families. They just wanted to sep-arate us."

"But you two were already together?" Jesse asked.

Ryo nodded. "Since we were fifteen. We went to board-ing school in Paris."

I thought of my parents and said nothing.

"The Collective recruited us, too, just like Ames," he continued. "But they said Élodie had turned and I couldn't get ahold of her at all."

"They did the same thing to me," Élodie said. "They said that Ryo had gone rogue, that he had stolen evidence, and they wanted me to help find him. But I knew he had not done anything of the sort." Her eyes blazed with anger and her fingernails were digging into the wooden table. Ryo must have noticed, too, because he reached over and covered her hand with his.

"So we ran," Ryo said. "And apparently the Collective didn't like that very much."

My mind was spinning at a furious pace, trying to keep up with the story and the connections to my life. "When was this?"

"The beginning of summer," Ames said.

"Angelo," I said, and all three of our new friends nodded. "He got you out."

"He smuggled me out of Dakar," Élodie said, "and got Ree into Paris."

"Ree!" Ames snickered, which made Ryo turn red.

"Why do you have to call me that?" he muttered to Élodie.

"Ignore that *sai sai*," she said, nodding at Ames. "He is an idiot. Angelo should have left him in Dublin."

"But he didn't, so the story has a happy ending!" Ames grinned, then looked at us. "So you're the safecracker," he said, pointing at me. "What do you two do? Angelo never mentioned that you might be joining our little soirée."

Roux just smiled at him. "I deal in sarcasm, punching people, and ordering takeout."

"I specialize in being a civilian who manages to find himself in life-threatening situations," Jesse replied. "It's a natural talent. Oh, and apparently I speak French, too."

Ames, Élodie, and Ryo all gaped at us. "You're civilians?" Ryo cried. "And they tried to kill you, too?"

Jesse nodded. "Blew up the building and everything, but Angelo got us out, too."

"This isn't the first time someone's tried to kill us, actually," Roux replied, helping herself to some cheese and bread. "Last year, Maggie had to break into this guy's safe and he was chasing us but I punched him in the nose."

Ames let out a laugh and looked at her in admiration. "I'd have *loved* to see that."

"Stick around." Roux shrugged. "I come in pretty handy."

"You'll never get tired of that story, will you?" I said, and she shook her head and smiled at me through a mouthful of bread.

"Well, we are safe here, at least for now," Élodie said. "This is Angelo's home, he brought us here. And the tunnels, of course, they are safe, too."

"You know about the tunnels?" I blurted out before I could stop myself.

Roux raised her hand. "Can we pretend that some of us haven't heard about these tunnels?"

"Good idea," Jesse added.

"You don't know about the tunnels?" Ames said, looking serious for the first time in our conversation.

"My parents told me about them," I said, sitting up in my chair. "You've been in them?"

Ames took a pencil out of his pocket and started to lightly trace the eraser end across the table. "There's a network of tunnels underneath Paris. Sort of the flip side of our City of Light, yeah? The tourists love it. But they're messy and damp and cold. Still, though, fun for the whole family." He grinned and I saw Roux grin back.

Oh, boy.

"But we use them a little . . . differently," Ryo continued as Ames and Roux continued to make googly eyes at each other. There was a soft *lump* sound under the table, and Ames winced and shot Ryo a dirty look as he rubbed his shin.

Élodie rolled her eyes. "You two take forever explaining this," she said. "I'll do it." She set her cup down and looked squarely at Jesse, Roux, and me. "When we went to school here, we used the tunnels under Paris to set up film festivals and art shows, and we snuck into old cultural buildings to repair them without the government's knowledge." She sat back in her seat, satisfied. "See? I did it in one sentence."

"What do you mean, you *repaired* them?" Roux asked. "What, like you fix their lights or something?"

"Or something," Ryo and Ames chorused.

"There are some buildings in Paris that will get attention," Ryo added. "The Louvre, for example. It's a massive tourist site and it has the *Mona Lisa*, of course, so the government will always pay for repairs."

"Its security is absolute crap, though," Élodie added.

"True," Ames said. "But Ryo is right. It's in fine condition. But we think that maybe there are other things that are also worth a bit of our attention. So we fix them up, show them a night on the town, and we do it all without even a thank-you. Rude, I know, but hey." He let out a sad sigh. "Being a merry band of artistic criminals has its own special set of perks."

"So you repair things and you use the tunnels to access buildings?" Jesse asked.

"Mostly, yes. We set up shop in different buildings." Élodie smiled to herself. "We used to have this little saying: If it's already been created, it must be possible to re-create. That is what we wanted to do, re-create parts of Paris. But then we joined the Collective and we came back and found that all of the work we had done in school was destroyed." She looked so sad. "We forget that not everyone sees things the same way, but *they* are the idiots. You can appreciate the past and still have an iPhone, you know. It is not difficult."

"Did you—I mean, do you know my parents?" I asked them.

"Your parents are so cool." Roux sighed dreamily. "Can we swap, please? Or can they just adopt me?"

"Oh, we've never met," Ryo assured me. "We've only met Angelo."

"He used to provide a bit of financial backing," Ames said. "For tools and such. And a nice establishment to stay in every now and then. We're very picky about our chandeliers, as you can imagine. No thief worth their weight in gold would settle for any old bulb."

Jesse smiled to himself and ran a hand over his eyes. "Maggie." He sighed. "We're never going to get bored, are we?"

I ignored his comment, though. I had never missed my parents as much as I did right then.

"Now it's our turn for some questions," Élodie said. "What did you do to piss off the Collective? Because if you're here with us, there's a reason."

"What did Angelo tell you?" I asked, not sure of how much to say. I had tucked the gold coins into my pillowcase, hidden from everyone else, but I could still feel their weight in my hand, the way they clinked together.

"That you might be here one day," Ryo said. "He didn't mention your friends, obviously."

"A very nice surprise," Ames added, smiling at Roux. "And you, too, Jesse, of course."

"Hey, no offense," Jesse said, smiling a little. "Feel free to keep eye-flirting with Roux. You're not hurting my feelings."

Roux groaned. "You're *such* a mood killer, Jesse, seriously."

"So you must have something of Dominic's," Ryo guessed. "Seeing as how you're the official safecracker of the group."

"I have several of his things that he wants back. But he stole them from someone else."

"Plural? Them?" Élodie asked.

I took a deep breath and dug my hands into my pockets. "Are you sure you want to know about this? Because if you do, we have to all be in this together."

Ames gestured to the table. "We already are. Breaking bread in Paris is a sure sign of team loyalty."

I stood up. "Be right back," I said, then came back a minute later with the velvet pouch. "Go ahead," I said, handing them to Élodie. "Be my guest."

She took it and shook the coins out, her eyes widening at the sight of them. "Are these . . . ?" she started to say.

"Yes," I told her, knowing the recognition in her eyes. "They are."

Ames's eyes lit up when he saw them, but Ryo just furrowed his brow. "The double-eagle gold coin," he said. "How do you know these aren't fake?"

"The fact that someone sent a crew of hitmen to try and kill us after I took them was kind of a tip-off."

"Shame, really," Ames said. "The Collective used to be so admirable." He picked up one coin, then rolled it over the back of his fingers before making it disappear into his palm. "Oops," he said, then made it reappear. "Gotta work on that one."

"How much are these worth?" Jesse asked. "Like, roughly?"

"About seventy million dollars," I said, and Roux leaned away from the table like the coins might suddenly bite her. "Roughly."

Ryo let out a low whistle. "And Dominic wants them back, I assume?"

"Yep," I said. "And since the Collective accused my parents of stealing the coins, my family and I probably won't be too safe if that happens. Not to mention *your* safety, as well."

"Right, so we're all dead, then," Ames said cheerfully. "Drink up!"

"So what we do?" Roux asked. "Call him up and say, 'Hey, let's arrange a trade.'" I knew she was kidding, but she had a point.

"I don't know," I admitted. "I've always taken things, I've never had to give them back before. And these are technically stolen material," I added, and Ryo nodded along with me. "Angelo said that they were taken from the US Mint in 1933, so that's partly why they're so valuable. The Secret Service has arranged stings to get them back before. So there's that, too."

"The fun just keeps coming, doesn't it." Jesse groaned. "What else, do they explode? Are they really tiny grenades?"

I made a face at him and he gave me a goofy smile in return. "No," I said. "They're just gold coins. That people really want. A lot."

"Has Dominic asked for them back yet?" Ryo asked me.

"Well, I don't know, we're not exactly on speaking terms right now," I said. "I mean, I lost his cell, then I e-mail him and it takes him three weeks to write back, then the next thing you know it's finals week and I'm just a mess."

Élodie smirked at Ryo. "I like her."

"What I *meant* to say," Ryo said, bumping Élodie's leg with his knee while giving me a sarcastic look, "was that he's going to find this place and come calling. It's more of a when than an if, innit?"

Ryo had a point. "Probably," I admitted.

"Angelo will know what to do," Ames said, picking up another coin and rolling it around on his left hand this time. "He'll make demands through someone."

"He called when you were sleeping, by the way," Ryo said. "He said that Dominic is not in Paris. Yet, anyway. That's all he knew. He knows you have the coins, though, and without you, he doesn't get them. So we're all right now, at least for a day or two."

I felt a small twinge of jealousy when Ryo said that Angelo had called, but I let it slide. "I can't imagine Dominic is happy about that," I muttered. "I don't think he's used to having his toys taken away."

"Yes, the Collective doesn't like to lose," Ames said, the first time I had heard a trace of any anger in his voice. "Look at Colton Hooper. He spent ten years trying to kidnap you."

"You heard about him?" I asked, and they all nodded.

"Can I just say that breaking his nose was so satisfying?" Roux chimed in. "Because I did. There was blood everywhere, like, *gushing* out—"

"Roux," I said, still wincing at the memory. Blood was not my strong suit.

"Good on ya," Ames said, smiling at her.

And then Roux did something I have never seen her do before: she blushed. It was faint in the low light, but her cheeks pinked up and she ducked her head away. Ames just kept smiling at her and I looked away, suddenly feeling like I needed to give them privacy.

"Can I see the tunnels?" I asked tentatively. I wanted to see where my parents had been, their old home back when they were my age. I wanted to feel connected to them in this crazy new world of ours where nothing felt safe at all.

"Yeah, enough about the Collective!" Ames declared. "We already know what our guests here do, breaking locks and noses and bread and everything in between. Let's show them how we travel through Paris." He held out his hand to Roux, who took it like he was holding out a lit firecracker. "It's time for a little show-and-tell."

CHAPTER 30

If you think I'm going down there, you're crazy."

Roux stood with her arms crossed in front of her, shivering a little in Ames's coat. I was standing next to her, wearing one of Élodie's sweaters while Jesse had his hoodie zipped up to his throat. "You don't exactly get to pack when you're on the run," I told Élodie when we slipped out the back door of the building, avoiding the front door entirely and instead going through a basement door that had the same archaic lock on it. Ames opened it in less than a minute, using a tiny tool that fit in his palm, and I watched in amazement as he clicked through all four locks as Jesse laughed under his breath.

"You need to teach me how to use that thing," I said, trying not to look too impressed.

"Relax," Ames said, patting me on the shoulder as we went through the door. "I might be able to pick locks, but you're still the safecracker."

The six of us went down the street toward a Métro

entrance, but instead of entering the underground station, Ryo took a right and went easily through what looked like a janitor-style door. Élodie followed him, and we followed her and found ourselves suddenly in a tight space that left little room to breathe and even less to move. It was slightly damp and very cool, much cooler than outside, and it took a minute for my eyes to adjust to the light.

"Is it a bad time to mention that I'm claustrophobic?" Roux asked, her voice small.

"You're claustrophobic?" Jesse asked.

"I didn't know that until just now," she said. "Are the walls moving? I feel like they're moving."

"Easy, darlin'," Ames said. His voice sounded so kind when he talked to her. I had never heard anyone speak to Roux that way before, and it was nice to hear. "We just need to go down this grate." He pointed at a small set of iron bars in the ground, a pool of water splashing underneath.

Roux looked at it for a bit. "Nope," she finally said. "I'll just wait here. If I see Dominic, well, it was a good run and I had some fun and—"

Ames bent down and moved the grate, only he didn't just move the bars, he moved the entire thing, water and all. It was an illusion, I realized, simply a tray of water designed to look like a normal hole in the ground.

"Rolling tray," he said. "It keeps others from finding our secret passageways. Not to brag, but I invented this contraption."

"Aren't they all secret passageways?" Jesse asked as relief crossed Roux's face.

"Some more than others," Ryo said. "Ladies first."

Roux and I followed Élodie down the rabbit hole and dropped into a much drier tunnel. This one had electric bulbs lining the ceiling and while it was still dirty, it felt almost civilized. "These are *our* tunnels," Élodie said. "Or I should say *your* tunnels. Your parents are the ones who found them."

"We are going to have such a serious talk when I see them again," I said, but the thought of when I would see them again made my heart twist and I shoved the thought out of my mind. *They must know where I am*, I thought. *This is as much my history as the Collective is. Home is where your family is, and my parents had once been here.*

We walked along, Jesse sometimes reaching up and tapping at the lightbulbs. "I didn't think there'd be light down here," he admitted. "I was picturing mining caps or like when we went down into that secret platform at Grand Central Station."

Ames turned around, his eyes wide. "You saw that? I thought that was just an urban legend."

"It's the real deal," Roux said. "We were there."

"What's it like?"

"Dirty."

Ames smiled at her and reached out to ruffle her hair, but Roux ducked away. "Careful," I said. "She knows tae kwon do."

"I'm missing my class today, actually," Roux said. "But this is way better."

"Ryo put in the lights," Élodie said, taking his arm and

finally answering my silent question of whether or not they were a couple. "He's the electrician of our group."

"And what do you do?" I asked, tucking my hand into Jesse's hoodie pocket as we walked along.

"Cartography," she said. "Mapmaking. I help map out the tunnels for everyone. Well, not everyone. Just a select few."

"And you?" I nodded at Ames.

"Your local horologist, at your service," Ames said, bowing a little.

"Your local *what*?" Roux said. "What did you just say?"

"*H*, not *wh*, darlin'," Ames said, but there was a twinkle in his eye. "And it's a fancy word for clock maker. I fix gears, get things going again." He wiggled his eyebrows at Roux, and she burst out laughing

"That's what they call clock repair people?" She giggled. "That's the worst name ever! That sounds like the scientific name for a pimp!"

Ames's cheeks had gone red all the way to the tips of his ears. "We can't pick the names of our calling," he said. "Unfortunately."

"I think I'll call you Gear Man," Roux said, patting his shoulder and making Ames go even redder. "That's much more flattering."

"A lot of people like to use the tunnels for partying or drinking, things like that," Ryo said. "Which is great and all, but we use them as a means to an end. The partying helps give us a nice cover, though." He shot a grin over his shoulder at us. "You should know something about blending in."

I grinned back. "All too well," I said. I had to admit that it was nice to talk to other people who knew about the Collective, who also had secret lives. I never got to discuss my life with near strangers before. "This is sort of a new experience," I said, "talking about spying and the Collective with you. I like it, it's different."

"In French, the word 'experience' means both 'experience' and 'experiment,'" Jesse said, and Élodie nodded in agreement. "I never really got that until now. We're experiencing an experiment."

"So you don't talk to this one, Maggie?" Ames said, pointing at Roux as she frowned at him and pretended to shove his hand away.

"Pointing is rude," she told him.

"So is breaking a man's nose, love, so don't go launching those stones out of your glass house just yet." He caught her hand in his and Roux smiled, hiding her face behind her hair.

"Of course I talk to her," I said. "Jesse, too. But they weren't supposed to know about all this."

Élodie, Ryo, and Ames all looked at me. "You know you have to tell the story now," Ryo said. "How did they find out?"

Jesse and Roux looked at each other, both of them smiling. "Go ahead, Mags," Jesse said. "Tell them how we met."

"Jesse was my assignment," I admitted. "Only it got a bit complicated and the case was corrupt and I needed his and Roux's help to solve it. So I kind of broke the rules a bit. Well, a lot, I guess."

"It's good to break the rules," Ryo said. "I met Élodie because we were in detention together one afternoon." He took her hand and kissed it. The affection ran deep between them, that much was obvious. "Rules were made to be broken, anyway."

"It sounds like it worked out well for Jesse, too." Ames grinned at us. "Am I wrong?"

"Not at all," he said, and I smiled despite myself.

"Jesse's a trooper," I said.

"Yes, I am," he agreed with a laugh. "Maggie likes to keep it exciting."

"Speaking of excitement," Élodie said. "We are here. You do not argue with the mapmaker about these things."

We left our coats down in the tunnel and climbed back up through the rolling tray (which, I had to admit, was sort of a genius invention) and out a side door onto the Paris streets. "Just a few minutes," Ryo warned as we went outside. "That's all."

The air was much warmer than in the tunnels and as we rounded the corner, I saw the Jardin du Luxembourg ahead of us. I had only been in it a few times, mostly when I was younger as we traveled through Europe, but I heard Roux gasp in surprise. "Wow," she said, her voice hushed almost like she was in church. "Paris is really beautiful."

Ames smiled at her and Jesse raised an eyebrow at me. I just shrugged, our secret language firmly in place. I knew we'd be discussing Roux and Ames later.

Roux and Ames. Even in my head, it had a nice ring to it.

"Looks like another locked park," Jesse said to me, nudging his shoulder against mine. "Is this our thing now? Locked parks?"

"Could be." I shrugged, then wrapped my arm around his waist. The sun had nearly set, and I could just make out my friends' features in the dark. Roux was smiling, saying something to Ames as we walked, and even in the near dark, I saw him grin back at her, his hands stuffed into his pockets.

I wasn't sure what was going to happen, but I was glad we were together.

All of us.

CHAPTER 31

By the time we climbed through the tunnels and back into the apartment ("Seriously," I told Ames as he undid the lock, "you need to show me how you do that"), we were all exhausted, especially those of us suffering from jetlag. Jesse and I fell into bed almost immediately, my head resting on his shoulder as we started to drift off, but I could hear Roux's and Ames's voices floating down the hall, soft as whispers.

"Do you think he's a good guy?" I asked Jesse, my eyes already closed. "Because if he's not, I'll rip his balls off."

Jesse ducked his head and I could feel him smile against my arm. "I think so," he murmured. "I'm pretty sure Élodie would have already kicked him out if he wasn't good."

"You can be a good thief and a terrible person," I pointed out. "Look at Dominic."

"I don't think it's quite the same thing," Jesse said. "Can we sleep now, please? Roux is fine. Roux can take care of Roux. If anything, Ames should be scared of *her*."

"She's not tough, she's gooey," I said, but my words were

already slipping away as sleep pulled me under. The last thing I heard before I fell asleep was Jesse's amused voice saying, "You are so weird sometimes."

When I woke up, it was nearly three in the afternoon. The clouds had parted by this point, leaving some hazy sunshine through the window, and I showered and went into the kitchen.

"Coffee's right there," Roux said, pointing at the French press on the table. "It's fresh."

"You know me well," I said, reaching for it.

"Well, it's not like you keep it a secret or anything." Roux smirked. Her eyes were tired but she looked at ease in her skin, which was something I hadn't seen on her, well, ever.

"You look . . . *happy*," I finally said.

"Are you accusing me of being happy? How dare you." Roux smiled at me over the rim of her coffee cup. "Be nice to me. I was up late last night."

I raised an eyebrow. "Oh, really? And what were you doing?"

"We were *talking*," Roux said. "Only talking, dirty birdy. He's nice."

"I don't think you've ever described anything as 'nice' in your life," I said.

"Well, it works on him. He's different. He's a clock maker."

"I thought it was technically a horolo—"

"Yeah, no, that word is never crossing my lips. But we just talked. He was raised outside of Dublin. His family still lives there."

The question hung between us. For all the times that Roux loudly brushed off her parents' absence, I knew it cut right through her, leaving her heart exposed. "Did you tell him about your family?" I asked, trying to sound as nonchalant as possible.

"I did," she said, her voice soft. "I told him about everything."

"Your parents?"

"My parents, or lack thereof, about Jake and Julia and everyone else at school, about how I met you. Ames knows everything."

"Wow," I said. "I'm surprised. You don't usually talk about it."

Roux just shrugged. "I talked because he listened. Most guys don't listen to me. They just want to hook up. But he listened."

I was about to say something when the front door started to open. My eyes shot to the hallway, then back to Roux. "Is everyone here?" I asked. "Did Ryo go to the store or—?"

"We're all here," Roux said. "I swear, all of us. Ames and Jesse are talking and Élodie and Ryo are—"

Élodie suddenly came running down the hall, her eyes wide and frightened. "Who is that?" she demanded. "Who is—?"

"Wait!" Ryo called after her. "Élodie, wait, it's—!"

The front door opened.

"So sorry for the disturbance, my loves," said a familiar voice. "I hope I didn't frighten anyone!"

No one moved for a second and then—

"*Angelo*!" Roux screamed, launching herself at him. "Oh my God, you're alive and they didn't kill you and try to use the body as a bribing tool with Interpol or anything!"

Jesse and Ames both came running at the sound of our cries. I was right on Roux's heels and I threw my arms around Angelo's neck as Roux continued with her half hug, half strangulation. "Angelo." I sighed, so glad for his familiar voice and face that I could have cried.

"It's me, it's me," he said, trying to disentangle Roux so he could hug her properly. "Here and in the flesh, I'm afraid. Sorry I couldn't give you any warning. Our communication is a bit compromised. But I am alive. Although I'm not sure for how much longer. Um, Roux, my love . . ." He coughed a little.

"Sorry," she said, immediately releasing her hold around his neck. "Sorry, I just get excited sometimes." Roux was wriggling like a puppy, but I still hadn't let go of Angelo yet. I hadn't really thought I would never see him again, but now that he was here with us, I realized how close I had come to losing him.

"I'm fine, love," he whispered into my hair as he patted my back. "Everyone is fine and I'm here now. Are you all right?"

"I'm okay," I said. "I'm just glad you're here." I looked over his shoulder as I pulled away. "My parents, are they here—?"

"I'm afraid not, no," Angelo said. "It's not quite safe

yet, and they are both working hard. You did hear that they were all right, yes?"

I nodded and tried to hide my disappointment. Roux was still hopping up and down and when Ames came into the room, she grabbed his arm. "It's Angelo!" she cried. "Angelo, the guy who taught me how to play chess!"

"Yes, I know." Ames laughed as Roux nearly tore his arm off. (Ironically, the happier she gets, the more dangerous she becomes.) "We've met before, remember? I've probably known him longer than you have."

It took a while for everyone to say hello to Angelo: he hugged Élodie and Ryo and Jesse, who looked as happy to see him as I did. "You're all right?" Angelo asked Jesse, clapping a hand onto his shoulder.

"Just a scrape, I'm fine," Jesse reassured him. "I'm tough, don't worry."

Angelo laughed. "Well, you should be, if you're going to continue dating Maggie."

We settled around the dining room table, just next to the nonfunctioning fireplace. I rested my legs over the armrest of the chair so I could put my feet in Jesse's lap. Across from us, Roux and Ames sat as close as their chairs would allow, and I reminded myself to quiz Angelo about Ames. If he was as good a guy as Jesse claimed, Angelo would know.

"So this is where we are," Angelo said by way of introduction. "Dominic is in Europe, but not Paris, and he is very angry with you, Maggie, to say the least."

"He's angry with me?" I cried. "*He's* the one who tried to kill *me*! And us! He doesn't get to be angry!"

Angelo held up his hand. "Yes, I am aware. I'm just report-ing the news. But as I'm sure we all know by now, Dominic quite enjoys revenge and it makes him decidedly less happy when things do not go according to his revenge plan. We arranged a truce, though, at least until Wednesday."

"A truce?" Ryo repeated. "You called a truce with him?"

"He wants those gold coins quite badly," Angelo said. "Bad enough that I think someone else might want them even more."

"He owes someone money," Élodie said as she realized. "It's not revenge; he needs those coins to pay someone off."

"The research points in that direction, yes," Angelo nodded. "We don't know who, but we can always bluff if need be. But I told him that if anything happens to Maggie or any of her friends, the coins would be melted down imme-diately and destroyed. So he has quite conveniently agreed to a sort of cease-fire."

"Until Wednesday?" I asked. "Then what? You dangle me on a stick out the window?"

"We could rig up a sort of pulley system," Ames said, which made Jesse laugh.

"Oh, thanks, loyal boyfriend," I said. "That's nice of you."

"*Vive la révolution!*" Jesse replied, but he squeezed my ankle so I decided to let him live.

"On Wednesday, we need to give the coins back," Angelo said. "Or what he thinks are the coins. That's why I'm here in Paris. Not only to see you all, of course, but to rustle up some facsimiles. Or make them, time permitting."

"Forgeries, I love it," Roux said, rubbing her hands together. "My passport was a work of art, Angelo, really. I could probably travel with it tomorrow."

"Well, I'm glad, my love. And keep it close; you very well may need it." Angelo looked tired, and I wondered where he had traveled from, how much he had been worrying. "I told Dominic that we would say where and when on Wednesday. Any thoughts?"

We all fell silent as we thought. Paris was vast, both above and below ground. "Let's keep it on this side of the tunnels," Angelo said, reading my mind. "Having Dominic underground with us could be quite disastrous, especially if some hapless tourist stumbled into our path."

"Well, that narrows it down to one of three thousand different tourist sites," Élodie said, but she sounded thoughtful. "We'll figure it out, Angelo. You just get the coins."

"I have to admit, though," Angelo said, "that's not the only reason I'm here. I would be bereft if I missed our Roux's birthday."

Every head at the table swiveled to Roux's direction.

She looked both shocked that Angelo knew and embarrassed that we had found out. "Um, surprise," she said, waving her hands a little. "I'm eighteen. Woo."

"Were you going to say anything?" I cried, immediately leaping out of my seat so I could run around the table and give her a hug. "It's your birthday and I didn't know? I'm a terrible friend, oh my God!"

"It's your birthday?" Ames looked aghast. "Oh, no, no,

this will not do at all. *At all*. We have to celebrate with something. Fireworks or balloons or—"

"No balloons," Roux said.

"—or something," Ames continued. "Stay here, all right? I'll be back." He grabbed his jacket from the back of his chair and started to run out of the room, then ran back and gave Roux a quick kiss on the cheek. "Happy birthday," he said, then hurried off.

Roux startled, her hand on her cheek as if to keep the kiss on her skin, and a slow smile spread across her face as the door clicked shut behind Ames. "*Iiiiinteresting*," Jesse said as he came around the table to give her a hug. "You and Ames, huh?"

"Oh, go away," Roux said, then slugged him in the arm. "It's my birthday so you have to be nice to me. That's the rule."

"So how did you know?" Roux asked Angelo that evening. We were still waiting for Ames, who had texted Ryo twice, but Ryo refused to show Roux any of the texts, even after both she and Élodie attacked him. "Jesse, handoff!" Ryo had shouted, and Jesse had taken the phone from him and held it above their heads until they promised not to read it.

"Well, it *is* public record," Angelo answered Roux. "And Maggie had never mentioned it, so I suspected that she didn't know."

"I didn't know!" I wailed. "I'm so sorry, Roux! I should have asked."

"It's fine, it's fine. My God, you have enough guilt to power the Vatican." Roux seemed amused by all the fuss I was making, but I felt terrible. "And you know, we've been a little busy," she pointed out. "I don't think I could handle a surprise party. This week has been exciting enough."

"Why did we never celebrate, though?" Jesse asked. "I don't remember any parties or anything."

"It's not during the school year." Roux shrugged. "It's right before the start of school, which is horrible, by the way, in case you were wondering. It really puts a damper on any celebrations."

Jesse and I were starting to realize the same thing at the same time, though. "Your parents didn't celebrate it," I said.

Angelo leaned against the kitchen sink and glanced at his watch. "Where is that Ames?" he said distractedly.

"It's not a big deal," Roux insisted. "They would call if they were gone, and they'd send these huge gifts with bows and paper. And I had nannies until I was twelve, so . . ." She trailed off, then snapped herself out of it. "Seriously, it's fine."

Ryo and Élodie looked at Jesse and me. "Your parents," Élodie said, slinging an arm around Roux's shoulders, "sound like absolutely horrific people."

Roux glanced up in surprise. "Well, that's because they are." She laughed a little. "And I did get a Fabergé egg and a ridiculous amount of money out of the deal, so it's not doom and gloom. And—"

"I'm back!" Ames cried. (I was starting to see why

Angelo had soundproofed the place.) "I'm back, I'm back! Everyone in the kitchen! Is Roux still here?"

"Where would I go?" Roux wondered aloud as Ames burst into the room, cheeks flaming and eyes sparkling. If a stranger happened to stumble into our apartment, they would have thought it was his birthday, not Roux's.

"Oh good!" Ames said, several bags in his hand and out of breath, like he had been running. It was incredibly adorable and Roux bit her lip when she looked at him, trying to keep her smile from getting any bigger.

"Please tell me there aren't any balloons," she said. "Or clowns. Do you even have clowns here in France? Oh, no, you have mimes, don't you? Please, don't tell me there's a mime waiting in the living room or I'll—!"

"No and definitely no clowns or mimes or anything else that's mute," Ames assured her. "It's your birthday, not a nightmare."

Ryo grinned at Ames. "Ames loves a good time," he told us. "And a good party."

"So does Roux," Jesse said. "Admit it, you love it."

"I do," she said. "I've just never had one before."

"Darlin', that is so tragic." Ames sighed. "We have to fix that." He set down his bags and clapped his hands together. "Might as well start now!"

An hour later, the small apartment kitchen had been transformed into one of the best parties I had been to. Ryo and Élodie had thrown cheap crepe paper streamers between the light fixtures, and Ames had made a playlist that consisted mostly of the Beatles, Jay-Z, and a French band that sounded amazing, even if I couldn't understand any of their lyrics. Roux could, though, and she danced in her bare feet as we ate everything I could find in the refrigerator that was party-appropriate. (Mostly cheese and olives and two baguettes, but Roux seemed fine with that.)

"Okay!" Ames announced as he paused the music. "It is *officially* nighttime, which means we can *officially* toast Roux's birthday." He produced two bottles of champagne. "Don't worry, there's more," he said, "but this can get us started."

Of course, Angelo had gorgeous cut-glass champagne flutes stored away in a hutch in the guest bedroom, and he pulled them out so we could toast properly. "These are never used," he said. "It's nice to see that they still function."

Roux had been silent this whole time, her cheeks pink from dancing and also, I suspected, pure delight. "It's not like this is my first drink," she told Ames as he made a big deal of handing her a glass that was half-full of Veuve Clicquot. "I hate to tell you, but you're not the only lawbreaker here."

"Yes, yes, but this is your first drink on your eighteenth birthday and you're in Paris, so this counts more than all the others combined. Now a toast!"

"Oh, God," Roux muttered, covering her eyes with her free hand. "This is so embarrassing."

"I'll start!" Jesse said, holding out his glass. (Jesse didn't drink, so his was filled with mineral water.) "To Roux, my oldest friend. I've known you longer than almost anyone else, ever since that first day of preschool when you stole my Transformers action figure and wouldn't give it back.

This wasn't quite how I saw our friendship going, I'll admit, but I'm glad it did. Happy birthday."

"Aww, Jesse, you're not supposed to make me like you!" Roux protested through her smiles. "That was so sweet!"

"My turn!" I said. "Roux, not only are you my oldest friend, but you're my best friend. You were the only person who would talk to me last year, and you've always had my back. Even when someone was shooting at it, which I really appreciate. I love you."

Roux just shook her head, and I could tell she was trying not to cry. "This is why I don't have parties," she said. "I get too emotional."

"Which brings it to my turn," Angelo said, his smile warm as he sent it in Roux's direction. "I'm sorry that our celebration is happening amid some international turmoil, but the fact that you're a part of it means that you're a part of our family now. I told you last year that you had been a wonderful friend to Maggie, and that has only continued. I know you don't hear this very often, but I love you very much, and you will always have a place in our homes and hearts and lives." He raised his glass up and winked at her. "To Roux."

Roux's eyes spilled over and she crossed the room to hug Angelo's waist as tight as she could. He hugged her back, kissing the top of her head.

"She didn't even spill a drop," Ames said, making everyone laugh.

"I told you this wasn't my first time," she said, wiping at her eyes as she pulled away from Angelo. Ryo shut off the lights, and Élodie came into the room with seven small raspberry tarts on a tray, the center one lit by a tall sparkling candle. It looked like a firecracker and Roux started laughing when she saw it. "This is too much," she said.

We sang to her, anyway.

When we were done, Ames stood behind Roux and held her hair back. "You have to make a wish!" he told her. "Hurry, before this thing launches itself through the ceiling."

"Spoiler alert," she said. "It already came true." And she leaned forward to blow out the candle.

CHAPTER 32

After the champagne was gone and the playlist on Ames's computer started to repeat itself, Jesse and I climbed out the window in Ryo and Élodie's bedroom and went out on the roof. Élodie had mentioned it earlier, how beautiful the views were, and she wasn't kidding.

"This is amazing," I said. "Almost worth being on the run, right?"

"Totally," Jesse agreed as he settled down next to me. The sky was a dark blue, not quite entirely black, and all of Paris shimmered below us. Off in the far distance, the Eiffel Tower stood at attention. "Is that a McDonald's?" Jesse asked, pointing at something, then chuckling when I slapped his other hand away.

"You're ridiculous," I said, then took his hand in mine and kissed the back of it. "Way too ridiculous for me."

"I try. I like Ames, by the way. He's really good for Roux. She's not so . . ." Jesse flailed his arms and made a crazy face. "You know, like that. She's calmer with him."

"Well, apparently she's eighteen now," I said. "She's an adult. I hope she'll still talk to us mere children."

"I wouldn't worry about that," Jesse said.

"Do you think Ames is a good guy, though?"

"Yeah, I do," Jesse said. "Look at it this way. Roux's always making a big deal about people, right? And things and just stuff in general. She gets excited about everything, but no one ever really makes a big deal about her."

I rested my head against Jesse's shoulder. "That's true. We usually just go along with her."

"Exactly. And somehow in less than two days, Ames figured that out and knew how to fix it. That's a good guy right there, trust me." Jesse paused before adding, "And if I thought he wasn't a good guy, I would drop kick him out the window."

I smiled to hear him be so defensive of Roux. "My hero." I sighed. "I'm very lucky."

"Yeah, you are," Jesse agreed. "Almost as lucky as me."

"Can I ask you a question?" I said, then continued before I lost my nerve. "Why do you keep dating me?"

Jesse turned to look at me, all joking gone. "Wait, what?"

"Why do you keep dating me? I keep putting you in these terrible situations and you stick around."

Jesse looked at me for a long minute. "You seriously don't know why I stick around?" he asked, almost incredulous. "Are you being serious right now?"

I nodded. I hated being vulnerable in front of him, asking him the questions whose answers scared me more than Dominic or any of his cohorts.

"Okay," Jesse said, settling back next to me and putting his arm around my shoulders. "Let's start with the *A*'s!"

"You aren't seriously going to—"

"Ambitious!" he said. "Beautiful. Caring. Determined. Eager to learn."

"That's cheating," I said, but I couldn't hide my smile.

"Shh, I'm trying to romance you on a rooftop in Paris. Be quiet. Where was I? Oh, yes. Fearless. Generous. Happy."

"I'm not happy all the time!"

"You have a happy spirit. Work with me, Mags, okay? This isn't easy. Ignominious!"

"I don't think that's a compliment."

"Jolly!"

"Did you just compare me to Santa Claus?"

"He's beloved by millions. You should be so lucky." Jesse tucked some of his hair behind his ear and pretended to think. "Where were we? Oh, yes! Kind! Loyal!" He stopped for a minute and looked down at me. "Very, very loyal. You never leave anyone behind, even when it means life or death."

We both had to take a deep breath then, and I remembered how his shirt had felt in my hand as I had pulled him to the ground as the shooting began, how his pulse had pounded against mine. "Magnificent," he murmured. "Nice. Opulent."

"I sound like a McMansion."

"There's a reason I didn't say optimistic for *O*. Pretty. Resourceful."

"You skipped *Q*."

"Damn. *Q* . . . *Q* . . . Queryful? Is that a word? Querying? *Questioning*, there it is!"

I was laughing too hard to answer, but I nodded my head.

"*R* was resourceful, so now it's *S*. Sneaky, which I like. Trustworthy. Undeterred. Valiant."

"Oooh, tough one coming up," I teased. "*X*. And if you say X-rated, I'll hurt you."

"*T* should have been Threatening. Um, okay, *X* . . . *X* . . . Xcellent!"

I pretended to applaud. "Well done, well done."

"We're rounding third and going home," he announced. "Yearning. And zealous. Boom!" Jesse thrust his arms in the air, as if all of Paris was clambering to their feet and cheering for him. "Thank you, thank you so much! The entire alphabet about how my girlfriend is awesome. *People* magazine should be calling me about their Sexiest Man Alive issue"— Jesse pretended to check his watch—"*any* minute now."

"You're insane." I giggled. "But literate. And very good with the alphabet."

"I went to kindergarten and everything," he boasted. "Plus I'm bilingual."

"Definitely worth a kiss," I told him, then cupped his cheek in my hand. His stubble was rough against my palm, and I kissed him gently, almost like he would blow away. "I love you," I whispered against his mouth. "You're my favorite. You're mine."

"And you're mine," he replied, kissing me harder. "I know you don't think so, but I'm lucky to have you."

"I almost got you killed."

"And now I'm in Paris, looking at the city lights with my amazing girlfriend. Ups and downs, babe. They happen to everyone."

We kissed a few more minutes, the emotion starting to deepen between us. Sometimes I felt like I couldn't kiss him enough, like I wanted more of him until there was nothing left to have, and I pushed him back a little so I could climb into his lap. His hand settled at the small of my back, holding me steady as I straddled him on the small terrace, and he leaned on his elbows so that I could rest against his chest as we kissed.

When we finally pulled apart, my cheeks felt scratched from his stubble and I was breathing hard. So was he. "Someone's probably watching," I said. "Or looking for us. Or waiting for us."

Jesse nodded, trying to calm his own breathing. His hand slipped under the back of my shirt and stroked the skin there. "I have something for you," he murmured.

I leaned away a little, raising an eyebrow. "Is that a euphemism?"

He grinned, his teeth white against the darkened sky, and pulled me back to him as we sat up. "Not quite," he said, "but I like your dirty mind."

I kissed his cheek as he dug something out of his pocket, then held it up between his fingers. It shimmered a little, reflecting the city lights below us, and I reached out to take it from him. It was a gold chain, so thin that it almost seemed invisible, with two charms dangling from it.

"If you hate it, that's okay," Jesse said, and I could hear the nerves in his voice.

"I don't hate it," I said, but those words seemed inadequate. "I don't hate it at all." I leaned in closer so I could see the charms. They were both tiny and gold, but I couldn't see what they were in the dark.

"I got it for you after we had that fight," Jesse explained, resting his chin on my shoulder as he talked so that his voice was soft in my ear. "I felt bad and I had been stupid, so yeah. This one's a compass." He poked at one of the tiny charms, then pulled something out from under his shirt. I saw a matching compass glinting on the edge of a chain. "I have one, too. It's so you always find your way back to me, and so I can always find you, wherever you are in the world."

It hurt to talk. It hurt to think. It hurt to even breathe, my chest was so full of love for him. "What about this one?" I asked, poking at the second charm, only an inch long. "Is that . . . is that a *knife*?"

Jesse grinned and nodded, kissing the spot right behind my ear. "It's for fighting the good fight," he said. "Which you always do."

I turned so I could look at him, resting my palms on either side of his face. "You are amazing." I sighed. "Absolutely amazing."

"Not all the time." He shrugged. "But I have a few moments every now and then. So you like it?"

"I love it," I said, tugging it over my head. "Why are you the best?"

"Because I learned it from you," he replied, then wrinkled his nose. "We sound so stupid sometimes. *'I learned it from you.'* Roux would puke if she heard us."

I leaned in to kiss him. "Bring on the stupid." I laughed, but Jesse stopped me, putting his finger to my lips.

"Shh," he whispered, and I looked over his shoulder. "Roux's busy, I guess."

Roux and Ames were in the dark bedroom, illuminated by only moonlight as they shared a kiss. Ames held her so tenderly, his hands on her hips as if he knew how fragile she could be, and Roux stood on her tiptoes to reach his mouth. It was so intimate that I wanted to look away, but my heart swelled to see Roux happy.

"Told you he was a good guy," Jesse murmured in my ear. "Not even getting handsy with her."

I kissed his shoulder and we snuggled together, waiting for Roux and Ames to leave before climbing back inside.

CHAPTER 33

The next morning, Angelo woke me just as the sun was rising.

"Whuzzat?" I said, sitting up. "Is everything okay?" Jesse was asleep next to me, one arm slung over his head and his face mashed into the pillow. (My boyfriend was many things, but he was not an elegant sleeper.)

"I'm so sorry to wake you, darling," Angelo whispered. "It's early, I know. And everything's fine. I just need the coins from you. I have to leave this morning for a few hours, and I don't want you to have the coins in case something goes wrong. It's too risky for you."

I reached under my pillow and pulled out the pouch. I had carried them everywhere with me, even the bathroom, for the very reason Angelo mentioned. I didn't want anyone else to hold them and have to assume that responsibility.

"Travel safe," I said, then collapsed back into my pillow and fell asleep before I could even hear the door click shut behind him.

A few hours later, we were all awake and gathered

around the kitchen table. "We need an emergency meeting place," Ryo said. He wore a different pair of frames every day. Today's were a dark jade green and they glinted in the late morning light. "But where?"

We thought for a minute. The problem with Paris wasn't that there weren't enough options, but that there were too many. Every third doorway had probably once housed someone famous. Or, as Roux kept putting it, "Marie Antoinette probably died there."

Now, though, she was deep in thought, her fingers drumming on the table in front of her. She and Angelo had re-created their long-standing chess game the night before, and now her eyes were glazing over as she stared at it.

And then she leaped up.

"I get it!" she cried.

"Jesus, babes," Ames said, clutching at his chest. "Warn a lad, will you?"

"Get used to that," Jesse told him. "Roux doesn't exactly keep her feelings to herself."

"Shut up, Jesse. I still have your Transformer, by the way. Anyway—"

"You do?" Jesse cried.

"ANYWAY," Roux continued, ignoring him. "Angelo's always saying this thing to me whenever we play chess: A knight on the rim is grim. And usually I'm all 'Angelo, what are you smoking?' but I get it now!" She looked absolutely delighted with herself.

The rest of us stared at her. "Well?" Élodie finally asked. "Are you going to tell the rest of us?"

"Look," Roux said, then picked up her knight. "Don't tell Angelo I'm doing this or he'll try to forfeit the whole game. So here's the knight, and he can only move in a certain way. Either one square, then two, or vice versa, right?"

We all nodded.

"Okay, so when he's in the corner of the board, he can only move in two directions." Roux demonstrated with Angelo's beautifully carved knight piece. "So that's bad. And then if he's on the edge of the board"—she slid him halfway down the board—"he can only move in four directions, which is better but not great. But if he's in the center, then he can move eight different ways. Eight different escape routes, so to speak."

Roux moved the knight to the center and set him down. "If you stay on the edge where it seems safe, you're more easily captured. But if you're in the middle of everything, even though it seems less safe, you have the most options. God, that was driving me insane!"

I just looked at her in astonishment. "Remember when you used to just call the knight 'the horsey guy'?" I asked.

"There's no shame in having a steeper learning curve than others," Roux said primly. "So wherever we meet needs to be open, in public, something like that. There's going to be seven of us; we need ways for all of us to flee without getting, you know, captured." She made air quotes around the last word, then dramatically dragged her finger across her throat to illustrate her real meaning.

Ames looked at her adoringly while the rest of us winced.

"Thank you for that, um, delightful interpretation of our fates," I said. "But good work, Roux."

"I aim to please," she replied. "But now we just have to figure out where."

We had Élodie's iPad on the table in front of us, a picture of the double-eagle gold coin blown up on the screen. It looked better in person, but the picture was still accurate, and I locked eyes with Victory once again. It felt like years since I had stood under her protection at Grand Army Plaza, but in reality, it had only been three days ago. Her engraved arms were spread out like wings and—

"Oh my God!" I cried, and Roux screamed and clutched at her chest.

"Sorry, sorry," I told her. "Actually, no, I'm not. That was payback for earlier."

"Fair enough," she said, taking a deep breath. "I was just thinking too hard. I think. What's wrong?"

"I know where we can meet!" I cried. "This coin was designed by Saint-Gaudens, right?"

Five blank faces looked back at me.

"Okay, just trust me, it was. He also designed the statue of General Sherman at Grand Army Plaza in New York—"

"Manhattan or Brooklyn?" Roux asked.

"Manhattan."

She nodded in approval. "Go on."

"That statue has the same figure on it, the figure of Liberty just like on the coin. But his original inspiration was in the Louvre." I grabbed Élodie's iPad and typed in a few key words, then flipped the screen around. "It was this."

I had pulled up the Winged Victory of Samothrace on the screen, one of the major exhibits at the Louvre. It sat at the base of a stairway, its huge marbled wings spreading throughout the atrium. Her head was missing, but you barely noticed that fact against the sheer size of the statue.

"We tell Dominic that if he wants these coins, he'll know where to meet us."

Ryo looked doubtful. "You really think it's a good idea to toy with him like that?"

I shrugged. "I don't care. He tried to kill me and my family. You know he's done his research on these coins. If I know that little fun fact, so does he. I guarantee it."

Roux wrinkled her nose, then nodded. "I like that it has Victory in its name," she said. "That's a good sign, right?"

"A good sign for *someone*," Ames said. "Hopefully it's us."

CHAPTER 34

Everyone was on edge the next morning. Roux sat at the kitchen, picking all the chocolate pieces out of her *pain au chocolat*, while Ames stirred his coffee again and again until it resembled more of a dirty whirlpool than a beverage.

Élodie and Ryo were packing up their things, getting ready to move out. "Where are you going?" I asked them. It was clear we couldn't come back to the apartment, even if our plan went according to, well, plan.

"Sydney, maybe?" Élodie shrugged. "Ryo hasn't been home in quite a while. Or perhaps London. Or maybe even—"

"Élodie, love." Angelo poked his head out of the office, where he had been working all morning. "May I speak with you for a moment?"

Ryo picked up the conversation after she left. "Élodie hates Australia," he said with a laugh. "I doubt we're going there. Maybe we'll just stay in Paris."

"So jealous." Roux sighed at the table. "I want to stay here, too."

Ames hid a smile. "Careful what you wish for, darlin'," he said.

"Seriously," I added, remembering when I told Angelo that I just wanted something to happen, right before too many things started to happen. "Let's just make it through the day, okay? Then we'll discuss jetting off to nowhere."

"Not to be negative," Jesse began.

"Oh, here we go," Roux muttered. "Mr. Positive."

"But do we have a plan if things go wrong?"

Ryo and I looked at each other. "It's not going to go wrong," we both said at the same time, even though I wondered if he fully believed that statement. I knew I didn't. I had been through enough over the past week to know that things could definitely go wrong.

I also knew that even if things went wrong, they could still work out.

"All we have to do is stick to the plan," I told Jesse, sitting down in his lap. He reached up to play with the necklace he had given me, the tiny knifepoint sharp against the pad of his thumb.

"This looks really nice on you," he murmured. "Very cool."

"This one guy gave it to me," I said. "I might keep him around for a while. Use him for his body, you know."

Roux pretended to make barfing sounds next to us.

"He sounds like a keeper," Jesse agreed, winding his arms around my waist. "Probably good with the alphabet, too. He could put *U* and *I* together."

There was a pause, and then—

"That was terrible!" Roux cried as I started to laugh.

"So terrible, Jess, oh my God! Pass me some crackers for that *cheeseball*!"

"Really awful, mate." Ames sighed, even though he was chuckling. "Mine aren't even as bad as that."

Jesse just smiled and kissed the secret spot on my neck. "Tension diffused," he whispered against my skin, and I hugged him.

"Yeah, I think I'll keep him for a while," I murmured.

A few minutes later, I went to get a sweater (the Paris apartment was beautiful and drafty) and heard Élodie and Angelo talking. The office door had popped open just a crack and I stopped, even though I knew I shouldn't eavesdrop.

But hey, I'm a spy. Eavesdropping is pretty much the first item in the job description.

Élodie and Angelo were whispering together in front of a huge computer screen, clicking through passport photos one by one. I saw Markus, Mathieu, Zelda, my parents, Ryo and Élodie and Ames. Then Angelo clicked something again and the screen filled with dozens more photos, all of them people I didn't recognize.

"Not for your eyes, my love," Angelo said suddenly, then turned around and smiled.

"But—"

"And shut the door behind you, please."

I did as I was told, but all I could think about were my parents' pictures, and why Roux and Jesse hadn't been included at all.

*   *   *

A few minutes before three, the cars arrived for us. All the tension that Jesse had managed to crack was back now, plus more. I couldn't see the drivers' faces as we piled in, and I wondered if Mathieu was one of them. The windows were all tinted, though, and I noticed Angelo breathe a tiny sigh of relief once the cars pulled away from the curb.

"Bulletproof?" I asked, pointing to the window, and he nodded.

"Of course. We're currently in the safest place in Paris," he replied, then glanced out at the street. Ames, Élodie, and Ryo were in the car behind us, gliding as smoothly as we were, and Roux kept looking over her shoulder, keeping an eye on Ames.

"He's fine," I whispered to her, taking her hand. "Ames could probably survive a nuclear fallout."

"Oddly not comforting, but thank you, Maggie."

I patted her hand in response.

Behind closed doors, I had argued with Angelo about using Jesse and Roux as part of the plan. "We can't involve them anymore!" I protested, my voice low enough so that they wouldn't hear me. "They've done more than enough! They're just civilians!"

"They're not civilians anymore," Angelo replied, which stopped me in my tracks. "Dominic knows who they are. The Collective knows who they are and, more importantly, what they know about us. Do you honestly think they're safer alone than without our protection today?"

I paused, thinking about his words and realizing he

was right. "I hate that I brought them into this," I said. "I really do."

"Sometimes, my love, we don't get to choose our team," Angelo said. "And Roux and Jesse are becoming seasoned professionals at this point. Jesse, especially, would do anything to protect you."

"That's the problem," I admitted. "I don't want him to do anything."

"Like I said, love," Angelo repeated, then bent down to kiss the top of my head, "sometimes we don't get to choose."

Now that we were in the car, I could see his point.

Still, I didn't feel any better.

We had arranged to meet at the Louvre at three, mostly to avoid the first rush of morning tourists and the last rush of evening crowds. It was still packed, of course, with the end-of-summer tourists crowding through the doors and into the halls, and most were Americans.

The six of us all had badges that designated us as a tour group from a local school. Angelo had a docent badge, which let him lead us past the heavy lines at security and into the museum.

Ryo just shook his head after we made our way inside. "Do you see?" he whispered to me. "Security is so lax. They didn't even check the badge."

On my other side, Roux had more pressing concerns. "If anyone asks," she whispered to me as she and Ames walked hand in hand, "I'm French."

"Got it," I whispered back. "I'm not sure anyone will be asking, but I got it."

Their voices rang up to the high ceilings and through the corridors, and my heart started to race. This wasn't my area of expertise. I needed something to open, to crack, to unlock, in order to feel better. All I had instead, though, were five friends and ten gold coins in my pocket.

We all had ten gold coins in our pocket, actually. It's just that mine were the real ones. Angelo had produced some amazing-looking fakes and distributed them to everyone else that morning. "We'll have about five minutes before the police arrive to keep Dominic at bay," he said.

"Assuming they don't decide to go on strike," Élodie grumbled. I could tell she had been in Paris for too long.

"We just need to keep Dominic in the museum," Angelo said. "As soon as you hear the police arrive, get out. Go, take the car, take the tunnels, I do not care. But go."

Ames looked around the room. "I'll just say it," he announced. "We're going to play keep-away with a criminal mastermind in the Louvre? That's our plan?"

"Yes," Angelo said.

"Deadly," Ames replied with a smile. "I love this game."

As Angelo led the six of us up the stairs toward the Samothrace, I hurried to catch up to him. "Angelo," I whispered, "this doesn't feel right. I think this is a bad idea."

"Don't worry, darling," he said. "This plan has many facets. And faces, actually." He smiled down at me. "Are you ready for a new adventure?"

I looked up at him, trying to read behind the secrecy. There was something big happening behind his eyes, bigger than a stupid plan of keep-away with Dominic and a bunch of fake gold coins.

"Third rule of being a spy?" Angelo asked me as we continued to climb.

"Don't look back," I answered.

"Good girl," he said, then looked past me at someone in the distance.

"Let the games begin," he said, and I turned to see Dominic Arment making his way into the museum.

CHAPTER 35

We stood on the stairs as Dominic approached, fanned out in front of the Samothrace. Angelo was in front and the rest of us were a few steps behind him, almost like he was our shield into battle. People shoved past us on the way to see the statue, their cameras out and ready, but none of us moved. It was as if the tourists weren't even there.

Dominic was wearing a suit. I suspected that he was one of those men who always wore a suit, even in these types of situations. It was hard to imagine him in an actual appropriate outfit, like maybe track pants and running shoes, but he looked clean-cut and like any other well-dressed Parisian. There were four men behind him, but I couldn't tell if they were security or henchmen or hired ankle-breakers. Maybe they were even part of the Collective.

"Hello, Dominic," Angelo said, as if he were greeting him over coffee at a café. "Lovely to see you, as always."

"You are always so smooth, Angelo," Dominic replied, his voice so deep and soft that it gave me shivers. "Except in

your plans, of course. I see you've assembled quite the ragtag bunch." He nodded in my direction and smirked.
"Maggie and Her Merry Band of Criminals. Where are my
coins?"

"Ah, yes, the coins," Angelo said, adjusting his watch
a little as he glanced at it. "They're very important to
you, aren't they? Suddenly everybody wants them: you, me,
Maggie, our friends." Angelo paused for a few seconds
before adding, "A few gentlemen in Russia are also quite
interested, from what I hear."

Dominic blanched only a tiny bit. "Stop with the non-
sense and give them to me," he told Angelo. "And we can
all go home."

"You tried to kill me in my home," I spoke up, and
Angelo didn't make a motion to stop me.

"You took what wasn't yours," Dominic replied. "Very
naughty, Maggie."

I felt Jesse tense up behind me, but I didn't look back.

"Maggie has a point, though," Angelo said, still so
calm and steady that it was eerie. "We give you the coins
and . . . what? You call off the Collective and let us go? Or
you hunt us all down and make sure we never talk again? I
know what I would do if I were you."

"Lucky for us, you are not me," Dominic said through
gritted teeth.

Angelo pulled his phone out of his pocket and pressed
a button. "I've just sent you three drafts of an e-mail," he
said. "One to Interpol, one to my contact at the Secret Service, and one to the Associated Press. Don't you think that
they would all be interested in this story? International

intrigue, scores of years spent slowly building one of the most secretive organizations in the world, only to have it fall to corruption? I name quite a lot of people in these e-mails. Everyone who attempted to use our good deeds for their own malicious intentions, in fact."

My heart started to pound faster. What was Angelo talking about? He was bluffing. He had to be bluffing.

"I think this would make a wonderful story," Angelo said. "The Collective finally revealed, along with all of its dirty misdeeds and indiscretions. Very naughty, Dominic." Angelo's voice ran cold as he repeated Dominic's words back to him.

"You would never reveal the Collective." Dominic laughed. "You are part of it. All of you are." He narrowed his eyes at Roux and Jesse, which made me twitch. "You *all* are," he repeated. "You reveal one of us, you reveal all of us."

"Well, that might not be true," Angelo said, then looked up and waved a couple forward. "Let's see what my cohorts have to say about that."

I followed Angelo's gaze and then let out a small sob because dashing up the stairs, slightly out of breath and hair tousled from the rush, were my dorky, ridiculous, wonderful parents. Behind me, Roux made a tiny sound that sounded like "meep!" but I didn't turn to look at her. I just watched as my parents came closer and fought the urge to hurl myself straight into their arms.

"Sorry we're late," my mother said. She sounded easy and breezy, but I was her kid. I could tell from her face that she was pissed and ready for a fight. Every kid could tell that about his or her own mom.

"Traffic, strikes, you know," my father said. "Dominic, hello. I think the last time I saw you, we were all in school together. And then you tried to kill my family."

Dominic looked from them to Angelo. "This is your plan? What, do you want to trade them for Maggie?" He began chuckling to himself. "Why have one useless person when you can have two, is that the logic?"

"Not quite," Angelo said, still looking a little bemused. "The Collective has become infested with people like you. We think it's time to remedy that."

I heard Élodie take a deep breath behind me, and I remembered how Angelo had called her into his office earlier. Did she know what was going on?

"If you turn in the Collective," Dominic said, still sounding unimpressed, "you turn yourselves in."

"Darling," Angelo said, turning to my mother. "Tell me. Was it hard to erase our identities from the database?"

"Not at all," my mom replied, smiling sweetly at Dominic. "I was trained so well by the Collective. So, *so* well."

"And you, sir," Angelo said, turning to my dad. "Did you have a difficult time finding people like us who were a bit exhausted by all these recent antics?"

"Of course not. They were more than happy to help us steal files."

The color was starting to drain from Dominic's face as I felt the blood pulse through my temples. It was as if the Collective had a termite infestation. Angelo wasn't just going to find the termites and kick them out: he was about to burn down the whole house.

Angelo held up his phone. "Once I send these e-mails," he said, "you'll have about five minutes before the police arrive to get the coins from us and get out of the Louvre. And if you don't, well, I'm sure the Russians would love to listen to your explanations. Or maybe the Secret Service. Or Interpol. It'll be a most interesting story either way. I, for one, wish I could be there to hear you tell it."

"There are security cameras everywhere in here," Dominic protested. "Like they would not see you."

"Ah, that reminds me," Angelo said, tapping his forehead. "Forgive me, I'm an old man now, I forget things. That's why I have friends like the lovely Zelda here." He beckoned someone out of the crowd and Zelda stepped forward, followed by Mathieu and Markus. "Zelda, love, tell us all what you did with the security cameras today."

Zelda held up her right hand and made a scissoring motion with her fingers. "Snip snip," she said, then grinned wickedly. "I'm so grateful for everything that I learned about replacing security film. I can never thank you enough, Dominic. Truly."

Dominic's breath was coming in short, fast gasps, and his men standing beside him looked like deer in headlights. Definitely hired help. They had no idea what the Collective was or why it had been important. And why it was about to go down in flames. "You wouldn't," he said to Angelo. "It would be a huge mistake for you."

Angelo held up his phone, pretended to examine it, and then pressed a button. "Oops."

Dominic took two steps and lunged for the phone, but

Angelo turned and tossed it to Ryo, who caught it and dashed up the stairs, Élodie hot on his heels.

This was the cue, I realized. This was the plan. It was time to run.

I grabbed Jesse's hand and we turned and flew up the stairs, taking them two at a time as we shoved past tourists. Ames and Roux were behind us, dashing up past us, and Ryo and Élodie went up the left set of stairs as we took the right. One of Dominic's henchmen followed them and I could hear the footsteps on the stairs behind us. Below, I saw my parents flying up after us, followed by Dominic, with Angelo hot on his heels.

The chase was on.

Jesse and I ran down one long hall filled with Impressionist paintings. "Do you know who has the real coins?" Jesse asked as we ran. I could see Roux and Ames darting past some sculptures and a long way away, I heard Ryo yell something unrepeatable.

I just looked at Jesse.

"Oh, great!" he cried. "Why is it *you*?"

"Because I don't want it to be *you*!" I cried as we came to a sudden stop as Dominic appeared in the next gallery. "Go back, go back!" I yelled. We had to hold him off for another three and a half minutes before the police arrived. As it was, it was getting difficult to avoid security, who seemed flummoxed as to why a tour group was suddenly racing through the museum. "*Madame! Monsieur!*" we heard as we ran down a hallway filled with portraits, away from the *Mona Lisa*. It was by far the most crowded part of the museum, like gridlock in the middle of a car chase, and we didn't want to get stuck in it.

I saw Zelda and Mathieu zipping by, followed by one of Dominic's hired men. Zelda had a huge smile on her face, like this was her favorite part of the job, and she waved at me as she ran past. I just spun around a corner, though, and saw Angelo and my parents running down a set of stairs back toward the first floor. We followed them, hurling ourselves back to the ground floor and around a corner. I had looked at a map of the Louvre, but now I was just trying to stay in motion, literally running out the clock.

Three minutes to go.

That's when I realized I had lost Jesse.

He wasn't behind me and I couldn't see him in the crowd. My heart, which had been keeping up a steady beat, seemed to skid to a halt, and I whirled around to look for him, but he was gone. "He's fine," I told myself. "He's fine. He doesn't have the coins." But I didn't feel any calmer, and my anxiety started to climb as I ran toward the end of the building, looking for any boy with curly hair.

And then I saw it at the end of the hall. Dominic stood in front of the elevator, his hand on Jesse's shoulder, squeezing just a bit too hard. Jesse was wincing a little and when he saw me, his face fell. "No, Mags," he mouthed, but I shoved my way through the throng of tourists trying to see the *Venus de Milo* and arrived in front of both the love of my life and my archenemy.

"You don't want him," I told Dominic. "You want me."

"You are so pathetic now that you are in love," Dominic

hissed at me. The crowd waiting for the elevator was deep and loud—no one could hear us whispering back and forth. "I've been watching you for years, Maggie. You used to be great. Now you're just useless." He paused for a few seconds, then added, "Why Colton wanted you, I have no idea."

I patted my hip, right where the coins rested in my pocket. "How useless am I now?" I said, trying to catch my breath after my mad dash through the museum.

Dominic's eyes widened when he saw the outline of the coins, but he tried to hide his nerves. "I knew you'd have them," he sneered. "You'd never let anyone else take the fall." He squeezed Jesse's neck hard and Jesse winced again.

"You want me," I said again, not wanting to see Jesse in any pain ever again. "Let him go."

A crowd of security guards came around the corner just as the elevator doors opened. All three of us took one look at the guards, then Dominic tossed Jesse away and grabbed me instead, hustling us into the elevator. "Mags!" Jesse yelled, and I saw my parents and Angelo round the corner, all of them watching in horror as the doors slid shut.

CHAPTER 36

The elevator was hot and stuffy with tourists and Dominic tightened his grip on my wrist. "If you scream or say anything . . ." He didn't have to finish his threat.

"Nice cuckoo clock collection," I muttered back. "I bet your mistress loves them almost as much as your wife does."

A muscle tightened in front of Dominic's ear. The bones in my wrist were starting to ache under his clutch, but I didn't say anything. I had only one minute now, and I knew Dominic was aware of the time as well. We both wanted this to be over with as fast as possible.

The minute the doors opened, Dominic shoved us out and down the hall, shifting his grip from my wrist to the back of my neck. I marched ahead of him but reached my hand under my shirt to grasp the necklace Jesse had given me, feeling the tiny knife and compass, cold against my fingers.

Dominic pushed me toward a set of doors that read NO ADMISSION. "Open it," he said.

"I don't have my tools," I replied. "I can't do it."

He shoved me hard and I bounced into the door, losing my breath a little. "Do you think I am kidding?" he asked. "Do you think this is a time to be funny?"

Dominic, of course, knew what we all knew: I would never leave without my tools. "It might not work," I said, pulling a pen cap out of my back pocket.

"Oh, I'm sure it will work," he said, letting my imagination run wild with all the painful possibilities that could occur if I didn't get the door open.

It took less than a minute, but I scrubbed it open and it popped with a click. Dominic wasted no time in getting inside, forgetting to shut the door behind him in his haste. It was an empty room, half-finished with construction, the paint fumes strong and definitely not environmentally friendly. "Here," I said, reaching into my pocket and thrusting the velvet bag at him. "Have fun with them."

"You think it's that easy?" Dominic asked, but he took the coins anyway, tucking them into his inside jacket pocket. "You think that's all?" He grabbed my wrist harder and I felt the bones grind together. "You think you just humiliate me, break into my house, ruin my security? You lead me on a chase around the world and ruin everything I have made? Everything!"

I whimpered despite myself, but the pain wasn't terrible. All I could really feel was anger, sheer, white-hot anger that coursed through me and numbed the hurt.

"You ruined everything I made!" I yelled at him. "That was my family, my home! You're like a snake in the weeds.

You just take whatever it is you want and you don't care who gets hurt! You tried to kill my family! You're as terrible as Colton Hooper!"

The reaction was exactly what I wanted.

"Colton was an amateur!" Dominic seethed, his hand tight on my skin, so tight that I could feel it pull together, and I flattened myself against the wall. "He didn't even realize what he had!"

"What, a job?" I baited him. "A job and a really bad plan to kidnap me?"

"Exactly!" Dominic spat. "That's all he wanted. You! You were a child! What could you possibly do for him? He had an army at his disposal and he goes for a *girl*." Dominic looked disgusted, his anger getting the better of him. My wrist was starting to burn with pain, but I ignored it.

"An army?"

"I kept telling him, mobilize! Mobilize!" Spittle was collecting in the corners of Dominic's mouth, he was so impassioned. "Take these people and use them! You have their lives in your hands, sometimes literally! Stop wasting time on documents and CEOs and go for the money, the power!"

"And why didn't he?" I asked, trying so hard not to wince. I sort of succeeded.

"Because he was scared." Dominic sneered. "And weak. He didn't know what he had, so I decided to show everyone what could be done." His eyes were nearly spinning; he was drunk on the idea of the sort of power that was at his fingertips. "Colton turned the Collective into a joke. I'm here to fix it."

"Pity you won't succeed," I replied. The anger was making my heart race and I could see the vein in Dominic's neck pulsing. "It's all over now," I said. "Angelo never bluffs. You're going up in flames."

"As if I would go without taking you with me."

"Yeah, good luck with that," I spat, then reached under my shirt, yanked hard on my necklace to break the chain, and twisted the knife in my fingers to bring it straight into Dominic's cheek while driving my knee directly between his legs.

He almost sank to the ground, one hand going to his cheek as he dropped my wrist. "Help!" I cried as I turned and started running down the hall. "I'm an American tourist trapped by a madman!"

Within a minute, the second floor of the museum turned into an even bigger sea of humanity. Museum workers came running, followed by security, followed by Angelo, my parents, enough tourists to fill the Eiffel Tower for a week, Roux, Jesse, Ames, Élodie, Ryo, Zelda, and blessedly, the police.

"He attacked me!" I cried, putting on my best wounded face. "I was just here to see the *Mona Lisa* and he attacked me! This would have never happened in Boise!"

Roux, sensing that it was her time to shine, threw herself into her role. "My friend!" she cried. "She's my friend, we're from America! WHO IS THIS MADMAN?"

My father was arguing with the security guard, flashing his docent badge as Angelo spoke French with a police officer, showing his own credentials. "Are you all right?" Jesse whispered, rushing to my side and grabbing my arm. "Did he hurt you?"

"I'm fine," I whispered back. "Go help Roux." All I really wanted to do was hug him until my arms fell off, but there would be time for that later.

Right now, we still had a job to do.

Jesse immediately waded into the situation, raising his voice as Élodie came over and started to translate his words. "He says that you are an American and you have been mistreated," she whispered as she pretended to console me. "And this sort of treatment will not stand! He has quite a gift for this language, do you know that?"

"He surprises me every day," I whispered, trying not to let my love for him show.

"Now Angelo says that you got separated from the group," she continued. "Your father says that this museum really needs to improve security or they will lose money—here, put on my sweater, you don't look traumatized enough—and Jesse, good boyfriend that he is, is still making a scene. As is Roux, of course."

I hid a quick smile as I tugged on Élodie's cardigan. In the throng of people, I saw Ryo and Ames slip away, no doubt heading back to the tunnels. Zelda caught my eye and held up her phone, showing me a quick glance of the actual security cameras, then winked at me and disappeared behind the boys.

My father was really letting the security guard—who seemed humbled by the screwup—have it, and Roux was still going on as Jesse joined her, shouting in French at the top of his lungs. "He just wants his beloved city to be safe for his friends," Élodie translated. "This world is too precarious for such dangers!"

"My hero," I murmured.

"Ow, my eye!" Jesse muttered quietly as he wrangled with Roux, who was trying to climb over him, her American angst in full effect.

"My friend could have died!" she wailed. "Will someone *please* think of the children?"

"Do they have Dominic?" I whispered to Élodie.

"Yes," she whispered back. "In handcuffs."

"Then go," I told her. "I'm fine."

Élodie nodded and pretended to go talk to some tourist. As soon as it was safe, she disappeared down the stairs. My mother caught my eye and I saw the emotion in hers before she too left behind Élodie. My heart twisted when I saw her leave, but just then my dad grabbed my arm and pulled me to him, still yelling in French.

"We will take her back to the group," Angelo said in English to one of the police officers. "We do not want to press charges. She is fine."

My dad's fingers were tight on my arm and I could feel him shaking a little with emotion. "I'm fine," I told the officer, but I was really saying it to my dad. "Can I see the woman with no arms now? I want to take a picture."

"They are lying!" Dominic suddenly screamed. "They are thieves, all of them! They are liars! Angelo! Angelo, I swear I'll kill you!"

"Delusional," Angelo clucked. "Let's get this young

lady back to her group, yes? Thank you, gentlemen. Too bad your security is not quite up to the same standards as your kindness."

My father ushered me toward the stairs. "No elevator," I whispered, and heard him laugh a little.

"Never," he replied, and we hurried down the stairs; Roux, Jesse, my mom, and Angelo on our heels; did a quick loop past the *Venus de Milo* in case someone was watching; and then slipped out of the museum to the screams of Dominic Arment echoing behind us.

Two cars were outside this time and my father hustled me into the one that had Zelda behind the wheel. Roux, Jesse, and Angelo got into the one behind us, but I ran back just before Jesse climbed in and kissed him. "Good work," he said, then kissed me back harder. "See you underground."

"Chop chop!" I heard Zelda yell. She was smoking a cigarette, her lipstick staining the end, and I nodded at her as I got into the car, still a little flushed from the excitement and kissing Jesse. "Thanks for keeping an eye on me, Zel," I said.

"*D'accord,*" she replied.

I crawled into the backseat, straight into the arms of my mother. She was weeping even before she saw me, and when she hugged me, I started to cry, too. "I was so worried!" She sobbed.

"I'm fine." I sniffled against her shoulder. "I'm really okay."

My father wrapped his arms around both of us, and

Zelda, obviously not one for sentiment, started the car and pulled away from the curb.

We sat hugging each other for a few moments before I sat up and wiped my eyes. "I'm fine," I said. "I swear, we're all okay. But where were you? What happened?"

My parents looked at each other over the top of my head. "We were destroying what's left of the Collective," my mother finally said, then shrugged a little. "We had been thinking about leaving for a while, ever since the Colton Hooper incident opened our eyes to what was really happening. But this solidified it for us."

"Your mother destroyed the records of all the innocent spies who had worked there," my dad continued. "We spoke to all of them, and those who hadn't already left were ready to leave."

"And those who wanted to stay, had a good reason," my mom added. "They were working with Dominic, stealing money, trading arms, the list went on and on. I'm sure you'll see it on the news, sweetie."

"You think?" I said. My head was still spinning. "So . . . where do we live now? We can't go back to the loft. What about school?"

"You can still go to school if you want," my mom said. "I have a feeling that anyone who wants to hurt us or our family will be in police custody in about, oh, two hours or so."

I sat back against my seat, trying to take it all in. "The Collective is over?" I finally asked. "For real?"

"It's the realio dealio," my dad said, reminding me that

even though I had missed him terribly, I hadn't felt deprived over losing his truly terrible sense of humor.

"So what's my name?" I asked. "Who am I?"

My mother smiled and pressed her mouth to the top of my head. "You are Maggie," she whispered, "and you are wonderful."

CHAPTER 37

The car eventually pulled up near the Pantheon, back toward the same exit and entrance we had used three nights earlier, and Zelda parked it, then threw the keys into the river before following my parents and me into the tunnels.

"About this," I said, as we moved the rolling tray. "We need to talk. You founded an underground society in Paris?"

My parents just smiled at each other. "You asked how we fell in love," my dad said. "This was part of it."

"We wouldn't want you to think your parents were *cool* or anything." My mom ruffled my hair, then dropped down into the tunnel like she had been doing it all her life.

Ryo and Élodie were there, along with Ames and Jesse, and Jesse grabbed me up in the tightest hug imaginable as soon as he saw me. "I was so worried!" he said. "Did he hurt you?"

"Just my wrist, a little," I admitted, then kissed Jesse right in front of everyone, parents included. "You were amazing, did you know that?"

"No, you were." He kissed me again, his hair tangled around my fingers.

"Ugh, smoochy smoochy, we get it," Roux said as she dropped down into the tunnel, with Angelo close behind her. But her eyes softened when she saw Ames and she ran right into his arms, a huge smile on her face.

"Really?" my mom asked. "Roux and Ames?"

"You know Ames?" I cried.

"Everyone knows me!" Ames grinned, pulling away from Roux just long enough to shake my parents' hands. "Lovely to finally meet you in person! Good work today!"

"Same to you," my dad replied. "Be careful with Roux. She scares us." But he winked at Roux and tapped her on the head.

"You're only scared of my amazing crossword skills," she retorted. "I missed you crazy kids, by the way. You owe me dinner."

"Yes, Roux, we'll get right on that." My mom pretended to be annoyed, but I knew she would make it happen within the week.

"So now what happens?" Ryo asked. "Élodie and I are going to London for a while, I think. Or maybe Barcelona. We haven't decided yet."

"You're not going to keep working here?" I asked. "But you still have so many things you want to do!"

"Here," Angelo said. "Maybe these will help." And he handed over two of the coins to Ryo.

Élodie gasped, covering her mouth with her hand. "Angelo, no, we can't!" she said. "Everyone is looking for these!"

"I had the fakes?" I cried.

"I figured once the police realized that Dominic had counterfeit coins, there would already be plenty of other charges to hold him." Angelo shrugged. "We might as well donate to the arts, yes?"

Élodie threw her arms around Angelo's neck, hugging him so tight that he gasped a little before laughing and patting her back. "Hold tight to them for a while," he advised. "Just until things calm down. We can see what adventures they bring in the new year, perhaps."

Ryo just shook his hand, pumping Angelo's arm up and down like a well. "Thank you so, so much," he said. "We can fix so many things, you don't even know."

"Oh, I have an idea about a few things that need fixing," Angelo said cryptically. "But I believe our flight is leaving in a few hours so we can discuss that later."

It seemed impossible to say good-bye to Ames and Ryo and Élodie, but I did reluctantly, hugging each of them as tightly as I could while trying not to cry. "You're amazing," I told them. "Really, it's incredible."

"Your family created our family so it makes sense," Ryo said. "I guess we are family now."

"Home is where your family is," I agreed, then stepped back so Jesse could hug them good-bye, as well.

"I'm not going with you," said a small voice, and I turned to see Roux standing next to Ames, both of their faces worried.

"Babes—" he started to say, but she cut him off.

"I'm not going back to New York," she said. "I'm staying here in Paris."

"What?" I asked. "Why? You can't, we have to go home. School starts tomorrow."

Roux just shook her head. "No, I'm not."

"Roux, my love," Angelo started to say, but Roux cut him off.

"I love you all, really, and I love New York, but there's nothing for me there." Her voice was getting wobbly, and I could see how tightly her fingers were intertwined with Ames's. "I'm better here. I'm happier here. I go back to New York and it's a cold house and people who call me 'slut' and 'bitch' and . . ." She trailed off and I saw a tear slip down her cheek. "I don't want that anymore. I want to be me, and I want to be with Ames."

Ames looked tortured, and he let go of Roux's hand long enough to rest his hands on either side of her face. "Babe," he said gently. "You think I'm not going to see you again? You have to go back to New York with them."

Roux's lower lip was trembling and Ames stroked her hair off her forehead, as gentle as always with her. "It'll be fine," he whispered. "I'll come visit. We just need to let things calm down. Wait for the waters to calm a little."

"But it's not the same," she whimpered, reaching up to wipe her eyes. "I don't want to be sad anymore."

"Things are different now," Ames told her. "It's a big world, darlin', and we've got a lot of time. We've already cheated death once today, yeah?" He smiled at her, making her smile back. "These lads love you and they'll look out for you."

"Yeah, Roux," Jesse said, and my heart swelled with affection for him. "New York won't be so bad this year. You'll see."

"Stop trying to be nice to me." Roux sniffled, but she smiled when she said it. "Promise me you'll visit," she said to Ames.

In response, he bent down and kissed her. All of us looked away, as if it were a private moment that we shouldn't be witnessing. "As if I want to be anywhere else except where you are," Ames whispered. "Now go. Don't miss your flight."

Roux nodded, kissing him again. I recognized the desperation in her, the need to hang on to a love that was all hers, and when she finally stepped away, I held out my hand to her. "C'mon," I said gently. "The car's waiting."

Roux took my hand as she let go of Ames's with the other, her eyes sad but resigned. "See you soon," she said, giving them all a small wave, and Ames's eyes sparkled once more as we climbed out of the tunnel and back into the world.

Only this time, they sparkled with tears.

CHAPTER 38

We took a private plane out of DeGaulle. I didn't know where it came from, since clearly it didn't belong to the Collective, but Angelo arranged it and I didn't feel like asking any more questions. My brain was already on overload, and I was afraid of what would happen if I got any more new information.

Zelda was our flight attendant, only this time she absolutely refused to give Roux any champagne. "But I'm eighteen now!" she protested.

"It's an American-bound flight. Twenty-one to party."

"But I'm brokenhearted and emotional!"

"So is everyone," Zelda replied coolly, then handed her a Coke instead.

"Woo." Roux sulked, but she popped it open anyway.

Once we were airborne, my parents fell asleep in the back of the plane, tumbled into each other. "Poor guys," I said to Jesse, from where I was slumped against his chest. "They're not young anymore."

"They're still pretty badass, though," Jesse said. "I guess even badasses need sleep."

"Good point."

I glanced up at the front of the plane, where Angelo was discussing something with the pilot, then back at my parents. "They're kind of like us," I said as I realized. "A little group of three, kicking ass and taking names."

"Not a bad legacy," Jesse murmured against my hair.

"You guys?" Roux asked. She was leaning heavily against Jesse's other side, a rare quiet moment between them, and he moved his arm to put it around her shoulders. "How did you know you were in love?"

I looked at Jesse. He looked at me. "I don't know," I admitted. "I just was. He made me laugh and he made me happy."

"It was probably her lying, seducing ways," Jesse said. "I'm kidding, don't hurt me!"

"Oh, you love it," I said. "Do you think you love Ames, Roux?"

"I don't think it," she replied as her eyes fluttered shut. "I know it."

"I guess it is that easy," I said to Jesse. "You just know. There's not a lot of explanation."

"Mags?"

"Hmm?"

"More sleeping, okay?" Jesse yawned loudly, and I grinned and curled up next to him. He and Roux were asleep within minutes, but even though I tried to close my eyes and match my breathing to his, I didn't feel like sleeping.

I still had some things to figure out.

I carefully moved away from Jesse, throwing a blanket over him and Roux before creeping toward the front of the plane. Angelo was sitting there with a scotch in front of him, *El País* open to the international section. "Well, hello," he said when he saw me. "Can't sleep?"

I shook my head and crawled into the seat across from him. "Do you want something to drink?" he asked. "Non-alcoholic, of course."

"No, thank you," I said. "Did you really turn in the Collective?"

Angelo took a deep breath and folded his newspaper shut. "I did," he said. "I'm sorry I didn't tell you about it. I didn't want to put you at risk in case it fell apart."

"Was it difficult, though? I mean, we've been around for almost a hundred years."

"Your mother was able to delete all the innocent files, so no, it wasn't difficult. It's terrible when something you love becomes a shell of its former self. Sometimes it's better to dismantle it before it gets destroyed. And what usually arises from ash?"

"A phoenix," I replied.

"Exactly." He smiled at me, then raised his glass to me. "Excellent work today, my darling. You make us all very proud. I look forward to our next project together."

I nodded. "Me, too. Angelo?"

"Yes, my love?"

"Élodie said something to me about the work they do. She said, 'If it's already been created, it must be possible to re-create.'"

Angelo merely raised an eyebrow. "An interesting thought. What do you think about that?"

I thought for a long minute before replying. "I think I'm excited to meet the phoenix."

Angelo smiled at me, and I smiled back as we sailed home through the sky.

ACKNOWLEDGMENTS

As always, thank you to my wonderful family for loving me, cheering me on, and making everything in my life more delightful than it has any right to be.

There's no limit to the amount of times I can say thank you to my agent, Lisa Grubka at Fletcher & Company. Thank you for taking the wheel and steering the car. (Is that too many car metaphors?)

Writing a book can be a difficult thing at times, so I'm fortunate to have lovely friends, fellow writers, and an excellent support crew who always say nice things at the right time: Adriana Fusaro, for the (gulp!) twenty-seven years of friendship; Maret Orliss and Johanna Clark, for being the loveliest village I could ever hope to have; Steve Bramucci, for the guac & talk; Megan Miranda and Yelena Black, for the 5:00 a.m. hotel lobby coffee; Nora Ray, for the grand crazy; Morgan Matson and Lauren Strasnick, for the Hollywood hikes; Dan Smetanka, for the Toast; Stephanie Perkins, for the epic phone conversations; and Amy Spalding, for sharing my affinity for caps lock.

A massive dose of gratitude to the phenomenal team at Bloomsbury and Walker: Emily Easton, Laura Whitaker, Patricia McHugh, Cristina Gilbert, Katy Hershberger, Bridget Hartzler, Erica Barmash, Emily Ritter, Beth Eller, and Nicole Gastonguay. You are all delightful.

Thank you to my foreign publishers who work so tirelessly on my behalf: Caspian Dennis at Abner Stein; Jane Griffiths and Kat McKenna at Simon & Schuster UK; Femke Geurts at De Fontein; and Céline Charvet at Éditions Nathan. Thank you also to my foreign rights agent, Rachel Hecht at Foundry Literary + Media; and my film agent, Stephen Moore at Paul Kohner, Inc.

To the fans, bloggers, librarians, teachers, and booksellers who support and champion my books every day, you have my endless appreciation. Writing books is fun, but having people read them is even better, and I thank you for reading mine.

© Lovato Images

ROBIN BENWAY

is the acclaimed author of *Also Known As*,
Audrey, Wait!; and *The Extraordinary
Secrets of April, May & June*. Benway's
books have been published in sixteen
languages, won international awards, and
been bestsellers in several countries.
Formerly a bookseller and book publicist,
she lives in Los Angeles.

www.robinbenway.com

@RobinBenway

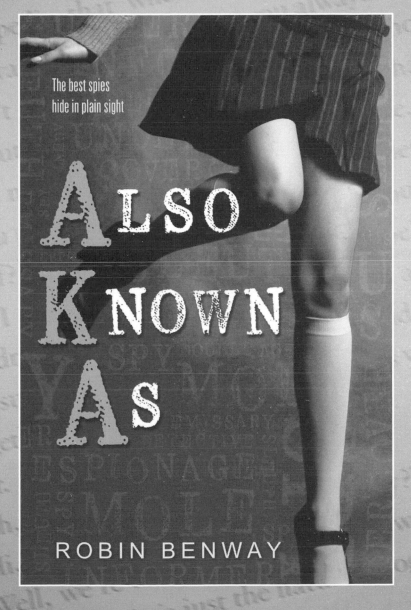

DON'T MISS MAGGIE'S
FIRST THRILLING ADVENTURE!

The best spies
hide in plain sight

ALSO
KNOWN
AS

ROBIN BENWAY

www.bloomsbury.com
www.facebook.com/bloomsburyteens